ALL I SHOULD NOT TELL

BRIAN LEUNG

C&R Press
Conscious & Responsible
Winston-Salem, NC

First Edition
1 2 3 4 5 6 7 8 9

Cover art by Matthew Revert
Interior design by Jojo Rita

Copyright ©2021 Brian Leung

ISBN: 978-1-949540-19-2
LCCN: 2021939658

C&R Press
Conscious & Responsible
crpress.org

For special discounted bulk purchases, please contact:
C&R Press sales@crpress.org
Contact info@crpress.org to book events, readings and author signings.

For Brian Yost, patient husband and most beautiful son of Louisville, for the city itself on its finest days, and eternally, for the lamp-lit sojourners of the passageways.

ALL I SHOULD NOT TELL

1

There are two kinds of boys in Kentucky as far as I'm concerned, those that like to beat the hell out of the other kind, and me, the other kind. Most days, at the least, I'm taunted, sought out to receive new variations of familiar insults. I call these school days. If you're reading this and you're that first kind of boy, I feel like I should apologize to you. I'm sorry that my father died and that for a long stretch I was grieving and weak. I'm sorry I don't have a mother who cares all that much. I want one who does. I'm sorry for being slight for my age. I'm sorry for having a crush on you even as you pummel me.

Would you treat me differently if you knew everything I should never talk about? Well, anyway, here—

2

In my thirties, I will be forced to confront the stories and accept unwanted addendums, but for now, I'm fourteen.

"We don't know what's going on at your house right now," Mark whispers, "but I'll tell you what, you're in a world of trouble if you go back." He runs both hands through his red hair revealing the whole of his freckled-moon face, a lit cigarette between his fingers traveling over his scalp like the smokestack of a locomotive. I'm just now fourteen and he's a year older, held back in fourth grade because he failed, but really because Charlie Pickney and Farl Smith said Mark slammed their heads together in the boys bathroom, which was true. Hard not to fail when you're taken out of school.

"I'm in trouble no matter what," I say. We're 8th graders, smoking in his room though we're not supposed to, exhaling out a window that launches an icy blade of air at us every time we crack it open; we're badasses within these blue walls covered in pictures of wolves, trucks, and one aging poster of ABBA, the four members glowing like white candles. I finally stood up to my stepfather, so he's going to kick my ass no matter what and I don't want him to bring that here. I don't want every fucking person in this town from the riverbank to Parson's Oak knowing what he's been doing. Cudge is the red-headed perverted maniac married to my mother, height of a Giraffe, moustache of a walrus. "You think it's bad now," I say, "being the town fag, you wait and see what happens if I don't go and calm him down."

"Conner, nobody thinks you're actually a fag," Mark says. "You just act like one." He cracks a nervous smile and passes me the cigarette for the final drag. He's trying to lighten the mood. Me and my little brother, Sammy, are over for the weekend to celebrate my birthday. That's the story, anyway. In twenty years, I'll be married with a daughter, but right now, besides Sammy, Mark is all I have. Soon, he will disappear, and when it's certain he's gone forever, that's when it will hit me that I will never be in love precisely this way ever again. "And what's this fight with Cudge?" Mark asks.

Damn. I shouldn't have said anything. I'm good at secrets, but sometimes I lapse like I did with Cudge. The thing I'm about to tell Mark starts like this. Last fall, Cudge was repairing the stairs to our porch, which he rammed with his van just to scare the shit out of me and my brother. After, he borrowed a rotary saw and not two cuts in, zzzhup, blood everywhere, and then "motherfuckingGoddamnitI'vecutmyfuck-ingfingersoffGoddamnmotherfucker." Cudge ripped off his T-shirt and wrapped it around his bloody gob, red running everywhere, down his arms, his painter's pants a spray of modern art. Then he was in the van and yelling out the window, "tellyourmotherfuckingmotherI'mgo-ingtotheGodamnedmotherfuckinghospital." Quiet; just me, the saw horse and my newly favorite bloody saw in the entire world. I looked to the ground and found the fleshy twig Cudge left behind. I was dis-appointed there was only one. "What I didn't tell you," I say to Mark, "is that I kept it. The finger."

He's clearly surprised, but there's mostly worry in his expression, like I've waded in a bit too deep. "No fucking way," he says, taking the extinguished butt from me and flicking it into the cold. His hand pauses for a moment, as if capturing a thought, thin pink fingers trailing outward like the claws of a jetting crawfish. A nervous expression washes over his face, holds him until he shakes his head and torso like a dog just out of a pond.

"Really," I say, almost in apology. "You know some of it. Saw his finger laying there on the ground caked in dirt, and I'm thinking he's going to need that. I stared at it almost forever, deciding on what I was going to do. Maybe it came to me quicker than that. But I ran in the house and called the sheriff. Told them they should come get Cudge's finger and take it to the hospital. They said to put it on ice."

"You just said you kept it." Mark is justifiably agitated. Usually I'm the one, fidgety little Conner thinking about when I'm going to get beat on next, or worse.

"I got a baby food jar, the tall kind, put Cudge's finger in it and took it out to the garage. I never had any intention of letting him get it back, but I had to look like I tried."

Mark is stunned, looks as if he's about to break into a sweat. He's got one hand pressed to his forehead, elbow on his knee as if forcing himself to look at me. "You told me a fucking dog carried it off."

"When I left the garage, I saw the neighbor's mutt sleeping in the sun in their back yard. Nobody was around, so I called it over and walked him around the sawhorse and sent him home." This is what I've become.

"You thought of that right then?"

I nod and sigh. "I guess. For the pawprints."

"Sometimes Conner, it's scary what an evil shit you can be."

I shrink a little because now it's out and it's all true, except for telling Cudge. A necessary lie. "He knows and he's pissed. Went after me, but I pushed him off."

Mark's eyes, dark blue in this thin light, go teary. "Man, this is fucked up. I've done some crazy shit with you Conner. I've done some even crazier shit *for* you." There he pauses and shakes his head again as if warning something away. It's true about the crazy shit, especially over these last few months when things with Cudge got worse. He looks to the carpet and clears his eyes with his forearm. "Pretty fucked up. You got a guy's finger in a jar."

I should feel worse about it, but that part I have to fake. "I know it's awful. That's why I've gotta go." I touch his arm and he looks up, light from the window streaking blue through his hair. He's agonized, so I say, "Now he's threatening to get after Sammy, and that can't happen. He says he wants the jar."

"That's even more fucked up."

"I haven't looked at it since, but I'll give it back. Maybe I can smooth things over." I feel awful telling this lie. I have no intention of appeasing Cudge. I have no intention of letting him hurt me and Mark. I've figured a way out of all this, which means something bad is about to happen.

"You know what smoothing over is going to mean?" Mark asks.

We both know.

He collapses around me and embraces me tighter than any other time I can remember. "You don't fucking deserve this," he says. This is the same Mark that got expelled for beating up two boys in the bathroom. The same Mark that beat more than a few boys down when they came after me. Of course, he isn't around every time I need him, but he's pretty good at squaring accounts. Nobody ever once thought of calling *him* a faggot. Pussies. We are lying on his bed, and tall, strong Mark sobs into my neck even though his mother could walk in at any minute. I'm small by comparison, a skinny, brown-haired geek feeling loved. I'm holding Mark and thinking I wish we could be alone like this forever. Maybe not crying, but all the rest.

After a while, clear-eyed, we go to the very yellow kitchen where I tell Mark's mom, Mrs. Callihan, I want to show them the hunting knife I got for my birthday. It's a lie that will be useful later. Then I go too far. I tell her that, anyway, Cudge wants us to check in and a call won't do.

She puts her hands on her hips. "Now that's ridiculous," she says. "You're here for your birthday. God bless that stepfather of yours." Mrs. Callihan is a tall woman who leans back when she's addressing someone, so much so that by the time my eyes clamor up the ski slope of her thin torso, I feel I've accomplished something in the summit of her kind, blue eyes. She snatches the phone and tries to call Cudge but to no avail, and when she hangs up she makes the sign of the cross. "And anyway, is that safe? A boy your age with a hunting knife?"

"It's okay," I tell her. "I'll leave it in the box."

Sammy runs in from the other room. "What knife?" There are almost too many moving parts for me to manage. My younger brother is a squat version of our late dad, with the same semi-combed brown hair and eyes that seem to never stop darting around.

I know I'm not coming back with the knife, but I keep lying. "The one Mom got me," I say as if I'm shocked he's asking. Sammy wrinkles his nose because he's never seen it. "She said you were too little to be around a hunting knife." I immediately stop myself and turn to Mrs. Callihan. "It's okay," I reassure her. "I promise. In the box."

Sammy is shaking his head. "I am *not* little," the childish formulation proving my point.

Mrs. Callihan looks skeptical but relents, even to the idea that I'm walking instead of letting her drive. "If I wasn't getting supper ready and expecting a call from Mr. Callihan," she says, and then, "Really Conner?" as she opens the door and cold air hits our faces like shards of glass.

"I'm staying," Mark says, and I thank him with a smile because it's Cudge, and I have to have a talk with my stepfather, alone. We'd fought before I left, and I know I'm in for more, but it can't be like this any longer. I'm certain my mother expects me to step up and set things right with her husband. And I know that no fourteen-year-old should be thinking this: by setting things right, I mean to use that knife on Cudge. Sammy's safe. Cudge is alone. I'm through with him and it's too late for anyone to stop me. That time has passed.

"I'm going," Sammy says, and he's already bundled up. "I want my rocket."

Shit. He saved box tops for months and our mother sent away for the toy. "I'll bring it if it comes," I tell him.

I lose, but maybe he'll be useful after all. I've learned to think fast. He can't see what's about to happen, and I promise myself I won't do anything that will get him hurt. If it's possible to feel a color, my insides feel black.

In minutes me and Sammy are turning the corner, leaning into an icy cold blast of February wind, our boxy two-story house looming a long half block away, almost glowing in this bright, gray day that smells of burning wood. I didn't want him anywhere near our house, but I also didn't want a show of making him stay at the Callihan's. And if it works out, I decide, if I can keep Sammy out of the house 'til it's over.... It's my job to keep him away from a very, very angry man. Angry at me. Maybe Sammy is here because I want a reason not to go through with this.

Then there's the business of returning Cudge's finger. Mark will ask me about that. I've no idea what I'm doing. Something worse, and as I think this, I feel a hardness in my chest. I'm not sure Mark can take what's coming.

Gritting my teeth as we continue up our frozen street, I see through the naked branches of a tulip poplar that the upstairs bathroom window of our house is open, a dark gray rectangle receding to black. It's a sure sign our stepfather is inside. The window ledge is fanged with a row of slender icicles except in the center, like a gap in a jagged smile. I hold out my arm to halt Sammy's progress, the two of us shivering and without any expectation or consolation that Cudge will have turned on the heat, at least to the extent that it does more than merely keep the pipes from freezing. "Do you think it came?" Sammy asks, a brown-mittened hand pointing at our mailbox, his eyes, also brown, shining with hope just above the sliver of space between the wool wrapped across his face and the too-big-for-him brown toboggan on his head. I shrug and continue on, tightening my jaw against whatever might come our way beyond the threshold of the front door.

It's me who's assuming the worst. Sammy's oblivious. For him it's just a bitterly cold walk home. He's more of a sensitive kid who can't yet see what's in front of him even if it flashes at him like hazard lights on a car. At the moment, it's a quality I'm grateful for. Years from now, when he leaves for California and never returns, I'll think differently, but for now, I'm happy he's living in his own head. Happy he has no idea the only thing standing between him and Cudge is me. And really, that's what this is about now. Why it's happening *now*.

When we reach the edge of our winter-gray, near barren yard, Sammy runs ahead to the mailbox and opens it. "Nothing, Conner," he calls. "It didn't come." I can't see his mouth for the scarf but I hear the frown under there.

"It'll come," I assure him.

Sammy's eyes brighten when he looks toward the house which stands in front of us like two weathered cardboard boxes stacked atop one another. He bolts to the foot of the steps where a young raccoon lays dead and frozen. Picking it up without a second thought, he shows it to me. He's a mass of brown wool, a bear cub. He reminds me of Mickey all covered in batter, from *In the Night Kitchen*, the Sendak Dad read to me at night. I call to Sammy, trying not to yell, but when it's clear he doesn't understand what I'm saying, I lower my scarf. "What the hell you gonna do with that?" I ask, looking up at the windows for fear Cudge has heard us. Sammy's younger than me by nearly six years and has increasingly little aversion to investigating dead animals like the road kill and almost-bloated vermin we sometimes find in ditches and on the banks of the Ohio River. Treasure, he calls it, which just might be the best indicator of our expectations from life. He has an action figure he named Flea. Nothing to worry over, I've been telling myself about his fascination with dead animals, as long as it doesn't get worse, as long as he doesn't move on to live animals. Maybe he's just being a kid.

A gust catches me from behind, pushes me a step forward. "Well?" I ask, still waiting for a response. "What're you gonna to do with the raccoon?"

Sammy closes his eyes until a second gust passes, then looks at the ice-caked animal dangling in his grasp. It's a sparkling, furry, oversized Christmas ornament. He shrugs and turns to me. "Guess I'll stab it," he yells through a scrim of wool. "Stab it good."

"You do that," I say, knowing we should be out of the cold at the Callihans'. I'm not at all anxious to be inside, not here at home, but I've got a job to do. To say the least, things did not go well with Cudge when we left for the weekend. The tail end of his orange van peeks from behind the house, so it's possible he's merely biding his time, waiting for me to come home. It would be like him. He knows I'm wracked and he's patient enough to let that play out so he can make it worse face-to-face. And it's too late in the game for me to run, to tell. He knows that too. I think of his catfish face and grow angrier.

I need time to check out the situation, and thankfully Sammy is content to run around the yard looking for a weapon with which to abuse the frozen raccoon. Sammy the Impaler I should call him. I'm surprised he doesn't have a ready stash of pokers and prodders, his own armory. The cold turns the sound of his footsteps crunchy, making it easy to track him in the yard without watching. I turn my attention to the front door. It's seldom a pleasant entry, particularly when Mom is away, as she is now, of course. Our dear mother. Cudge is unpredictable in her presence and very predictable out of it.

I take hold of the doorknob with more than the familiar dread. It feels like a ball of ice even through my glove. Sammy's found a length of rebar and is thoroughly puncturing his frozen prize.

Cold as it is, and the wind picking up, I can't bring myself to turn the knob. Stepping back, I look again at the weathered door that seemed so tall and heavy when I was younger. Before this moment, when was the last time I thought of myself as a child? Aren't I supposed to feel like that even at fourteen? When I go to the Callihans', I get a taste of what it feels like to be taken care of, but never here. *This shit can't keep going on,* I tell myself for the millionth time. Maybe just plunging in is worth the risk no matter what.

There's no denying I've changed over these past few months— breaking into houses, thinking of every possible way to get Cudge out of ours. I've often imagined a moment like this when it wouldn't bother me in the least, for me and Sammy and for Mom as well, if one day I opened the door and found Cudge dead in his flowery recliner. I've thought about it, in fact, more than is healthy. In the most recent version I imagined the scene down to a half-eaten pimento loaf sandwich in his hand and a daytime rerun of *The Beverly Hillbillies* on the TV. I could almost smell the warm tumbler of Mountain Dew sitting on the coffee table next to him. But on this freezing day coming from the Callihans', I'm hoping to see Cudge alive. He'll be pissed at me sure as shit, and if it's necessary and I can't do it inside, I'll hold him off. There's the knife, after all. I'll stand outside with Sammy and let Cudge scream at me for all the neighbors to hear. I'll let him make it worse for himself. I can count on his temper and I can count on self-defense.

I turn the knob and push the door open harder than I intend. What feels like a waterfall of light washes in front of me. I take one step inside and stop. The living room is not just colder than usual; it's freezing and near silent, sharp gray light from outside filtering through the curtains. I'm barely fourteen but my shadow stretches into the room as the flat length of a fully grown man. Everything is the same as when I left, stacks of archery magazines around Cudge's yellow peony recliner, a jar of pepperoncini on the coffee table looking like a green wad of embalmed fetal mice. But, on the opposite wall, near the stairs, there's something new. The thermostat dangles from a thin wire below the silhouette of old paint where it was once affixed. I'm cautious. "Cudge?" I whisper, walking deeper into the silent house. At the foot of the stairs, I call out a little louder with no response. I'm an idiot. If Cudge is upstairs, he's between me and the knife. I go to the kitchen and take out the heavy blade Dad use to whetstone sharpen. All told, it's the length of my forearm, wider. Again, it comes to me, as it has more and more in the previous months, the image, almost a wish, of finding my stepfather sprawled out on the floor, dead. Then maybe we could go back to the way it was before he came, a life that wasn't perfect by any means, but which, at this moment, I would trade the world for. Someday I will have a boyfriend. Someday I will have a wife. Someday I will have a child. But right now I'm living day-to-day, in love with Mark, learning to say things at school like "she's a fox," and round-the-clock seething with hatred for my stepfather who I want not just gone, but dead.

Cudge isn't a pushover, not the kind to make it so easy, and I'm not as eager to locate him as I was when I left the Callihans'; when he and I fought earlier I wasn't thinking, just reacting, when I told him about the finger. Which is why I was certain he'd show up at the Callihans' door.

I'm about to pick a fight, about to place a foot on the first stair when a loud thud comes from something hitting the outside of the house. My heart leaps and I cringe, looking up the stairs ready for the angry sight of Cudge. Then it occurs to me he might be outside, and I think of Sammy. I run to the porch just as my brother heaves the frozen raccoon against the house a second time, knife behind my back. "What the F?" I yell. "Scared the shit out of me." My wooly, brown pear of a brother laughs and picks up the animal again but doesn't attempt to throw it. "You want Cudge to come out here and warp the both of us?!"

I look behind me at the open door and wait. If Cudge heard Sammy he would've thudded out of the house all red-faced and raptor-armed.

Sammy drops the coon and walks toward the house. I'm not ready for him. "Wait," I say. "Throw that thing in the trees." I point toward the back of our property where gangly maples stand gray and bare. When he complies, I run inside, briefly checking the hanging thermostat, now useless, as I head up the stairs. For the rest of my life I will remember what I'm about to see as if it takes place over hours, rather than seconds.

The bathroom door in the hallway is open, the window opposite, open as well. Near the threshold, a thin layer of ice cracks under my shoes. When I look up from the sound the first thing I see is Cudge's red and green tattooed foot and his gray leg propped over the edge of the clawfoot bathtub, the limb held by iced-over bathwater. The knife falls from my hand. Sharp, cold air surges into my lungs. *It's already done.* The tattoo is a cherry-headed phoenix beneath a scrim of tangerine leg hair, now in frozen recline.

The front door closes. Sammy. *Shit.* "Don't come up," I yell. "Hear me, Sammy?" I think he asks why the house is so cold, but my attention returns to the frozen body in front of me. I've wished it true. *One push can do all that?* The son-of-a-bitch is dead. Feelings I won't understand for years sink through me as if I'm being force-fed ball bearings, a weight drawing down so heavy and strong I'm not certain I can lift my legs. *This is my doing,* I think. This is the man who months ago stood in front of me and opened his arms and said, "It's okay now, little man. Everything's going to be okay from now on." He held me and I believed him. This is a man who has a flavor I never wanted to know. Now he's dead.

It's as if all sound has dropped away. My gaze turns to the bathroom's open window, normally propped with a length of rebar, but somehow standing free. My breath fogs in front of me, and then I find half my face, a boy's face, in the medicine cabinet's swung open mirror. A comma of brown hair sits on my forehead beneath the white "K" of my blue University of Kentucky toboggan. I look exhausted and startled all at once. Heart thudding in my chest, I half expect Cudge to lurch out of the tub. That isn't going to happen. This isn't the movies. He may as well be a mannequin or a toppled statue. Something odd in these seconds of absolute stillness; I understand that Cudge is dead. That is, it's clear he's gone, but I *understand* it. He's finished, expired. He isn't a person. I think of my father who ceased not unlike this, immersed in the Ohio River. My head lightens and I fall back against the door frame. I have to get back to Sammy and figure out just what I'm going to do now.

Standing up straight, I pat discs of cold above each cheek. I stare at my dead stepfather whose body is motionless beneath a thin layer of ice, his head submerged to the eyes, gripped sharp and exact by the freeze as if his lashes are orange-tinted reeds extending over the winter-blue shore of a lake.

3

Sammy's not at the foot of the stairs nor in the living room, and the front door remains open. Before I go down, I think like Dad, think about the house that I hate but can't do without. I run back to the bathroom and turn on the faucet which offers up a slow drool. Then I rush down to the kitchen and put the knife back in the drawer before turning the faucet on there too. I do the same to the downstairs bathroom, and then I pause and close my eyes. For a second I think to call the sheriff but just as quickly something else occurs to me, maybe the worst thing a son could think. *Mom*, I'm thinking; *it was her.* As much as I know I should, I can't call the sheriff, and besides, I'm not certain. But it would be like her to leave a thing half done, to leave it for me to take care of.

It dawns on me; I'm not supposed to be here. My plan isn't part of *her* plan. Me and Sammy are at Mark's all weekend as far as anyone's concerned. She isn't done, and if she isn't, what if she's coming back? *Shit.* And if it wasn't Mom.... I look around. Except for the dangling thermostat, nothing's been moved. Nothing taken that I can tell. Someone went out of their way to kill Cudge.

I bolt and find Sammy in the cold yard where it feels like shards of ice are penetrating my skull on all sides. He looks up, the short, brown woolly mass of him having just driven the rebar through the raccoon's eye socket. I have to talk to Mark before anything else. He'll know what to do and he's the only person I can trust right now. Without saying a word, I back quietly away from the house, turn and lean into a new wind, waving for my brother to follow as he pleads with me to tell him why I'm walking so fast. "Not now," I half growl, half whisper.

"Tellllll me. What about the knife?"

At the end of the driveway I stop and take him by the shoulders. "Cudge said no."

"Oh," he says, as if it's the one thing I could say that makes absolute sense to him. We're on our way again, but I walk slower, realizing Sammy has to feel like everything is absolutely normal. I don't say another word because I'm thinking about Mark and the Callihans and what this is all going to mean. What happens when they find out Cudge is dead? What if they think it's too dangerous for Mark to be near me? What if I never see him again? What if it turns out that even dead Cudge has figured out a way to ruin everything? What I imagined would feel like relief is anything but.

We're blocks away from our house and Sammy turns to head towards the Callihans'. "Wait," I say. I look to the river, just beyond the little strip of businesses that pass in Orgull as our town center. It's a sight me and Sammy see almost every day, usually more than once. Not much to look at, a gray and frozen main street leading down to the river ending in a battered dock and wood pilings sticking out of the water, all remnants of when the place had a purpose. The street is lined with businesses that neither look thriving nor ready to board up, the Red Bud advertising "Lunch 'n' Supper" in chipped gold leaf on a plate glass front, Max's Tavern, and Pattitson's Hardware with its rusty, oversized hammer dangling above the entrance. The redbrick monument that is Maine Mercantile, standing silent and empty, will, in a couple decades, find itself a burned-out shell after a meth lab explosion. Then there's the wrought-iron-fronted shop, which has hand-painted black letters on a white door: "Knives-Ammo." That's where my knife came from and it's not a place I care to pass just now, so I move to the opposite side of the street and tell Sammy to follow me.

"I'm freezing. Let's go," he says, pointing in the direction we should take.

"Didn't seem that cold when you were working on that racoon."

"You're acting weird, Conner."

I can't afford to act out-of-sorts, but I can't find another gear. "Just come on," I say. The wind gusts in freezing, inconsistent pulses. I've never felt the air so sharp, and the earth beneath me is cold and hard. It's as if my feet are marble and the ground is marble too, every step a heavy, clacking thunk. It takes just a couple minutes until on one side of us the Ohio River is a white-capped soupy green, and on the other our decaying town, Orgull, and, quickly, the beginning of a blocks-long limestone rock face, cut at a time the town mattered enough to run a two-lane road to Louisville, a time nobody alive remembers. Columns of ice, thick as a man's arm and cauliflowered at the tops, hang from random parts of the rock face where the seep has frozen. Sammy knocks off the lowest hanging of these with the rebar he used to stab the raccoon. The rebar that held the bathroom window open until what? On another day we might have used pieces of the ice for short-lived sword fights, but today, facing increasing blasts of frosty air, I have other things on my mind. I have to get us out of this situation. My only hope is that it wasn't Mom, but that feels like a razor-thin prospect. I need a moment to think before we go back to the Callihans'.

"I wanna to go inside, Conner," Sammy says, holding his body cross-armed. We've arrived at what we consider *our* bench, a lonely installation at the edge of a mostly dirt and gravel park that looks out over the Ohio. I could have found some building to step into, but I don't want people to hear us. Sammy holds the rebar across his lap, the tip thinly frosted with raccoon flesh and hair. His weapon makes me increasingly uncomfortable. There's a reason why it fell from the bathroom window. When the right moment comes around, I will insist that we ditch it. Even through my toboggan the cold latches onto my ears until the pain turns into something like the sound of distant trumpets.

I'm seeing my brother, not hearing him, and this is when it comes to me. He thinks I've just spoken to Cudge. Sammy is a witness to me being the last person to see Cudge alive. *Well, no officer, I lied about that, Cudge was already dead when we got there. Why didn't I call the sheriff? Um....*

More and more I'm feeling like Mom has screwed me over. I feel it. I can almost read her mind. Who would blame the boy? My son was defending us.

In a fit not long ago, Cudge slapped her on the neck. I heard it. I doubt it's enough to justify a frozen corpse.

My head is spinning. If my brother doesn't say just the right things…
He tugs on my elbow. "I'm hungry, Conner. I'm cold."

"We'll go in a minute," I say, "but I want to ask you…." I pause
longer than I should. I don't know how to say what needs to be said
outright and I don't want to put unnecessary thoughts into Sammy's
head. I want for him what I want for myself, to feel safe, which is never
going to happen in our fucked up family. I wonder if Sammy feels the
differences like I do, the way the Callihans live compared to us. It isn't
like at our house, where at times it's as if Mom and Cudge live in their
dark cave and me and Sammy in ours, coming out only for meals like
grunting, somnambulant bears. The Callihans are different than us. They
use their furnace when the weather cools, and it's a home where they sit
down together every night for dinner. They go to church on Sundays. It's
not money. They're only slightly better off. Mr. Callihan is a maintenance
man, and Mrs. Callihan a cafeteria worker.

I have no idea if Sammy has any real memory of how it used to be
at our house before Cudge, when our dad hadn't yet given over to his
troubles and drowned himself and Mom was, if not always a mother
filled with kindness, then at least capable of her own brand of affections.
Every Halloween she made us beer-can jack-o-lanterns, and because she
remembered a childhood tire swing, she had Dad make one for us. She
could be okay. Sometimes I wonder if it's just me. I want more.

"Sammy," I begin again as the gusts calm, "what do you think of Cudge?"

He's looking at the choppy river, one hand raised over a scarf-cov-
ered cheek to block the wind, the other tapping his rebar against our
bench. "We talllked about this before," he whines. "I don't like him
anymore." We're both speaking through our scarves, our voices
muffled like prisoners communicating through cell walls. Growing up
in Kentucky we've learned to live with bouts of extreme winter weather,
but no amount of experience steels a person against the reality of bitterly
cold air.

"Yeah," I say, "me either. But I'm talking about something else."
It's terrible what I'm hoping to hear. Self-serving even. But it's a way out

for both of us. There was a time early on when things were much better and Sammy really took to Cudge. We both fell for the show. Cudge gave us candy and made breakfast, generally put on a real good performance for Mom about what a fantastic father he'd be to us. I was skeptical, but eventually I bought into it...briefly. What kid who'd lost his father wouldn't?

"Why did Mom marry him anyways?" Sammy asks.

What I want to say is, *that's the question I asked before they got married. Remember when I was the bad guy for telling Mom I wasn't interested in seeing her re-marry? I was shot down and now look.* I want to say all this but what I offer is, "I guess she was lonely." It's true enough, though it isn't where I want the conversation to head. A man is dead in our house. "But Cudge," I say, "I mean, did you ever see him hit Mom or anything like that?" There are other, worse things I could ask, but I won't. For months I've done my best to keep track of Cudge being alone with Sammy, trying to keep him safe from that, but there have been times when it just wasn't possible. I'd come home and the first thing I'd do is find my brother, talk to him up close, look him over, and he'd seem fine. It wasn't scientific, but I'm fourteen. I was thirteen. "Or, were you guys ever alone?"

Sammy looks at me, his brown eyes leading a quizzical expression, the remainder of which is hidden beneath his scarf. "Mom told me not to."

A feeling colder than the wind shoots through me. "Wait. When did she tell you that?"

Sammy fidgets. "It's freezing, Conner. I want to go." He smacks the rebar on the bench even harder.

"Hey," I say, pointing to the metal bar. "That's not safe."

"It's not supposed to be," Sammy says, widening his eyes in exasperation before bringing the metal down in a final emphatic thud. "It's my stabber." I hold out my hand, but Sammy tightly grips the metal rod. This is absolutely not a weapon he can carry around. Something happened upstairs and that slim length of steel is proof.

"Give it," I say, and after a moment of thought, he reluctantly complies. "It's dangerous, swinging this thing all over the place." I stand

and look around before heaving the rebar into the river. It's so gusty I don't hear the flunk where it disappears with a diver's splash.

"Hey," Sammy yells. "That was mine. I'm gonna tell." He hops off the bench, arms crossing his chest again, looking like an angry brown gnome.

I may have made things worse. "Sammy. That was from upstairs. Do you know what's going to happen if Cudge finds out we threw his bar in the river?"

"*You* threw it in the river."

"*You* took it. So we're both in trouble if you say anything." He's young enough that I can get away with such a ridiculous threat, but I hate to do it to him. "You have to promise you won't tell." Sammy crosses his arms tighter and narrows his eyes, not looking at me as he sits again on the bench. He's such a bundle of woolen pudge he goes from gnome to human-sized Weeble. "Promise," I continue. "It's got to be our secret. Okay?" When he doesn't move a muscle, I up the stakes. "Soldier swear," I say, extending my arm. It's something we made up, a gesture at important moments where we grip each other's wrists. Sammy unfolds his arms slowly and reaches out to seal his promise. I sit back down and pull him close. "Warmer?" He nods. There are still things I need to ask. "When did Mom tell you not to be alone with Cudge?"

"I don't know. Right before he moved in."

Whatever coldness I felt is replaced by a rising heat. Mom has never said a word to me about warning Sammy against Cudge. There have been times I thought we were working together and other times I suspected that maybe she was working *me*. "She tell you why?" He doesn't respond. "Sammy?"

Finally, he turns and glares. "Yessss, Conner. Because she said he wasn't used to little kids."

Cynical as it is, I doubt that's the reason, and it's not useful. There's something that worried her about Cudge, worried her enough to warn Sammy away from him. She's *never once* pulled me aside the way she has Sammy. That's what she thinks of me. But fine, if she was that concerned, maybe *she* can take care of this mess. The fact is I really don't know anything. I don't know the facts of what's happened at our house in the last twenty-four hours. It's palpable, this age where the truth has started to go gray. The world has been, if not lying, then fibbing all along. Indians and Pilgrims? Those great masses of bison I thought were still on the plains? My mother is looking out for me? Everything has changed and I know it will change again. I ask myself if I would have done it. If Cudge weren't already dead, would I have gone through with it? Have I really become that? Because I'm thinking, now, if anyone else finds Cudge, I'm in trouble; I've got to get his body out of there if it means thudding him down the stairs like a dead giraffe. And then what, when I've got a man's frozen body flumped on our porch?

I don't know myself and I need someone who does. I arrive where I started. It's Mark I have to talk to first because he'll make sense of all this and because he has to know I didn't murder Cudge, though he'll have reason to think so. Even I can't escape feeling that somehow it's me who set Cudge's death in motion. I could have prevented all of this. But, for the first time since Dad killed himself, life felt like it was coming together. With Cudge and Mom engaged, a lot of the gloom at home lifted.

I should have known. Cudge got strange fast, and I didn't say a word. The first sign: Cudge was at the wheel of his van, a 70's, burnt orange Dodge Tradesman with double doors on the side and back. I was in the passenger seat looking out the window into the night's dark fuzz of tree filtered light. It was a trip Mom insisted on. I'd played along with her dating Cudge, but she wanted more, a pre-packaged assurance I was on board one hundred percent.

We'd met Cudge half-way between his apartment and our home, and she handed me off as cheerily as if he were taking me to my first Boy Scouts meeting. On weekends, Cudge ran a booth at a flea market across the river in Indiana. "The boy in his complex can't help him this time," Mom had insisted. "It's a great chance for you to get to know each other better before we get married. Just you two. Make a little money." When I relented, I didn't understand that I'd have to spend the night, and that Cudge and I would have to get up at 4 a.m. to load the van.

That was hours away. For now, we were driving to who knows where. "You ever been to a flea market?" Cudge asked. "Ain't no fleas at a flea market, you know." I rolled my eyes, resigned to the fact that he was marrying Mom. But more than anything I didn't want Cudge to keep *trying* like that. I'd gotten on board with the engagement. Wasn't that enough? "Well, now, come to think of it," Cudge continued, "there's a few of them look like they got fleas." Yellow light shifted over his face and ran across his moustache like a brushfire.

"I thought you lived in Louisville," I said as the van turned onto the bridge crossing the Ohio toward Clarksville. To one side were the massive red fluorescent lines of the Colgate Clock. We obviously weren't headed to his apartment. "Don't we have to get up early?" From the passenger side, only upriver was visible, a dull wide strip dark as fresh asphalt with a slow-moving barge marked by lazy blinking of lights tracking in our direction.

"Do. But I got a guy might buy some of this shit." Cudge pointed behind us with his thumb. The space was mostly dark except for what light came through the rear windows. "You'd be surprised what people pay for. Sometimes I'll be driving down an alley and I'll see some old piece of something lying next to the trash and I'll toss it in the back and sure enough, next day someone'll give me cash money for it."

In the back of the van, I made out what looked like four kitchen chairs covered in pea green vinyl, though in the dimness everything appeared as if it might be pea green: a chest of drawers, its knobs offering the dull gleam of pewter, and three large cardboard boxes that rattled with the movement of the van. Outside the rear window, the cluster of high rises that marked downtown Louisville offered rows of static light like a collection of giant robots at rest. I came back to the contents of the van. "Lot of junk."

Cudge laughed. "Like I said. It is. But that's what the world runs on. Hell, I bet if a guy could measure it, he'd find out half our time is spent transferring our old junk to someone else to make room for new junk *from* someone else."

"Profound," I said. I'd heard a guy on television say it in the snotty way I was trying to imitate.

Again Cudge laughed. "College words and sass. Alright little man. I see what I'm working with." We were coming to the end of the bridge and Cudge fell silent, took a pack of cigarettes out of his pocket, bit one with his lip, and pulled it from the package. When the pack was offered to me, I reached for it without thinking. I snatched back my hand as if it was possible to erase the gesture. "Thought so," Cudge said, putting the cigarettes back in his pocket. "Knew you were a smoker the minute I saw you. But I'm sure your Mom doesn't know. Does she?" I stayed silent and looked ahead into the stretch and glare of the Indiana side of the river. "Thought not," Cudge said. "Bet there's a lot of shit she don't know about you. I was a kid once."

It was hard to imagine, this tall, big, mustached man had once been my age. I was small for thirteen, young-looking, so much so it was a triumph of sorts when Cudge started taking us out and I realized waitresses weren't pointing me to the child's menu any more.

"Oh, sure," Cudge continued, "used to get into all kinds of shit. Guess I was a little terror."

"I'm not like that," I said.

"Hope not. I got so bad the old man wrote me off. Come to think of it, I was about your age." Cudge grew quiet, and I saw something was playing in his mind as he took a drag on his cigarette and blew smoke upward toward the cracked-open window. "Shoulda just whipped me instead, that bastard. Mom stuck with me, though. For a while. She's the one dragged us to Kentucky."

It was more than odd to hear Cudge talk like that. It wasn't the way I thought of him, as a guy who'd once had a family. After all, he'd more-or-less landed in my life like some sort of alien, like he'd said, "take me to your leader," and Mom brought him to our house.

When Cudge pulled off the interstate, minutes passed without a word between us. The beginnings of the molded plastic chain store signs that in years to come would dominate that side of the river slowly gave way to trees in silhouette and starlight. Here and there farmhouses announced themselves with the glow of blue and yellow rectangles, but mostly the landscape was variations of gray and black. I looked into the side mirror, watched as the last of town disappeared. "Cudge, where are we going?" I asked. I didn't know what our destination was, but where we were headed felt too out of the way.

"Told you already, little man. Got a friend." He pointed again to the back of the van. "And, do me a favor. No more of that Cudge shit. From now on it's Dad."

I didn't want to believe what he'd just said. "I'm not fucking calling you Dad."

"Hey, hey, there. What happened to the college words?"

"I'm not calling you Dad. I had a Dad."

"Shit," Cudge said, swerving onto a dirt road, or was it a long driveway? I couldn't tell. It was bordered by trees on either side, the van's lights leading us into what looked to be only more darkness and more road, a gray line ahead of us thinning to nothing. "I didn't ask," Cudge insisted. "It's Dad, Conner." A new, unlit cigarette appeared between his lips, glowed bluish, a miniature Light Sabre. We came to a stop and Cudge cut off the engine and headlights. The darkness was capped by the swath of star-black sky above us as Cudge's face flared yellow when he lit his cigarette. "It's Dad, Conner," he repeated, punctuating each syllable with the cigarette's orange ember which moved as if it were the bouncing ball from a cartoon sing along.

"Real glad Mom wanted us to get to know each other better. Can't wait to tell her what a fucking good time we had."

Cudge unrolled his window, took a drag, then hung his cigarette hand outside. "You do that, little man. Tell her, little bad ass. But let me tell *you* first. We have the same goal, you and I. We want your mother to be happy. Cudge and Conner don't have to like each other, we just have to pretend, just like I know we've been doing. So, you're right. You're not my son and I'm not your dad. I'm certainly not some fucking, selfish son-of-a-bitch that didn't give two shits for his family and jumped off a bridge."

I reached for the door but Cudge grabbed my free arm. "Better know where you are before you run off into the woods. Never know what might happen out there." He had large hands but his fingers were thin, bony, and surprisingly tight gripping. I knew the feeling from being beaten at school. "Like I was saying, bad ass. We only have to make your mother happy. And take care of your little brother, too. Be a family. And a family starts with a dad. Got that little man?" He'd put his cards on the table. All that making nice had been an act.

"What's wrong with you?" I yelled.

"What's wrong with me? I'll tell you what exactly. I have a son got taken away. Not by the law or anything. By his bitch of a mother. Six years old and she hauls off down to Mexico to live with her parents."

I had no idea where this conversation had come from. Five minutes earlier we were on our way to sell some junk and suddenly I was getting a story that sounded like he was trying to replace one family, the one he lost, with ours. "What's all that got to do with me?"

"I learned you have to read the signs. If I'd paid attention...." When he trailed off, I thought for a second that whatever fuse had been lit was extinguished. But then, he turned to me. "That answer your question?"

I should have stayed quiet, but I was trying to make sense of what was happening. "If you knew where she took him, why didn't you try to get him back?"

"Try? I fucking drove my ass all the way down there. Didn't sleep didn't stop except for gas and to take a shit. Ate jerky and Cokes. That's it." He paused as if he'd come to the end of his story, then sat back and stared through the front window.

I waited, but nothing. "Are we going to go or what?" I asked.

Cudge narrowed his eyes but didn't turn. He fell into a strange quietness. "And so I got down to Camargo, and I don't speak Mexican, but they speak English pretty much when they want to. And then I start asking around about my boy, only that's when *suddenly* no one's speaking fucking English. A day goes by and I'm sleeping in my fucking truck and morning comes and I finally get someone to take me to the house where my girlfriend's parents live. Only they're not there. The house is locked up and no one knows when they left or when they're coming back."

I couldn't figure the man out. A minute earlier he was practically yelling in my face and now he'd devolved to what even I recognized as a racist whisper. "You never found him?"

"Paid a guy to watch that house. Nothing. Two years. Nada."

"That blows." I was genuinely sympathetic, confused by why this had all come down on me at this moment, but I didn't think it was right that his son had been taken from him. I was thinking of the kid, too. He probably didn't have any choice in the matter. I wondered if he even spoke Spanish. Did he end up down there hearing people talk to him, and him not understanding a word of anything that was being said? I looked to the passenger window hoping to find my reflection there, but nothing.

"So yeah, Conner," Cudge said, growing louder. "That's what's wrong with me. My boy was taken away from me and it fucking broke my heart."

It seemed like my mind was only capable of generating questions. What was I supposed to think about Cudge now that he'd opened up? His kid was taken from him, more than that, he'd disappeared. And it didn't sound as if his childhood had been that great. In some ways, I understood what he was feeling. I was so unsteadied by the moment it felt like someone was tossing firecrackers into my skull. A few minutes earlier I was ready to jump out of the van, and now I found my grip on the door handle loosen.

Cudge must have sensed this because he reached toward me, making me flinch. "It's okay, little man," he said, placing his hand on the back of my head. He rubbed my hair a couple strokes, gave me a light pat and then pulled his hand back. "Sometimes I get emotional." He started the van, turned around through the weeds, and set off back toward the main road.

"What about the stuff?" I asked. "We still going to meet up with your friend?" I was coming to.

"Fuck it," he sighed. "Big day tomorrow. We'll just head back to my place and hit the sack." When I didn't respond, he mumbled something and squeezed my knee as he spoke. "Then it's a plan." Later that night he'd be lying next to me, naked, one hand sliding across the sheets.

I'm about to tell Sammy we're heading back to the Callihans' when a car horn blows, startling me to my feet. It's George Gunnel in the mustard and white Ford pickup he won in a contest in the fall. *Shit.* Ever since he got that truck he's driven around Orgull seemingly non-stop, showing off the prize and bragging to anyone who'll listen. He pulls up at the edge of the park, rolls down the passenger window, and calls to us. "You boys oughtn't be out in this cold." I wave and he flutters a fat gloved hand, signaling us to the truck. George is a harmless middle-aged guy with a fat red nose, was a drinking buddy of Dad's. Lonely, though, since his only daughter left with her husband to live in Nashville. He probably has no good reason to be driving around Orgull in the dead of winter except for the hope he might come upon someone to talk to. I take Sammy's hand and walk to the truck where George has already rolled up the window and turned on his radio. It's Johnny Cash, though I don't yet recognize the song.

As we near the truck, I note the slush frozen in the wheel wells and the general dark splatter along the bottom edges. In a couple years, maybe even a year, salt from the roads will make rust. I wonder if it's worth it, George finding this temporary happiness in the form of a new truck that's certainly already rotting. Isn't it better, safer, to just buckle in the hurt, stay off the icy, salted roads, and keep the truck in the garage until spring?

I remember the mess that was his old truck, that he hid booze in a toolbox lashed to the front of the rusty bed. He kept an ignition key inside the left wheel well. Two or three times Dad was called to pick him up at Max's, and if George couldn't come up with his keys, there was always the spare.

He gestures for us to open the passenger door, Johnny Cash's thick voice tumbling from the cab fat and full as logs from a flatbed. As usual, George is unshaven, and he wears his toboggan rolled up high on his shiny, red forehead. It's the kind of look I see so often in Orgull that I assume it's where I'm headed, too. "Get in," George says over the music. "Ride you up to your place?"

"We're going to the Callihans'," I say, trying not to sound nervous. George thinks for a moment and then nods another invitation. Sammy is cold and as conflicted as me, but I have unfinished business and I need to get to Mark. This will be faster. So I hoist Sammy into the warm cab and climb in behind. The passenger window is scraped clean, but George has only bothered to take care of his side of the windshield so that everything in front of me is an icy blur.

"Wagon's ho!" George says with a sincere eagerness-to-please in his voice. I notice a black-on-red Reagan bumper sticker lying on the dashboard. I'm guessing he can't quite bring himself to paste it to his new truck even though in the corner it says "easily removed with gasoline."

Sammy and I are doing the very thing they taught me in elementary school not to do. They showed us a film about dangerous situations to avoid. *Pet the barking dog that looks friendly?* A red Stop sign flashed on the screen as the answer. STOP! *Accept popcorn from the adult who randomly takes the seat next to you at the movies?* STOP! *Accept a ride home from the nice middle-aged man in the wood-paneled station wagon?* STOP! When I told Mom about the movie, she was nonplussed. "Little man," she said, "those kinds of things only happen in the city."

She was right. I don't know what it's like anywhere else, but Orgull is the kind of place where two boys can climb into the truck of a man we casually know on the simple offer of a ride home, at least til Cudge came along. I can think of other situations where a flashing STOP would be useful. Mom could have used a few of those in her own life. *Take off on your parents when you're seventeen?* STOP! *Let your life get so desperate and lonely you'll marry someone like Cudge?* STOP! If she *had* stopped, I wouldn't be in a truck with my little brother heading to the Callihans', trying to figure out just how I'm going to tell Mark about Cudge. And I wouldn't be the cause for the flashing STOP that I am now.

"That fella there," George says, accelerating and pointing at the radio as the tires search for traction, "he ought to be a national hero. Speaks for the common man, that's sure. Kinda guy that'd drive one of these." He slips off a glove with his teeth and pats the dashboard with a knotty, chewed-nail hand, as if anything else would be less sacred.

"Good ol' hippie-whomper is what this is. Find one of them on the side of the road with their thumb out and thump thump." He hops in his seat as if both sets of tires have run over someone. "You boys best take care you never get in with that crowd. All that dope and such."

I've never seen an actual hippie in person, and I doubt George has either. More and more I'm annoyed by the things people fear and want me to fear. George has no idea, so I'm happy this ride will be short, accompanied as it is with a strange mix of praise for Johnny Cash, hit-and-run fantasies, and a retelling of the TV movie George once saw in which Johnny Cash plays a Georgia sheriff investigating a murder. Getting to the Callihans' is creeping up on me as an even more urgent necessity. The thing I wanted most has happened. Thought I wanted. What now? There's a dead man at my house!

It almost doesn't matter that me and Sammy are in the truck, because George isn't looking for someone to talk with as much as talk to. He prattles on with a lot of gossip about people in town, including an old babysitter of mine who apparently doesn't keep her curtains closed. "I mean, the woman is walking around buck naked every time I drive by." He offers this as a complaint, but I'm wondering why he keeps driving in front of her house. Off-in-his-own-world as he is, I feel a kind of sympathy for this man who's desperate for any kind of company, even two boys who've hardly a thing in common with him.

Things change fast. Now me and Sammy are in George's truck and Dad is gone and Cudge too. It wasn't all that long ago Dad and George were sitting on the tailgate of his previous banger throwing back whatever George could sneak and Dad could afford. "Pretty sure this is it," George says as we pull in front of the Callihans'.

I don't respond because I see Mark's anxious face in the living room window. He'll want to know every last word that passed between me and Cudge. It will be a short conversation.

I thank George for the ride and just before we get out, I lock onto his keychain: a dangling bundle of faded, dyed red rabbits' feet, house keys, and miniature tools and pocket knives. I could use a rabbit foot. We hop out of the cab into the open air, which feels like stepping into a walk-in freezer. "Bet you're gonna be a real lady-killer," George says, pointing and winking at me. I'm stunned by the phrase, but I know I have to say something. When they find Cudge they'll ask George about me. I have to sound normal, like nothing's wrong, but I can't decide what normal is. "Johnny Cash is pretty cool," I say, and then, patting the door, "Nice truck. Try not to whomp too many hippies. Hard on the tires." I think that's done it, because George offers a wide, satisfied smile as I shut the door. As he drives away, the rectangle of the truck bed calls to me, is the unlit fuse I should not engage but will. Big enough for a body.

Sammy runs to the house and just as he reaches the door, Mark opens it and rushes toward me. He's not wearing a jacket, just a white t-shirt, skin cast nearly blue in the cold gray daylight. "What did he say?" Mark asks, brushing the hair from his face. He's fidgety and checks me over, looking for injury.

"You know how to drive?" I ask, and of course Mark gives me a strange look. I want to tell him what I saw, but Mrs. Callihan comes to the door and in an instant my courage has been sucked away.

"Mercy," she says loudly, hand at her hip. "Mark Michael Callihan. You boys, get out of the cold. She rubs her arms for emphasis even though she's changed into a sweater and an apron printed with the fat white face of a Snowy Owl which glares at me and Mark as we squeeze by her. "Just look at that," she says, pointing to the unbroken row of icicles hanging from the eve. "You two'll catch your death." Mark and I look at each other but say nothing. It's as if the world is playing one big joke on me. "No knife, Conner?" Mrs. Callihan asks. I stare at her blankly. "The one you were going to show us?"

I'm trying to think exactly what I told Sammy. "Cudge didn't think it was a good idea." As I say this, I realize there are now three people who will think I've just spoken with my stepfather.

"Seeing's how my son doesn't ecven have sense enough to put a coat on, he might be right." I want to talk to Mark but Mrs. Callihan strips me and Sammy of our coats and herds us into the kitchen for thick-slice baloney sandwiches which she serves to us at the counter. She makes the kind you see on TV commercials, everything fat and layered and too big for the bread slices.

"Can I eat this with cartoons?" Sammy asks, not waiting for an answer as he takes his plate into the living room.

I look at Mark to see if we can get away, but he shakes his head and shrugs an apology as we watch his mother begin making a birthday cake. My cake. The phone rings and we both jump. "Goodness," Mrs. Callihan says. "What's that all about?" She takes the receiver from the cradle, pinching it between her shoulder and ear. Holding a green mixing bowl in one arm, she immediately returns to stirring the contents as she silently mouths "It's Dad" to Mark.

As soon as his mom turns from us, Mark asks, "Is everything really okay?" When I offer a convincing "yes," a look of relief washes over him and he's suddenly playful. His bare toes pinch at the end of my sock, slowly pulling it off. He's trying to make me smile and normally I would, but it's not going to happen today. He has no idea. Mrs. Callihan follows up with a concerned expression, as if to ask her son *what's wrong with Conner?* I'm sure he thinks he knows exactly what. That Cudge and I have fought again.

"Okay," Mark whispers, "let's have a smoke." His red hair is a tangle over one eye, the other a tired blue gem doing its best to get me to buck up. I'm closer to him than anyone else I know except maybe Sammy, who's in the living room eating and giggling.

It's been this way with Mark and I since the Third grade. The Callihans had just moved to Orgull and he didn't want much to do with other kids at school when they started calling him Strawberry because of his freckles and that mop of red hair. After days of that, and seeing how it worked on him, I felt like I needed to do something. During lunch, I watched as a few boys wadded bits of napkin and tossed them at his hair. Mark did his best to ignore them, and even though I didn't really know him he looked at me from across the lunch room, his hair decorated like a Christmas tree, and something inside me made me leap up. Without thinking, tiny me crossed the room and punched one of the main bullies. I was sent to the Principal's office and it didn't do much for me with the other kids, aligning myself with Mark, but who needed them anyway?

He takes a last tug on my sock which brings it almost all the way off, and I crack. He's being oddly playful, free. He wins and a smile does come. "Cigarette," he pleads in a whisper. And then, softer, "Did you give him his finger?"

We must have smoked an entire pack last night. I don't think my lungs can take even one more puff. If I knew that this is the last time we'll be this tight, that soon the Callihans will move, I'd take him up on the cigarette and lean on his shoulder the entire time. But I don't know that in just days he'll be stripped from me. "Nah," I say. "It's too cold blowing smoke out the window."

In minutes, I'm hearing, but not listening to, Mrs. Callihan as she continues to talk to Mark's dad on the phone and pour cake batter into two round pans. I've always liked the sound of her voice because it's like drizzling butter, something that starts thin but eventually makes everything feel warm. It's love, which is a sappy thing to say, but it's true. It's what a mother should sound like. She's facing us at the kitchen counter, wearing that well-used owl apron and presiding over the tidy mess of her from-scratch recipe. The yellow phone cord stretches from the wall, hangs low, twisting and bobbing in the middle as if its own dance partner.

I can tell Mrs. Callihan wants everything just right for my birthday, which is why me and Sammy are here for the weekend, why our parents didn't make us go to school yesterday. It's like Mrs. Callihan stepped out of a women's magazine just to make me happy, so I have to keep pretending it's not the worst Saturday of my life.

I turn to Mark who's never stopped looking at me. He's making fish lips and mimes a cigarette drawn to his mouth, the same hand coming to rest on my shoulder.

"Fine," I say, taking his hand away, but not letting go when our grip is out of sight below the counter. It's time to tell him about Cudge. As if on cue, we hear Sammy's chittery laugh from the other room, and then Porky Pig ending a cartoon.

Mrs. Callihan startles me by setting the emptied mixing bowl in front of us and I let go of Mark. She hands me a spatula, and him a spoon. I can tell she's purposely left batter in the bowl. "Dad says he loves you," she tells Mark. "And the interview went well." Mr. Callihan is in Indianapolis applying for a job at a meat packing plant. His call couldn't have come at a worse time because I need Mark. He can't move away. He can't.

I guess Mrs. Callihan sees distress on my face. "Oh, sugar," she says, "I don't think she's going to call. Let's just enjoy ourselves." She points to the oven where my cake is baking. Happy birthday to me. She thinks I'm waiting to hear from my mother. Of course Mrs. Callihan would think this because that's what mothers do on their son's birthday. Okay, yes, and mothers bake their son a cake. It's not that Mom doesn't love me and Sammy, but she's just not built that way. Mrs. Callihan knows me and my mother well enough to make the assumption this is what's on my mind. *Poor kid, won't get a birthday call from his mother* she's thinking. She kisses her index finger and touches it to my nose. I could set the record straight, *well, no, actually I'm more worried about the fact you're going to think I killed my stepfather.*

I can't hold it in anymore and I start crying. More than that, I'm bawling. Mrs. Callihan rushes around the counter and holds me close. There are so many tears that I practically turn her messy apron into salt and chocolate. "Sugar," she says. "We love you." I feel Mark's hand on my back. It's a warm star, a maple leaf, a healing, and suddenly I understand what this is. I'm not crying because Cudge is dead and that I don't know what to do, and I'm not crying about my weak mother. I'm crying because I want a family.

4

I stay awhile in Mrs. Callihan's arms until I calm down and then Mark takes me by the elbow. "We're going to my room for a while," he says, pulling me forward. Neither of us wait for her response or look back, and once in the hallway, we both run for his door. He closes it so fast behind him that his Yoda calendar nearly swings off its nail, the furrowed green face tick-tocking above his head. "What the hell was all that?"

"I wish I lived here."

He nods with understanding. "Me too. For real." Then he walks to his dresser and turns on the radio. It's the middle of "Pretty Little Thing Called Love," but he shuts it off immediately. "Can't take that shit."

I sit on his bed and sigh because I have to tell him. "About Cudge," I begin. "You have to promise not to tell."

His eyes go wide with concern, and he's instantly just as anxious as I am. "What?"

My mouth opens without sound.

"What?" he asks again, only this time there's an urgency that breaks through.

I start slow, but I tell him exactly what I saw, the length of Cudge crumpled beneath frozen bathwater. Some details I didn't even know I saw flash from my memory. There was the great dug-out callous on the side of Cudge's big toe that he sometimes cut away with a pocket knife, and his hair, the comb over, an icy zig-zag over a pink-blue scalp.

"Did you touch him?" Mark asks, quickly sitting next to me. "You know for sure he wasn't breathing?" He's rising toward frantic.

It occurs to me that I've known what TV dead looks like but not real life dead until now. They wouldn't even let me view my own father. "Sammy doesn't know, but Cudge is dead," is all I can say.

Mark puts his head in his hands and then flops back on the mattress. I join him. "That's fucked up." He says this five or six times, each iteration sounding more breathless.

I take one hand away from his face. It's wet. Now *he's* begun to cry. I understand it's about me. It's like him to be that concerned. He always is, but this is my mess. And because he's the only other person who knows, I'm able, finally, to come to a boil. "The other thing is," I blurt, not holding back an ounce, "I think it was my mom. Only, she's off the hook because who was the last person to talk to Cudge?"

"Could be lots of people."

He doesn't get it. "Just one," I say. "And you, Sammy, and your mom know who."

I see in his face that now he understands. "Shit. So much fucking trouble." He's shaking.

I suddenly recognize my mistake in telling him anything, and not just now. It started when I had this stupid idea of setting Cudge up by breaking into houses and I asked for Mark's help. I hate being *that* kid but it's who I've become, the winner in a contest of who could be the bigger monster. "Cudge is *my* problem. Your job is to know nothing."

"But...."

"I know," I say. "It's too late for that, but you have to pretend." I hesitate, but I have to tell him the rest, offer what years later I will understand as one of a long line of impossibilities that right now ring so plausible in my ears. "I've got to get rid of Cudge's body. I'm going to steal George Gunnel's truck...."

Mark's mouth becomes a pink "O" of concern. "Are you nuts?" he says. "Are you fucking nuts? You're afraid of being accused of killing a guy, and dumping his body is your answer?" He stands, shakes a cigarette out of the bottom of a Godzilla piggy bank, and walks to the window. "I've gone along, Conner, but this...." He takes a drag on his cigarette and blows the smoke out the cracked open window. A beam of cold strikes me as he continues. "This is bad. You have to stay away from that house or it's going to be worse." He invites me over by extending the cigarette, insists. When I take it and inhale the warm smoke, he slides the window back open. "It wasn't you," he says as I exhale. It's a statement of disbelief or a question.

"It wasn't," I say, handing back the cigarette and returning to the bed. I don't say somebody beat me to it. I have enough to worry about without Mark thinking I've killed Cudge, though this morning that's precisely what I set out to do. I need the Callihans. I need Mark. "I can't call the sheriff. You know that, right?"

He hesitates. "I was going to say. You could. You're innocent."

"What if Mom isn't?"

Mark shakes his head. "You really think your mother had something to do with this? Man, if I thought it would work, I'd say we should just get on our bikes and ride out of this fucked up town." This is the Mark only I know.

When I'm married and in my thirties, I will look back and have no idea why I thought this was possible, but I'm out with it. "I'm going back tonight, Mark. I'm getting Cudge's body out of that house."

He flies to the bed. "Are you crazy?" All I can offer is a sigh because maybe the answer is *yes*. It's confusing. If I don't do something about the body tonight, tomorrow we'll go home after mass. I know that. And Mom will be home shortly after. And then what? I wouldn't put it past her to accuse me. I'm not walking into that, not when I'm a step ahead. In the meantime, there will be cake and candles, and from the aroma filling the house right now, fried chicken. Two very different homes. "I don't have a choice," I finally say. "I've got to get him out of there."

"Man, Conner, you aren't thinking. How tall is Cudge: six something?"

"Six-eight"

"And you're going to do what with that?"

"I'll figure it out. I'll get George's truck and...."

Mark places his hand flat on my chest. "You'll make it worse. You can't move a dead body. You can't steal a truck. And why would you do that anyway? You've got Cudge's van right there." As he says this, Mark brings his hand to his mouth as if he could shovel that suggestion back in. "Shit."

Months of lying and stealing have prepared me for a steady moment. I look at Mark, and it takes no effort to say, calmly, "Help me." When I'm married and have a daughter, I'll pray that she'll never be as desperate and naïve. And if she is, I'll hope she has a Mark.

He doesn't respond but we both know his answer. Reluctantly, he scooches over and pushes me back on the bed, laying his head on my belly and negotiating my ribs until he's comfortable. We calm. "*Maybe* two of us could," he says. "I can't believe this." We stare at the ceiling where he's pinned a constellation of photos of shirtless athletes torn from the pages of magazines. His parents are sweet but blind. "I'm sorry, man," he says, softly.

"For what?"

"All this shit you've been going through."

"I don't look like any of them," I say, trying to change the subject at least for a moment.

"What do you mean?"

"Up there. The guys."

"No," Mark half laughs. "Not at fucking all. But they didn't look like that when they were fourteen either."

"Oh, yeah," I say as if it's something I already know, and then, "So, Cudge's van, we could—"

"Let's not get to that yet." Mark checks the door, then rolls over and looks at me directly. We both have things we want to say and not hear.

"Cudge," I say, "there were times—"

Mark doesn't let me finish. "No," he says, raising a finger parent-like, as if to say "not another fucking word." He returns to his original position, head resting on my torso. Not even Mom can get away with shushing me, but somehow Mark can.

He takes my hand and I close my eyes. It reminds me, the warmth of his palm, of when this began. When my father drowned himself a couple years ago, more than anyone, Mark helped me through. We shared, I guess, that first kiss.

There was no viewing. I know now that Dad's face was too torn up, but Mom insisted on a visitation, insisted that me and Sammy be by her side for the entire six hours. It was as if she wanted the world to prove to her that the three of us mattered. A quarter of a day sitting next to a closed casket. The only thing that kept me from breaking down entirely was knowing the Callihans were coming, that Mark was coming.

Dad's casket was plain looking, dark wood with brass handles, and bulky. It wasn't the one he'd be buried in. We couldn't afford it. I remember that the size of the casket made me feel very small, as if I were sitting next to Noah's ark.

Not many people came to the visitation, friends of Mom and Dad's and a few of his relatives, all of them not knowing what to say to me and Sammy, so they pretty much offered a version of "you boys holding up?" Pats to the cheeks. Softly touched shoulders. I could stand it, but I felt bad for Sammy who sat teary-eyed and stiff in a too-big blue suit and fat black tie that looked like an open-jawed snake going after his tiny neck. He was a very sad ventriloquist's dummy waiting to be filled with words. And then, after hours of silence, when Mom stepped out of the room to smoke a cigarette, he asked, "Is Daddy really in there?" We were alone.

"He is."

Sammy pulled his tie away from his neck and thought for a moment. "It's not too dark?"

I looked around the room with its white-on-blue felted wallpaper. "It's fine," I said.

"No." Sammy pointed at the casket. "Inside."

I suddenly understood. My brother didn't know what dead meant. I wanted our mother to walk through the door right then but no such luck. "You keep your eyes closed in there," I said. "It's like sleeping."

"When will he wake up?"

"I said it's *like* sleeping, Sammy. He's not going to."

Sammy stared into his lap and spoke softly. "Ever?"

I started to cry. Dad was gone. "Ever," I said. Sammy looked at me with sad eyes but I saw he was still processing the finality I was trying to express. I understood the confusion. Years earlier, when my kindergarten teacher passed away, I remembered a scene from *Journey Back to*

Oz when Dorothy revives Pumpkinhead with one of her tears. It didn't work for me.

Mom walked back in on one crying son and another who was just beginning to understand he'd never see his father again. "Fix your tie, sweetums," she told Sammy, as if she didn't notice our grief. "We've got visitors." Seconds behind her was Mark and his parents.

I patted my wet cheeks with a tissue and shoved it in my pocket, not wanting Mark to see me like that. We'd been friends, but something different was happening inside me just then. I'd begun thinking about him a lot, wanted to be near him, got jealous when I saw him hanging around kids without me. He stood out in a crowd because of that bright red hair, pale skin and peach-blushed cheeks. There were times, when I was alone in my room, I lay on the bed and conjured elaborate scenarios in which Mark stumbled into me on the stairs, on the school lawn, in the cafeteria at school; and in each we fell into some form of embrace. Sometimes, when we sat on the couch together, watching TV, I convinced myself that his occasional brush of the knee was intentional. It wasn't something I could ask about; it wasn't even something I was supposed to feel. I knew that much.

When Mark and his parents approached us at the funeral home, Mom turned and accepted a hug from Mr. Callihan, who wore a shiny brown suit and a tie the same aqua as his wife's neck scarf. In a full embrace from Mrs. Callihan, Mom began to cry, as she had each time someone new came in. Me and Sammy stood as well, with Mark directly in front of us as his mother gave Sammy a puppet wave, then put her hand on my cheek. "Ahh, sweetie," she said. "It's hard, I know, but it's going to be okay." I nodded. Mrs. Callihan had a reassuring quality about her that my mother could never manufacture, and I doubt she ever tried. Mrs. Callihan turned and took Mom's hand, both of them walking to Dad's casket, Mr. Callihan right behind.

Mark stayed with me and Sammy. I hadn't seen him in almost a week, and even though it was a difficult day, I found a smile in myself. Mark's hair, usually an unruly red mop, was combed down, and he wore a white long-sleeved shirt with a tie nearly identical to his father's.

"Hey," Mark said.

Me and Sammy replied almost simultaneously. "Hey."

"Can you go outside for a minute?"

I looked at our parents but they were standing at the casket as Mom wound down her tears. "I guess it's okay," I said. "You coming, Sammy?" He shrugged and shook his head no, which is what I hoped for.

Outside, Mark led me to the rear of the funeral home and ducked in between two large boxwoods. Confined by the shrubs the two of us stood face to face, and even though we'd been alone many times, something about this made me nervous, but not in a way I'd felt before. This was anticipation. "I just wanted to say," Mark began, but he cut himself off, and looked down, extending his freckled hand.

I hoped that what I was about to do was what was being requested, so I slowly reached out and took Mark's hand. We were nearly the same age, but his hand was larger and more substantial than my own, warm. The pair of us looked into each other's eyes for a few seconds, his a deeper blue than I'd recognized before.

"I'm really sorry about your Pop," Mark said.

"I can't believe he did it." Then I said something that surprised me. "Fuck him."

Mark held my hand more firmly. "Mom said when we talked I should make sure you aren't blaming yourself. Kind of stupid, I know, but I promised I'd check." His hand felt strong. It might have been the first time I felt such unity with someone, even Sammy and Dad.

"It does kind of make me wonder," I told him, "why we weren't good enough to stick around for." Mom had been small comfort on that point. The fact was, lost in her own confused grief, she said very little to us. Just days after the funeral, she would give me and Sammy the chore of putting nearly all of Dad's clothes in plastic bags and dragging them out to the porch where a woman we didn't know came to pick them up. I remember the fat white cluster of shining plastic sitting there, patient blobs of discardable memory. When I joined these with one final bag filled with Dad's sweaters, it sat upright for a moment, then rolled to its side as if falling from despair. "I know Dad loved us," I said. "But not enough."

Mark nodded like he understood, looked to the ground, then back up at me. "Um," he said, "there's something...." Instead of finishing, he waited a second and then leaned over and kissed me on the cheek. A start shot through me, but it wasn't fear, and I know I was supposed to be grieving, but all of that fell away. There was no dead father who was drowning long before he leapt, no bereft mother or profoundly confused brother. This was something I hadn't felt before, something deep and whole and it gave me permission to pull Mark toward me and sink into his shoulder. Finally, someone.

I return to the men on Mark's ceiling and my eyes lock on the oddity of a broad-shouldered silhouette. We're quiet for a while, figuring out what's next. I put my hand on his soft red hair. I don't know it, but this is the last time he and will be alone together in his room.

That's what Cudge looked like today," I say. "Hercules." I point at the photo that looks less to me like a mythological hero than the chalk outline at a crime scene, white lines tracing the periphery of the muscled figure. I've seen it dozens of times in old movies, the police standing over the vacant figure, throwing out theories, sometimes a teary-eyed woman, everyone playing their part. That's what the bathroom is. A crime scene. I have a role in this production but I stepped in too early and I didn't see it through. I'm *supposed* to find Cudge. I'm *supposed* to call the police. I'm supposed to understand it's my way out; our way out. But I do not trust my mother. I'm lost in a sea of changing, shifting theories.

Mark turns his ear to my torso, the side of his face a distinct oval of warmth. "Your heart is beating a mile a minute, Conner."

"Yeah," I say. "Tomorrow morning Mom is going to be pissed."

5

Mrs. Callihan turns in early, so a little after ten, me and Mark bundle up and jump out of his bedroom window. We're good at this now. These past months we've run off in the middle of the night to break into a bunch of houses. We go the back way, through the woods, the leafless trees allowing in just enough moon. The air is still, making our winding trek among the blue-black trunks an unusually silent experience. I hear Mark's steps behind me, but nothing else. No clacking of branches nor whisper of breeze. Above, the bright three-quarter moon seems to look up and away from us. Nothing to see here. Permission.

Boys do ridiculous things. They jump off balconies into pools, get drunk too young and drive their parents' cars through the woods where there are no roads, sneak calves into grocery stores, bat mailboxes off their posts. Boys do ridiculous things that seem to them possible but not ridiculous. What we are about to do is possible.

When we reach the back of my house, we find a familiar sight, the metallic night-glow of clapboard interrupted by four black rectangles. At the corner sits Cudge's van, ready for loading. His prized Barracuda is parked in front of the van so that the car can't be backed out. Cudge's anti-theft system. Through the trees I make sure to observe that all our neighbors are down for the night. "This is freakin' me out," Mark says, teeth clacking. He's bunched up close to me. Bundled as we are, it feels like we're two marshmallows pressing together.

"We've done this before," I say. "And at least this time I have a key."

"Man, Conner," he says, shaking his head. "We never stole a fucking *body*."

I have no idea if this is going to work, but what choice is there?

We have to haul Cudge out of the bathtub and get him down the stairs and into the van. Then we have to ditch it or...? Cudge is tall, pudge-lanky, and frozen solid for all I know. "The river," I say. "We're past the dam. He'll chunk up who knows how many miles from here in a bunch of driftwood. Nobody's going to be out on the water this time of year except maybe barges, and they aren't looking for bodies on the riverbank."

"I hate this," Mark sighs, "but you're probably right about getting him out of there." Without another word, he stands and dashes for the house, becomes a dark flail that I'm compelled to follow. The moon feels like it's hovering inches over my shoulder, and by the time I reach Mark at the house, seconds later, I'm so scared it's as if we've run through all out daylight and sirens. At least this time won't be like the other houses, no jimmying open a window and hoisting ourselves up and in. This time there's a key and a back door. "Fuck," Mark whispers. "We really doing this?"

"Have to." I put the key in the lock and push slowly, pausing when the hinges squeak. But then it dawns on me. There's no reason for us to tip toe in. At this point nothing is going to wake Cudge. The kitchen is dark and silent except for cubes of moonlight and water trickling from the faucet. I feel Mark's hand on my back as we walk to the stairs where we pause in the dark. The sound from the bathroom, more dripping water, marches through us. Slow bullets. The house is absolutely freezing, feels heavy. "You okay?" I ask. Mark is trembling.

"What's with all the water," is all he manages.

"I didn't want the pipes to freeze."

"You found a dead body in your bathtub and you were worrying about pipes?"

I take out my flashlight and shine it on the stairs. "You ready? It's really bad. Mark nods but I'm not convinced. He needs preparing. "Ice. It's all over the floor up there. And Cudge is in bad shape." Maybe it's because I know what we are about to see, but I'm surprisingly calm, enough so that I'm thinking about just exactly how all this is going to work. At first I thought we'd drag Cudge down the stairs, but why go to that trouble? And we'd leave a trail of ice. The window is a better option; heave him out. What difference does it make now? It'll take two of us, probably, but then it's nothing to get Cudge's body into the back of the van.

I tell Mark my new plan, window, van, back to his house.

"That's fucking heinous," he says.

This is not how I want to hear Mark describe what we're doing. I shut off the flashlight so that, other than moonlight, me and Mark are in darkness. "Evil is up there," I say, pointing. "That man is evil. If we don't do this there's a whole new mess in front of me. My life will never be normal." It's a few seconds of me and Mark saying nothing, just looking into each other's eyes. The fact he's taller than me by a few inches is partially why I feel safe around him. But right now, it's me who's strong, and I feel this role reversal palpably. There's a frozen monster upstairs, but I take a moment and gently pull Mark into me. "We're this close to being done, and, and...I love you."

Any other time that last part would be a mind fuck, something two Kentucky boys would never say to each other. But just now it feels like the *only* thing to say.

"Man, that's another mess we'll have to figure out. The love thing. Fuck." He's so bundled up, coat, scarf and gloves, that I struggle to detect a Mark at the core, though I feel his warm breath as he sighs and lets go of me. No words are required. He doesn't want to go upstairs.

"Stay here," I say. In this light, we're ghosts. I pad up the steps and stop when I hear a crackle. "What the hell is that?" Mark whispers.

"The floor," I call back a little louder than I intend. "Ice." Cudge is just as I left him, and when I shine the light in his face, it's not like the first time. He's solid.... "Okay," I say to myself. The portion of Cudge's head above the ice is a creamy blue and the curved strands of his comb over are frozen rat tails. He looks ancient, like a creature half-excavated. I know I should feel shocked, standing in front of his dead body, and maybe it says something awful about me. But the thing is, it's different when you're prepared and you *want* the person dead.

Standing next to the tub, I shine the light across my project. The ice seems thicker than this morning, enough so that Cudge's body is a smear beneath the surface. The Phoenix tattoo on his leg looks dulled, nearly extinguished. This is something I hadn't thought of, it's not just a body. He's encased. As if I was a thread pulled from a sweater, I feel a sudden unraveling. I shine the light where Cudge's leg emerges from the ice. It's got him clamped, but I'm not sure the entire tub is frozen. I'm afraid to touch him, to alter a single thing unless I'm going all the way.

I take Cudge in again, the grotesque angles. If he's stiff as a board, there's no way to get him out of the window, and anyway, all the ice everywhere. I didn't think about that part, the aftermath. It's too much. *Fuck.* I head for the door, but turn and take a last look at Cudge without light. His leg is a thick black branch reaching from the tub. *What was I thinking?*

I race back down to Mark. "It's not going to work."

His face is cast in a geometry of grays, he looks at me like this is what he expected all along, or maybe it's relief. "What's plan B?"

"Mom's in charge of plan B. Our part is to go home and pretend we weren't here."

"It's better that way."

He doesn't get it. "Unless she blames it on me."

Outside, I pause next to the van which, in the winter darkness, looks to me like an outsized, blue brick. The Barracuda sits just in front. a big dark fish sitting next to a big blue brick. "When did you learn to drive that?" Mark whispers.

"I can't. It's a stick."

"You're kidding. You expected *me* to drive? I can't drive a stick."

"But you said your dad was teaching you."

"In *Mom's* car."

"Holy shit," I say, looking back at the house. What have we just averted? I'm imagining the broken wreck of Cudge's body on the ground beneath the open window. And then what?

When we get to the edge of the woods behind the house, Mark puts his hand on my shoulder. "The finger. You sure you got that hid?"

"It's in the garage where nobody can find it, but why does that matter? There's an entire fucking body in our bathroom."

Mark shakes his head like he can't believe he's just asked this question. "I guess I want to tell you, I mean, in case anything happens, I'm glad we know each other." I begin to respond but he plows through. "And I know at school I don't pay much attention to you, which is shitty, but if I did—"

"—the other kids would think you were a fag just like me." It hurts to say this out loud but we have both lived this unspoken rule.

He takes me by both shoulders and looks at me full on. "I'm sorry," he says.

"It's where we live."

For a moment we've removed ourselves to a place we don't think exists, some river island perhaps, where boys can love each other and still not be far from home. But, Mark brings us back. Pointing to the house and then to the garage, he says, "A dead guy up there, and part of the same dead guy over there. Man, this is one fucked up piece of property."

This is my first love story, which I will understand later but can never speak of, at least not for years. I want a cartoon calendar, pages, months tearing away in explosive wind, years passing, time sped toward that day when I can say the only thing that mattered to me was Mark.

6

Mass takes forever, and me and Mark can barely keep our eyes open. I'm eager to get home and get this over with. Cudge is waiting, dead, and I have to "find" him. We're not Catholic. We're nothing, but the Callihans are pretty devout, and so me and Sammy sit through all this getting up and kneeling down, the weird group prayers, the communion we're not allowed to take, and the overly sincere soprano who sings past the piano and guitar. The entire time, an alabaster Jesus on the cross looms over me, head hanging in what, sadness? Resignation? I can't stop looking at him, especially at his closed eyes which appear so lightly shut they could blink open at any moment. I know it can't happen but the thought unnerves me. In the past 24 hours I've seen a dead man twice, but it's a statue of Jesus on the Cross that gets under my skin.

Mark elbows me. He's wearing a short sleeved white button up with an awkwardly knotted green tie. Most Sundays he's one of the altar boys, but he's taken this sleepover weekend off, which explains the outfit. I'm guessing he never wears a tie under the robe. Sammy and me have gotten away with just button ups. "What are you staring at," Mark whispers in my ear.

"The Jesus," I whisper back. "That must've really hurt."

"That's when he's already dead."

I look again toward the crucifix, only I can't see Jesus any longer because now it's Cudge's naked body that comes forward, the sprawled, frozen length of it waiting for me at home. There will be no ascension, no rolling away of a stone. I imagine the sound of ice cracking beneath my feet on the floorboards and the ticka ticka ticka of our rotary when I call the police.

The young, black-haired priest stands and raises both hands, his simple white and green trimmed robe a thick, loopy dangle surrounding him as if he's an extinguished candle. "The Mass is ended," he says. "Go in peace."

I look at Mark who understands the impossibility of the command. He knows what's next for me. There's no turning back. Mrs. Callihan stands with Sammy at the end of the pew waving me and Mark to go ahead of her. She's wearing a yellow pant suit with a gold butterfly broach and her hair is done in a perfect crown of strawberry braid. As I pass, she puts her hand on my shoulder and walks just behind me, but close enough that I feel the wholeness of her presence. The priest had spoken about Jesus, Mary and Joseph. He called them an "improbable little family meant for big things." Mark walks in front of me, his curly red hair an unruly failure of the taming his mother insisted on before we left, and then, in a happy sigh, resigned to. Mr. Callihan will be home soon, and I sense how eager Mark and his mother are to see him. I feel him so close, Mark, and Mrs. Callihan so close as well, and why can't I have this? As I walk to the back of the church, Mary watching me from above, locked in her stained-glass perch, the priest shaking the hands of his parishioners, I'm only asking, isn't there something better in store for me, and how is it that these fourteen years of mine have amounted to a third rendezvous with the body of my dead stepfather?

It takes a while for us to get out of the parking lot, longer than I planned and I'm getting antsy, but Mrs. Callihan knows a lot of people and she's involved with her church. Easter season will require the annual cleaning and decoration, a family whose father died needs help with a memorial dinner, and where is Mr. Callihan today?

When we're finally on the road, if I have a schedule, I figure I'm an hour behind. On the drive to our house, I'm mainly quiet, barely hearing Mrs. Callihan's recounting of the homily about the sacrifices of the Holy Family. The irony of it is, as she does this, I'm ticking off the list of things I'm about to do: keep Sammy downstairs; find Cudge in the bathroom… again; manufacture surprise and run down stairs; call the sheriff; wait for Mom to say "good job" or "what have you done?"

"Don't you think, Conner?" Mrs. Callihan says. Mark pokes me. I've no idea what she's asked me.

"I'm sorry," I say, "I was daydreaming."

Sammy is sitting up front and I can barely see the top of his head. He cranes his face upward so I can hear. "She was talking about how Mary was a great mom."

"I mean," Mrs. Callihan says as we slow down near the end of our driveway, "to raise a perfect son, she'd have to be." When we stop, all four of us instinctively look up the gravel driveway to the house as if there'll be some sort of greeting. We should know better. It just sits there, cold and quiet. "Okay, sweet ones," she says. "You're home." She's looking at me in the rearview mirror. I'm sitting next to Mark, resisting the urge to hug him. "Hope you had a nice birthday, Conner. I guess your Mom will be home soon." Isolated in their reflection, I recognize Mark's blue eyes in hers.

"It was," I say, and I have to apologize. "I forgot the shirt you gave me."

She smiles. "I'm sure you'll be over soon. You and Mark are practically brothers." She has no idea.

"Let's go, Conner," Sammy whines. "It's cold." He's already out of the car holding the white trash bag containing his clothes and pillow. With his plump, brown winter garb he looks like an oversized chocolate chip.

I'm not sure what to say, so I thank Mrs. Callihan and slide out of the car into the ice-cold air, but before the door is closed, something slips out. "I love you guys," I say.

Mrs. Callihan smiles. "Sugar," she says, "we love you too," and Mark adds "Yeah."

As if in replay, and with the cold surprisingly ignored, Sammy checks our empty mailbox then picks up a stick and runs off to retrieve his mutilated raccoon. I'm happy enough to see him forget the cold for the moment because I feel a little dazed as I approach the house. Why was I so convinced I found a way to get Cudge out of our lives? This moment is my fault, though Mom was no help, and it's all I can do to remind myself there are reasons for that. She's going to be home pretty soon, so I have to find Cudge and call the police because who knows how she'll react. I walk again to the front door. At least there'll be no Cudge storming down the stairs. We haven't gotten along this well in months.

Cudge made a mistake. He didn't like it, but he'd agreed to let Mom go to Cincinnati for the weekend to visit, she said, a friend in the hospital. I have no doubt he said yes because it'd be just him, me, and Sammy in the house. But Cudge threw a fit when Mom told him he'd be alone for the weekend. "Can't fucking believe you're taking off on your son's birthday weekend," Cudge said when she was at the door. "Some fucking mother you are." I felt the whole heap of our lives falling in my lap when she looked back at me walking down the porch steps, telling me with a glance *Happy Birthday son. Here's your chance.* Maybe I can't read her as well as I think. Just before the door closed, Cudge told us not to be surprised if the house was burned to the ground when all of us got back.

I watch Mrs. Callihan's car turning the corner at the end of the street, the pink dot of Mark's face looking back at me. If I had my preferences, we would have stayed with the Callihan's tonight and just gone to school Monday morning from there, let Mom finish what she started. But, for this all to work out, I am resigned to the job in front of me.

This time I don't bother with caution. I walk straight to the front door without caring how loud my footsteps are. A cold wind follows me inside, and my eyes lock on my destination, upstairs. I flunk down my trash bag and pillow and get one foot on the first stair and then gravel is popping on the driveway. Back at the front door in a flash, I crack it open, hoping it's Mrs. Callihan, but knowing even before my eyes confirm that it's Mom. Sammy is already at the car's side jumping up and down and looking like a ground hog on its back legs. Mom steps out of the car and flips newly bleached blonde hair behind both shoulders. I've never seen it this color or this straight. I've never seen the crisp orange winter coat she's wearing either. It hangs past her knees covering the tops of a pair of shiny black boots. I'm trying to get Cudge's body out of the house and she's getting a makeover?

I meet her and Sammy at the door and she must detect some form of terror in my expression because she slings her arm in front of my brother like he's in a passenger seat and she's slamming on the breaks. "Go get mommy's overnight bag," she tells him. "I brought you boys a surprise." Once he leaps off the porch, Mom takes a step closer. "What's wrong?"

I'm not convinced but I go along and though I'm cautious, I don't mince words. "Cudge is upstairs in the bathtub," I say. "He's dead." She surprises me as being genuinely startled, and then taps her teeth with the nail of an index finger, which I see, like all of her nails, is newly manicured, pink with a shiny white tip.

She looks past me immediately, jaw tightening and nostrils flared. "That son-of-a-bitch" she says. "Keep your brother down here." She brushes by me and jogs upstairs. Her footsteps abruptly halt and I don't have to guess why. She's standing, as I was, in front of the corpse of her dead husband, though I'm suspicious if it's really a sight she's seeing for the first time. The door closes behind me, Sammy with Mom's bag. "Not nice, little man," she calls, and then she's slowly thudding down the steps, one hand on the rail, the other holding her coat. Something's happened to her over the weekend. I don't recognize anything she's wearing from the bright orange A-line skirt, to the white ruffly blouse that exposes her arms to the shoulder. If she wasn't my mother I'd think she was pretty. "Why would you do that?" she says, looking directly at me.

For a moment I'm confused, but I catch Sammy out of the corner of my eye and I'm not falling for anything she says. "What are you going to do?"

"Beat your little ass, is what."

"What'd you do, Conner?" Sammy asks, and without waiting for an answer he begs Mom for his promised surprise.

"Sure, sweetums," Mom says.

That's when I notice it. The thermostat is back on the wall. Mom's taken off her coat. The house is cool, but not cold. I don't hear the faucet running.

Mom glides down the remaining steps in her new hair and clothes, crossing over to me as if she's decided she's a movie star. She turns to my brother, "Can you give Conner and me a minute? Dig around in my bag if you want your surprise, but in the kitchen." When he's gone, she turns to me less calmly and speaks in a quiet hiss. "What the hell was that?"

I'm stunned. Our timing is off but I hoped I'd gotten close to what she'd wanted. "I haven't called the sheriff yet."

"About what?"

Now we're in a stalemate so I put it right to her, pointing above me to emphasize her responsibility. "About Cudge?"

She looks at me with angry concern. "Little man, are you one can shy of a six pack or is this some stupid game?" She checks that her hair remains behind her shoulders, and I don't know what to make of this new vanity. "Cudge isn't up there and I don't appreciate your little joke. I liked to've fainted."

I'm half convinced. Enough that I run upstairs where I find the bathroom, not sparkling clean, but clean. A pair of Cudge's white underwear sit on the floor as if he's just stepped out of them, and the window is closed, as is the bathroom cabinet, and most importantly, the bathtub is empty. I go to my bedroom and look out the window, my breath fogging the glass. Cudge's Barracuda is where it should be but the spot where his van was is merely an empty rectangle, a gray rash in the frozen ground.

I sit on my bed, trying to make sense of what's happening. What's been set in motion and where along the way have I missed something? It's like someone's cut out random frames from the movie of my life. Was it really just a month ago when Mom gave me the knife? I'd found her sitting on our front steps smoking a cigarette. We were enjoying a few days of relatively warm weather for winter so she was wearing jeans, a white T-shirt, and Dad's brown, stretched out deer head sweater, the only piece of clothing of his she kept. This meant she didn't expect Cudge home anytime soon. I sat down next to her and she did something unexpected; she passed me the cigarette. I must have looked confused. "What?" she said, "you think I can't smell it on you?" I was hesitant, but I took a drag as she asked me the next question. "What's your brand?"

"Whatever I can get my hands on."

"I used to like those too," she said, laughing to herself. I couldn't recall the last time I'd seen her this relaxed.

"What's up? You look like you're planning a picnic."

She surveyed the yard. January, gray and uncomfortably cold looking despite the decent weather. "Your dad always wanted to put in a real lawn." Without the leaves on the trees and shrubs, our street opens up, the neighboring houses on all sides more visible. Dad had a lot of plans he didn't see through, I thought, and one he did but shouldn't have, drowning himself in the river. Mom stared at the end of her cigarette. "A lot of things could have been different, ya know, little man?"

"Why'd he do it?"

Mom nodded to herself. "Just didn't want to be the man of the house anymore." She flicked the half-finished cigarette onto the gravel drive, a sinew of white smoke curling upward. "I thank the lord I had you around, little man, or I wouldn't have gotten through it. You'll make a good daddy someday."

It was a rare moment of kindness, and I knew enough to be wary. "Hell no," I said, "I'm never having kids."

She patted my knee. "Sure you will. Wife. Nice family. If anyone's meant to be the man of the house, it's you." I couldn't think of the future that way. I could think of Mark, and me and him, in any given hour, but beyond that, I couldn't forecast much of my life. "No doubt in my mind," she continued. "I see how you handle Cudge."

If I didn't exactly freeze on the outside, I was seized up on the inside. "What are you talking about?"

"Sometimes he seems afraid of you, little man. That says something right there."

I shook my head slowly. She was clueless. "How about one of those cigarettes?" She hesitated as I held out my hand. "Man of the house?"

"Getting there," she said, sliding the pack and lighter next to me. "Won't be long." She stood and told me she'd be right back. She had something for me.

Is this really how it starts, I wondered, the whole man of the house business? One day your mother just pops off with a prediction and you're anointed? You come home to find her in a strangely wistful mood. She acts like a teacher who's decided you have a kind of innate talent and on the basis of that she predicts what a bright future you have. You know enough to keep your mouth shut. that the whole thing's a sham. She got the exams mixed up.

In this case, Mom returned with her version of an early diploma. "Cudge won't be home for a while, so now's a good time," she said, sitting next to me. She held a brown paper sack a little larger than the kind for lunches. "Snuck some money out of the stash," she said, handing the bag to me. "Didn't make sense to wrap it."

Was she really giving me a sack of money? I perched my cigarette on the edge of the step where there were dozens of burn marks from where Cudge and Mom did the exact same thing. The sack was too heavy to be cash, I thought, and then I knew what was inside before I pulled it out, the bowie knife I'd asked for, a Case XX Kodiak Hunter. The white box was illustrated with the namesake golden bear standing on his hind legs, teeth bared. Inside, the knife was mounted against a blood red interior with white lettering. I removed it from the box. The blade itself was stamped with an image of another Kodiak bear, this one gleaming on all fours with a snarl equally fierce as the one on the lid. It was attached to a sturdy brown stag horn handle, tannish-white at both ends where it'd been carved down.

"You have to find a good place to hide it, and you can't tell Cudge," Mom said. She held out her palm in request, and I handed her the knife. "Pretty." A streak of refracted light blazed across her face as she turned the blade from side to side and examined it closely. Then, waking herself as if from a trance, she shook her head and held the knife out to me. "Really, Cudge can't know about this thing," she reminded me.

Like I would tell him or leave it lying around, I thought. But I was confused. "Why all the sudden?"

Mom snatched up what remained of my cigarette and stood, leaning on a post supporting the stair rail. She drew one of her arms across her midsection where she rested her other elbow. "Been thinking about it, little man. It's time." She wasn't looking at me. Her eyes were focused somewhere off in the barren trees. "Like we were saying, man of the house. This'll get you a bit further down the road."

I stared at the knife, not believing I was actually holding this thing I'd prized for so long. I couldn't imagine where she got the money. What was her "stash?"

She tossed away the cigarette near where she'd thrown the first, where the gravel was a sprawling cemetery of butts. Her eyes narrowed and she brought her hands together up to her chin like someone might if they were about to pray. Dad's sweater sagged from her arms. "It's not a toy, little man," she said. "It has a purpose. I don't want to see your initials carved all over town. There are laws." Her voice grew low and moody. "I expect when you have occasion to use it, you'll know what you're doing." Then she walked toward me and tussled my hair, smiling. "Guess they'd go easy on you if you did something stupid." She was looking directly into my eyes and I saw in them a command and a get-out-of- jail-free card. From that moment I knew I was supposed to kill Cudge.

I'd wanted that knife ever since I walked into Knives-Ammo with Dad and I saw it in the glass case. I wanted it not because I had any particular need for it, but because I was a boy and it looked cool. *I* would look cool possessing it, walking around with it in the brown leather case attached to my belt. And with something like that, maybe some of those morons at school would leave me alone. The longer I didn't have it, the more important it grew in my mind, and when I walked by Knives-Ammo I could almost feel it calling to me.

Then from out of the blue came the day when Mom gave me a cigarette and the knife. What "occasion" did she think a boy might man-ufacture for using such a gift? For a second, I considered the idea that maybe this was Mom pushing back against Cudge, taking a little control. She'd done something that would piss him off. A small, if secret, victory. But I knew better.

Regardless of what was true, or what I manufactured, there was the thing I thought she meant, that she could never say directly, and that's what stuck in my head. My body felt like a hot block of cement and I was held to the spot where I sat. The knife gleamed in my hand. My mother had put her faith in me and I hated her for it. I'd come up with fantastic schemes of my own to get rid of Cudge, and just then it felt as if life was asking me why I was dilly-dallying around. I put the knife back in its box and replaced the lid. The upright bear glared at me. The ferociousness I'd first seen in him now seemed cartoonish, hardly announced what was inside. Mom was right. I was not holding a toy. I was holding a weapon.

It occurs to me I don't actually know how Cudge was killed, but I'm guessing Mom does. When I get back downstairs she's in the kitchen having a cigarette at the table where I join her. "I never mailed the damn thing," she says, blowing smoke up toward the light. I know what she's referring to, the envelope containing Sammy's box tops that that were supposed to earn him a water rocket. He's running through the house with a new plastic spaceship, a Star Wars knock off. "Figured I owed him." She taps her finger on the table to get my attention. "And that was a fool ass practical joke back there." I don't say a word. It's her game but I can play as long as she can. She walks to the sink and runs water over the remainder of her cigarette. "Son-of-a-bitch knew I was coming home. Think he'd be more specific." She taps a torn open envelope on the counter and shakes her head, holds the scrap up, reading it with a scoff in her voice. "Back in a few."

"Let me see that," I say, and as the words come out of my mouth I realize she's won this round. She hands me the envelope and looks back at me as if I'm some sort of strange creature. It's Cudge's printing. Four words penciled in uneven block lettering.

"Then again," Mom says, sitting down, "s'pose neither of us gives two shits when he gets back." She smiles and holds her hand out for the envelope. "How was Mark's?"

"I *saw* Cudge in the bathtub," I say, and it comes out in a near growl.

Her chair flies back and hits the wall as she stands and leans over the table. "What the hell kind of game are you playing, little man?" We both hear Sammy running toward the kitchen, so she speaks tight and fast. "I don't appreciate any of this, and if you've done something stupid, your brother better not get hurt."

Sammy flies in with his spaceship. "What was that?" he asks, barely looking at either of us.

Easing back, Mom retrieves her chair and sits down. "Arm wrestling." It's a ridiculous response but Sammy pauses, looks at the two of us, and laughs.

"Mom won," I say. He laughs again then shoots us both with the imaginary lasers of his spaceship before telling Mom he's hungry. "There ain't no peanut butter and jelly in space," I tell him, which earns me another round of lasers before Mom tells him to wash his hands. He blasts off into the other room and to the upstairs where dead Cudge isn't.

"Want one?" Mom asks, dangling the polka dotted Wonder Bread bag of bread in my direction. "PB and J?" She seriously thinks what we need right now is a sandwich? The half full plastic bread bag sags in the air between us, the dots swaying in front of me as if my mother were a hypnotist. When I don't respond she plops it on the counter and crosses her arms. "Okay, Conner," she says sternly. "Enough. You're acting a little crazy. I know this isn't the best situation with Cudge, but I'm trying to figure it out. Until then we all just have to find a way to get along. Got it?" I can tell she doesn't really want a response, and I'm not certain what to say anyway. She crosses to the refrigerator and pauses, looking down at her clothes. "I've got get out of these," she says, and then, brightly, "You didn't say anything about the new duds."

"I noticed."

"It's a change," she says, crossing the room. Before she leaves, she pauses behind me and puts her hand on my shoulder. "Can't say I didn't half wish it was true. He'll be home in a little while. Do your best, little man."

Sitting alone in the kitchen I'm thinking, *I know what I saw.* At least I think I do. I close my eyes, and Cudge is there and he's dead but other versions of him appear as well and in those he's alive. I don't know how people go crazy but maybe this is it. It's a ridiculous thought, but what if in minutes Cudge walks through the front door with a new pack of cigarettes or six pack of beer, and if that happens how can I ever be sure if anything is real? I imagine Cudge reviving, struggling out of the icy water. It's just not possible.

I return to my room because I'm going to be prepared for whatever happens next. On the back of a dresser drawer is the duct tape cocoon encasing the knife Mom gave me. I slowly open the drawer, trying not to make noise. It's a mosh of unpaired socks and underwear and on the back of the drawer are the remnants of the tape but no knife. I pull out the two drawers below it to see if it's fallen. Nothing.

Jesus. I think, *I'm being screwed.*

7

By night time, Mom looks genuinely nervous. I haven't said another word, not about Cudge or the knife or anything. I'm just playing the game. If I could call Mark, I would, but Mom wants the phone kept free, and I rule out sneaking away, so I decide whatever's happening is going to happen without my help. Mom sits on the couch pretending to watch television with Sammy at her side, both of them phantoms in the blue light from the screen. I don't know what she's told my brother but he doesn't seem at all concerned that Cudge isn't home. That might be the one normal, understandable thing; none of us really want Cudge to return. I wonder if I'm truly the only one in the room who knows he's not coming back.

There's school tomorrow but Mom doesn't seem anxious about getting us to bed. We're watching *One Day at a Time*. Something about Bonnie Franklin being attracted to a guy, or the other way around. I haven't paid enough attention to know why. Sammy thinks it's funny. When the credits roll over the theme song telling us to "hold on tight, we'll muddle through," Mom looks to the phone and then at me with an expression I read as "What have you done?"

Right back at you.

I suppose if someone were to look in the window, Sammy curled up next to Mom, me with my feet pulled into the chair, we'd look cozy. We look, maybe, like I imagine the Callihans right now, except for the Dad spot. The emptiness of Cudge's recliner looms nearly as large as his presence on any night before this one, which is not how it felt at first.

There was a day I could have spared Cudge's life. Me and Sammy met him for the first time over fried fish sandwiches at Mike Linnig's fish camp. You would have thought we were being taken to an interview. Mom bought new-to-us jeans from the thrift store with money we were told we didn't have. She asked me to iron the t-shirts we planned to wear, but when she saw Sammy's *Super Friends* and my white Fruit of the Loom, she made us get out the itchy knit shirts we hated. She even made me part Sammy's hair because he couldn't get the line right. By the time we were ready it looked more like we were headed to church than an outdoor restaurant. "What's he going to be like," Sammy asked.

He managed a level of excitement I couldn't manufacture. Nobody could replace our Dad and I knew this is what Mom was up to. But I love my brother. I love him smiling and happy. In some ways, since Dad died, I've thought of it as my job to keep him that way. "Cudge'll be great," I said.

Now I think of meeting Cudge as an audition. The roles? Two perfect looking boys with just a hint of mischief. Like Barbara and Julie on *One Day at a Time*, or no, *Those Fabulous Graysons*. Starring us. It's still not clear to me whether or not Mom truly didn't understand that's exactly what she was doing. For certain, though, it was about her. It was really *her* audition.

When we got to Mike Linnig's, Cudge had already taken a seat at one of the outdoor concrete picnic tables which, in the summer heat, gleamed like the bleached white ruins we studied in school during Ancient Greece week. The surrounding oaks were tall, but thin enough to let in the brightness. "Is that him?" Sammy asked, pointing. There were dozens of people scattered around, but somehow my brother picked out Cudge, who was wearing a blue t-shirt, sleeves rolled up, showing the distinct border where his upper arms rarely got sun. An unlit cigarette dangled from his mouth, the butt end lost in his moustache. He looked much older than Mom, or, I thought at the time, he'd just had a hard life.

"That's him, boys," Mom said. "Isn't he a man?" She bent down and reminded us both how important this was to her and for us to be on our best behavior. We had no idea what was about to happen. I knew she was dating, that she'd had an eye out for a *someone* in her life, but nothing had come of it up to then. Once, at a baptism for her co-worker's baby, she pointed out a guy with shoe polish hair and a dusty black polyester suit— Abraham Lincoln clean shaven—and said she thought he was handsome, arching her eyebrows for emphasis. I remember thinking what bad taste she had in these new men, so I wasn't worried. No one who looked like that could possibly take my dad's place. When I saw Cudge for the first time, I thought Mom's taste had gotten worse. I'd seen carnival ride operators I would have preferred.

"Now, make your old Ma look good," she said, hands on our backs, pushing us forward. She leaned close to my ear and spoke softly, but about as earnestly as I'd ever heard her. "Help make this happen for us, little man?"

Cudge offered an over-eager wave with his simian arm, and me and Sammy shared a look, confirming between the two of us that, on first impression, we didn't think much of this guy we were about to meet.

"Where's your ring?" Sammy asked when Mom took his hand. I hadn't noticed. Her finger was bare.

"At home, sweetums," Mom said, "soaking."

She wasn't an outdoor person, but the white shadow on her finger was distinct enough. Cudge's arms, her finger. If she wanted my help, she was moving pretty fast. "It better be," I said.

She took me by the arm and got close to my ear. "This is what we're doing, little man," she said. "Don't mess it up." The bell was rung. Mom had flung us into the ring, boxing or circus, we could take our pick. That was the moment it struck me she'd been extra careful with her makeup. Not too heavy on the eyeliner and her curled hair as perfectly set as she could make it, which is to say that her sandy brown locks lolled but didn't sag. No dramatic changes, but enough that it was clear she'd made an effort. A new look for a new man.

We arrived at the table Cudge picked out and Mom became even more animated. "Sorry we're late," she cooed.

"Know you well enough to build in lady time," Cudge said, clapping his hands tight, then rubbing them together as if something big was about to happen. "Line was pretty long, Betty-doll, so I went ahead and ordered the grub." He stood and kissed Mom on the cheek, his moustache pushing against her skin walrus-like, making her giggle. Again Sammy and I looked at each other. It was true that she'd lately been in a better mood, but I don't think either of us would have described her as a giggler.

"Well, boys," Cudge said with arms raised and wide open as if to say "here I am." *Dork*, I thought about this man who, months later, would somehow resurrect himself from our bathtub.

Sammy stepped forward, a bit shy, but smiling. "Hello Mr. Cudge," he said, while I merely offered a half-wave and the best indifferent grin I could conjure.

We sat down just as a woman brought our food. It took Sammy five seconds. "It's fish," he said. "Mom, it's *f-i-s-h*."

She looked at the sandwiches, six-inch slabs of darkly fried fish extending well beyond the edges of each puffy bun. Plucking a fry, she looked at Cudge, then at Sammy. "Don't you think it was sweet of Cudge to order? Maybe it's time you started trying new things," she said.

"He doesn't like anything that swims, Mom," I said. Though it wasn't something I'd normally notice, I was keenly aware of the strong fish odor encasing us like an invisible fog. Why she'd agreed to have us eat there I couldn't fathom. My brother had long established his dislike of anything that came out of the water, with the exception of frogs' legs. And that, maybe, because Dad had taken him gigging and he loved the stabbing.

Mom sat opposite us, close enough to Cudge that he switched from holding his sandwich in his left hand to his right. "And *I* think he needs to try it," she said with manufactured sweetness. "There are all kinds of good things won't come your way if we don't experiment now and then."

"Betty-doll," Cudge said, "I didn't know. Hell, why didn't you say something when I suggested this place? I can get the boy something else." He sounded genuinely conciliatory, the entire act of trying to impress replaced by a desire to get a little boy some food he actually liked.

"It's a waste." She looked at Sammy. "You'll do what Mommy says, right sweetums?"

Sammy tightened his lips, paused for a second to stare down his sandwich, then nodded. "Okay."

"I'll make it up to you," Cudge said to him. "You boys pick the place next time. You like barbecue? We can have barbecue. I know a little place'll knock your socks off." He looked at both of us to see if he'd made any progress. "Spaghetti? Little Italian hole-in-the-wall up to Bashford Manor

I could take you to. Got some real Tony's over there doing the cooking."

Neither me nor Sammy responded, but I was thinking, *next time?* It wasn't a shock that Mom might continue going out with Cudge. What was sinking in was that me and Sammy were part of the package.

"Chinese?" Cudge asked. "Oriental House way up on Shelbyville Road. No? Hey, how about pizza then?" Sammy offered a shy smile. "There we go."

"Conner loves pizza too," Mom chimed in. "Isn't that right, little man?" She was putting it on *me*. "And we hardly ever get up to Louisville."

They're trying too hard, I thought, but I also hadn't seen my mother this lively in a long time. I didn't like any of this, but if Mom was actually happy maybe there was something I didn't understand. And after all, the man was doing his best to make us happy. "Sure," I said. "Pizza." I think now, for his own sake, Cudge would have been better off if I'd said no to all of it. He'd be alive.

Cudge clapped his hands. "All right then. Next time it's pizza on me." Then he took a bite out of his uneaten sandwich, crumbs of bun and fish catching in his moustache which he pinched away with his fingers, inspecting the bits before letting them go. "Little man," he said almost to himself before looking at me. "I like that. Fits you. I see it. Your Dad'd be proud."

I confess to warming, if not yet being won over. There was just something creepy I couldn't pinpoint.

"He gets knocked around a fair bit at school," Mom said, pointing to the faded bruise on my arm where I'd deflected James Hiekamp's attempt at slugging me in the shoulder. "Maybe you could help him with that."

"You betcha," Cudge said, kissing Mom on the cheek with his push broom of a moustache. "Scrappy little guys can fight too. Toughen you right up."

"I'm fine," I said.

"What'r they hittin' on you for?" Cudge asked with a big, fat, hairy grin. "Stealing girlfriends?" His accent went in and out in a way that made me think he was going for folksy.

Ten minutes went by about like that, Sammy picking at the top of his sandwich bun, hoarding french fries, and passing the time to look like he was eating. The fries were clearly the only part of the meal he was going to touch. I kept my mouth full of fish and chewed slowly, trying to avoid their getting-to-know-each-other routine. "So, Betty-doll tells me you boys like baseball." "Cudge does Archery. You want to learn how to shoot bows and arrows?" To these and other questions I offered polite, if indifferent, replies. Cudge and Mom didn't seem to notice. She ate little and kept her arms wrapped tightly around one of his. It was a gesture largely unfamiliar to me. I didn't have many memories of my parents being as intimate.

"Got one other question." Cudge paused long enough that both me and Sammy looked at him directly. A ray of light sifted through the trees and over Cudge's shoulder, glaring in my eyes until I could position his face between me and the sun. It was a large face, freckled, moist, and ledged by the front end of his comb-over. "So, how 'bout if I marry this here gal?"

"Gal?" Mom play-slapped his shoulder. "How about *lady*?" This ask of Cudge's clearly wasn't a surprise to her. It was as if an entire counterfeit history had spilled out in front of us, a sack full of cubic zirconia.

I looked at Sammy and then at Mom. She hadn't warned us. It was only just a little over two years since Dad jumped into the Ohio from a bridge; from when his body washed up on the Indiana side. And now, already, I thought, she brings this guy around for the first time and they're getting married? It was one thing to date. "What are you talking about," I said, looking more at Mom than Cudge. "What about Dad?"

"I told you," Mom said, turning to Cudge. "Give us a second?"

He kissed her on the forehead, stood, and reached into his pocket. "Not before this," he said, pulling out a slim gold band set with a small diamond I doubted was real. He slipped it onto her finger and kissed it. "Back in a few. I'll bring us a couple beers and some more Cokes. Give you three some time to talk." He looked at me and winked as if he'd just played a practical joke at my expense. Then he opened his arms. "It's gonna be okay, little man." I almost bit, my heart nearly overriding my mind as if any man's embrace might be Dad's embrace. If I hadn't been on the opposite side of the table, I might have rushed into Cudge's arms and I can't express exactly why except that I was tired. Since Dad died, I'd taken on a lot.

Between home and regular beatings at school I was near ground down. If it weren't for Mark.... I loved Sammy, but I couldn't be a kid and be his Dad at the same time. I was ready to retire. But then Cudge said one thing too many. "Betty-doll here says you need a Pop."

A switch flipped. He had no right. I waited until Cudge was out of earshot. "What was that?" I was furious.

"That, little man," she said, "is going to be your new dad."

The possibility clicked with Sammy. "Really?" he said brightly, catching me off guard. This brother of mine who'd been staring angrily at a fish sandwich since we sat down was strangely excited about the prospect of Mom getting married.

"No, Sammy," I said, turning to Mom, "*Not* really. You can't do this. You can't."

Mom reached across the table and placed her hand on my cheek. "I knew you'd be the hard one," she said looking off toward Cudge. Then she looked back and forth between me and Sammy. Her blue eyeshadow and pink lipstick shone brightly.

"Boys. What I can't do is go it alone anymore. I've been telling you."

"You're not. You got us," Sammy said.

She smiled. "And you'll always have me, sweetums. But your old mother needs a little help."

I knew she was worn. She said as much almost every day when she asked me to make dinner, or pack Sammy's lunch, or throw in a load of laundry, whatever it was that she was just too exhausted to do. I thought I resented it, but just then, with Cudge on the precipice of being our stepfather, it felt like something was being taken away from me. "It's not right," I said. "What if one day I went to the shelter and came home with a Saint Bernard without asking?"

"That's different. I'm allergic." She didn't get it.

"I mean I just bring this big, hairy dog home and that's that. No discussion."

"I'd be wheezing *and* upset," Mom said. "But there's a difference, little man. The dog didn't ask to be part of your family. And the dog doesn't bring home a paycheck."

"What do you think?" she asked Sammy as if there was no objection on the table. "I'd like the dog."

Mom laughed. "No, sweetums. What do you think about Cudge and me getting married?"

Sammy cocked his head and pointed to his plate. "Would we have to eat fish sandwiches again?"

"I'm sure we can work that out," she said, stifling a relieved laugh. It was as if the two of them were having a talk over strawberry ice cream.

"Then it's okay," Sammy agreed. "We could use a dad again."

"Yes, we could."

I didn't want to believe what I was hearing. They were making a decision as if buying a can of soup. "I know you're tired, Mom," I said, "but we've been doing pretty good." I looked toward Cudge who was almost at the front of the drink line. He was watching us from the corners of his eyes, the part in his hair that defined his comb-over looking like a creepy pink smile running the length of his head. *No way*, I thought. I wasn't having any of Mom's reasoning. "You act like the whole world is on your shoulders since Dad died," I said. She held up her hand, signaling me to lower my voice, and I complied. "It's not like we don't help. In case you haven't noticed, I hardly do anything but come home and take care of you and Sammy."

Mom offered a sympathetic smile. "That's right, Conner, you've given up a lot. That's exactly my point. You should be a kid, not a full-time babysitter. Don't rain on my parade, little man," she said quietly. "Please." She touched my cheek again. "Give Cudge a chance."

I was frozen. What was I supposed to say? *Yeah, go ahead. Dad didn't matter. Just go ahead and marry some guy we're meeting for the first time.* I might have saved the man's life by putting my foot down right then. Then again, some lives aren't worth saving. Right at the top of that list are men who try to stick their dicks in little boys' asses.

"Do you love him, Mom?" Sammy asked.

"I will, sweetums, you bet."

The indirectness wasn't lost on me, but I also understood that my leverage was slipping away. When Dad jumped off that bridge he'd not only abandoned two sons, he left his wife as well, left her with two boys to raise on a 25-hour-a-week gas station job. My head was exploding, throwing back and forth all kinds of conclusions. I told myself to pretend Cudge wasn't all that bad. It was probably our mother that'd made him try so hard at being friendly. But there was another voice inside me that said something wasn't right, what she was doing wasn't good for us. Yet looking at her eyes, which seemed, yes, tired, but eager, I found myself simply nodding, telling her "okay."

"That's my little man," she said, petting my hair.

I looked at Sammy to reassure him, forgetting I didn't need to, but he was picking pieces of bread, almost surgically, from the top of his otherwise untouched fish sandwich. Then, unexpectedly, he pinched off the tip of the breaded fillet, popping it in his mouth and offering an almost immediate grimace. "No fish," he reminded our mother.

The smell of bacon wakes me. For the moment I stare at the ceiling trying to get my bearings in this house of the missing body. I've just come out of a dream where Mark and me were riding three wheelers through the woods. The odd thing was that there was no sound. I felt wind on my face but I couldn't hear it, nor the motors from our bikes either. Mark sped ahead of me, his hair a wild red flutter when he turned, smiled, and spoke soundless words I couldn't interpret. Now, awake, as I picture him, us, and try to focus on his lips, I realize I'm changing the dream and what he might have said. It's no use.

But I hear actual voices downstairs. No, *a* voice that starts and stops at random intervals. Mom on the phone. Rubbing the sleep from my eyes I see that the clock says it's too early for school. I know I haven't dreamed the weekend. That only happens in the movies, but if Mom is downstairs cooking breakfast, Cudge is home, because she wouldn't be doing that for just me and Sammy. So, I have no idea of exactly what's happened over the past two days, what sick hoax they've played on me nor why. It's just not possible I've dreamt all this.

Sammy remains asleep in his bed, wrapped in his covers from the chin down like a caterpillar in a cocoon. I quietly make my way into the hall. Cudge and Mom's door is open but there's no movement. They're both in the kitchen. I pad lightly toward the stairs, cringing as the floorboards complain in thin creaks. I hear it more distinctly, the sound of Mom on the phone. She's saying goodbye and immediately dials another number, the rotary tumbling in a rush. When I get to the bottom of the stairs, I peek around the corner where I can just see my mother pacing back and forth with the receiver in one hand and a piece of bacon in the other. She's in her thick, blue terry cloth robe, and other than the new color, her hair is nearly back to its random twists and turns, each side held back with a barrette.

I get the gist from her side of the conversation. Cudge hasn't returned. She's on the phone with the sheriff and she sounds genuinely frantic. Sitting on the bottom of the stairs, I listen, waiting to find out that I'm in big, big trouble, waiting for my mother to give me up because I can't change the fact I've told her I saw Cudge dead, and now he's vanished.

There are problems which startle me. Cudge has taken his keys and wallet. He left a note. It hasn't been 24 hours. "I don't know if he was drinking," Mom says. "We weren't home. Two boys." She answers a series of questions all of which amount to a final word from her before she's dismissed. "But...."

The house is warm. I think about going to the kitchen but it's not necessary because my mother appears at the bottom of the stairs, one side of her hair fallen. "What the hell is going on?" she whispers. "Where's Cudge?" I stand in front of her in a t-shirt and pajama bottoms so loose around the waist I have to tuck one side into my underwear to keep them up. All I can do is shrug. We're in a stalemate of suspicion and shock. "Tell me you and Cudge are up to some fool-ass joke. Or you done something so shitty you've scared him off?" I can't believe this is the same woman who practically gave me permission to drive a knife into her husband's chest.

Her eyes are urgent and near tears, her brow pinched as if she's in pain. Either she really doesn't know anything or she should win an Oscar for this performance. It doesn't take me a second to know what I have to say. "Okay. It was a joke. I didn't see Cudge dead."

She puts her hand to her forehead in exasperation. "Yeah, I know that," she says, looking upstairs then mouthing "your brother," finger over her lips. She signals me to follow her to the living room where she drops into Cudge's recliner. "So then, where is he?"

I shrug. "I promise I don't know." I hate this, but I have to tell her about coming home over the weekend to get the knife she bought and how he stopped me and wouldn't let me take it to Mark's. It's a full on lie but I have no choice because this is the story Mark's mom and Sammy know, and as I speak it I'm almost able to believe myself because it feels no less plausible than the story I'm living out.

She looks confused. "Wait. You came home Saturday to get the knife when I told you Cudge couldn't know about it?"

"He was getting ready to take a bath," I say, watching her closely. "I didn't ask. I thought I could sneak it by." This is the test. She doesn't flinch but she tests back.

"You come home to get your knife, tell me you saw Cudge dead, and now he's nowhere to be found." She leans forward and glares at me. "Conner, what the hell did you do?"

She's got me, but not for the right reasons. "Mom," I plead. "He wanted to know why I came home and I messed up and told him about the knife. I swear. He was pissed off when I wouldn't say where I hid it. I went back to the Callihans' and that's all I know." I decide not to tell her the knife is missing.

"Hell," she says. "He's taken off because he thinks we're planning to kill him."

This is where we are? I've seen Cudge dead only he's really not dead, but he's afraid we're plotting against him and he's gone. What choice do I have?

Mom looks at me with suspicion, then points to the couch where I take a seat. "This is a damn sure can of worms," she says, pausing, eyeing me for a few seconds. "Can I trust you, little man?"

"Yes."

"I mean really trust you?" I nod. "It's going to look bad. I wasn't in Cincinnati. I don't know, that's why maybe he left."

"What are you talking about?"

"I was with Larry."

She doesn't have to tell me who this is. They work together, and I met him once at a picnic. This news confirms something I suspected since I saw them kissing in his truck. And she's right. It *will* look bad. A fire rises within me for being put through this, but before I can accuse her of anything, she stops me with an open hand and points toward the phone. "Just now told him we have to cool it, but it's worse."

"No kidding," I say, thinking she's about to tell me how she did Cudge in. But what comes next is something I don't expect.

"Remember," she begins, "that morning you heard me and Cudge yelling at each other down here?" I know exactly what's she talking about. I was upstairs and couldn't make out much except for him saying, "*Your* handwriting, bitch," just before a loud slap and shattering glass. The front door slammed, the sound of boots on the steps confirming it was Cudge who'd left. When I heard his van rumble to life and pull away, I ran downstairs where I found Mom crying on the couch, rocking back and forth. I saw the place on her neck where he'd slapped her. On the wall not far from her was a spray of wet. I knew what it was because the room smelled of Cudge's pepperoncinis. I saw that the bottle had fallen onto a ceramic platter decorated with a wild Tom turkey. The platter was broken in two. I went back to the kitchen and got a foxtail and dust pan to clean up the glass so Cudge wouldn't have something else to yell about if he came home. "Leave it," Mom said. "I'll do it." Then she noticed the platter. "Tom. He broke Tom." She started crying again, which made me angry and frustrated. The platter was worthless, won in a church picnic dime-a-try game. The wall was a splattered record of Cudge's fury, and the floor beneath it a mess of wet glass and pepperoncinis like little green zygotes set amongst diamonds. She had a welt on her neck and she was concerned about the plate?

Now, in Cudge's chair, she suddenly looks as damaged and vulnerable as she did the day he hit her. "I'm in so much trouble, little man," she says. "So much trouble."

"Just say it, Mom. What's going on?" She joins me on the couch and I ask her four or five times before she responds.

Holding my face with both of her hands she says, "It's bad and I don't know what to do." I feel a kind of heat come off her that I've never experienced before, as if the entirety of her insides is hot coal. "He's got all the money," she says, beginning to sob.

"What money? What are you talking about? Did Larry take money from you?"

She stands and paces the room, fingers trembling at her lips. "Oh, God, shit, I'm in so much trouble." Picking up the phone receiver, she stares at it in her hand as if on its own it will provide her with answers. After a moment she sets it back down and lifts her fists near her ears as she begins pacing again, her pinched expression making it look like she's trying to squeeze out a solution from deep within. Her face is so red I'm certain she's going to pass out, so I run to the kitchen and bring her a glass of water. "Cudge can't be beating on you," I say as firmly as I can without yelling, and then, weakly, "It's against the law." I hand her the glass which she looks at skeptically until I tip it toward her from the base and she drinks. "I don't care what you did, Mom."

"No, little man, you don't understand. It's not something *I* did. It's something *we* did. Cudge and me." She plops down in his chair and plants her face in her hands, elbows on her knees. "I really fucked up. He threatened me."

I beg her to tell me what's going on, but all she can do is ramble about being in trouble as if she's on some sort of taped loop. She stops crying but can't sit in one place for more than a few seconds before getting up and moving around. I take her by the shoulders and sit her back down on the couch. "Mom, look at me." I speak slowly, enunciating each word. "Exactly what. Kind. Of. Trouble. Are. You. In?"

"Little man," she says. "I don't want you mixed up in this." I don't relent, asking her again with the same intensity. My eyes shift back and forth between hers, looking for a sign that a person who can think straight is in there. "Hell," she says, finally, "I got drunk and wrote down everything. He has the paper. It's my handwriting."

The details pour out of her, and it's not at all what I expected to hear. A while back she and Cudge had gotten drunk at a bar and someone took his wallet and her purse. Combined they'd lost maybe forty dollars, but Cudge acted as if they'd lost every dime to their name. He complained about people who had it better than them, would always have it better. Mom let it slip that the man who owned the gas station where she worked came by early every Monday morning, parked at the rear entrance, and picked up cash for deposit. The man owned four other stations besides the one she worked in. He was a stupid, greedy old man who didn't trust his managers, she tells me. Her station was the last stop, and when the old man got there, Cudge was waiting with a gun. It was Mom's job to be scared and panicky. Cudge took the man's case and all the money locked in the trunk of his big green Buick.

"Jesus Christ," I say, "that was you guys?" It was in the newspaper and on TV "You and Cudge fucking stole four thousand dollars?" I'm startled, but not so much that I don't look around the living room and wonder why there's nothing to show for the heist. I've seen *Bonnie and Clyde*. Mom is no Faye Dunaway, but maybe Cudge has come to an end about like Clyde.

Mom shudders and scratches her hair with both hands as if waking herself. "Little man, it wasn't four thousand. The old guy had nearly thirty. Cudge said it had to be dirty money because there was no way five stations make thirty thousand dollars cash in one week." She raises her hands in the air in surrender. *There it is*, she's saying. *All my cards are on the table.*

I want to be sympathetic, but I can't believe she's been this stupid. "What was he hitting on you for," I ask, trying to contain how upset I am with her.

"I told him I was quitting the station. I was too nervous. I was sure they could tell I had something to do with it. He said if I quit, that's when they'd get suspicious, but I wanted to leave the station anyway. He went upstairs and got that damn paper and waved in my face. He told me if I did anything that fucks him over I'm going to jail, too."

"He's gone with the money?" This is a game, and I don't know the rules. Was this entire weekend about someone screwing us over? I saw him in the bathtub in iced-over water. I try to put it together. "Dead or gone," I conclude. It's all the same. "That's what we wanted, right?"

She looks at me like I'm being callous, and I understand that I have to be careful. I'm almost off the hook for whatever all this is. "It's not that easy," she says. "The Barracuda. He wouldn't leave that. I expect he'll turn up sooner or later and it won't be pretty when he does."

I'm 100% sure I saw Cudge in the bathtub. I've also just told my mother he was alive the last time I saw him. I've got no wiggle room. "We'll call the sheriff again," I say.

Mom knocks that suggestion down almost before it's out of my mouth. "That'll get me locked up. I shouldn't have told you all this," she says, wiping tears from the corner of her eyes. "You got to promise me you'll keep quiet."

"I'm not saying anything. But Jesus, Mom."

"I'm so sorry, little man," she said. "I thought this was going to be a whole new start for us. Wanted my boys to have a dad again. I needed somebody. And I know you tried to tell me something was off about him. I wouldn't listen."

"No you wouldn't." There's plenty I haven't told her. I can't. There's no need because the catalog is pretty full. "Like the paint?"

She nods slowly and looks to the floor. "I guess that *was* bad."

"You Guess? The man wanted Sammy to wash his dick for him." I remind her of how Cudge got the idea he was going to freshen up the living room walls. He had a ladder and 2 gallons of paint. Once again Mom conjured a bonding experience for her sons and new husband, leaving us alone under the pretense of needing groceries. Cudge had already given me reason to be on edge, and once he moved in he made awkward, transparent attempts at appearing friendly. I had this sense that he was two different men living in one body and I wondered why only I noticed. When he handed us paint brushes for the molding, he gave us a warning, but with a smile. "Don't you little rats go dripping on everything," the tone almost as if he were mussing our hair. This was his way, what kept me off balance. I'd start thinking that really it was me who was over-reacting, half-convinced myself if the three of us could make Cudge happy he'd settle down and be normal and then we could have what Mom wanted. The mouse keeps going back for the cheese if the trap doesn't snap.

As we painted, Cudge played a Creedence Clearwater Revival cassette full blast. It wasn't music we were familiar with, but it was a new energy. I, more than Sammy, was aware of how quiet the house became when we lost Dad, and Cudge was definitely not quiet. A half hour into painting, "Up around the Bend" played at a window-shuddering level. Cudge was drinking beer, and both me and Sammy each had our own Cokes, a treat. But then Cudge stepped off the ladder and tripped over a paint can, fell backward, catching the ladder with his foot and bringing a second paint can down on him. His upper torso, face, and hair were splattered in white paint. At first, we froze, but Sammy laughed. "You look like a cinnamon roll," he said. I laughed too. Cudge, stood up awkwardly, almost slipping back down on the vinyl tarp, a fourth Stooge. He looked at us, though under the dripping paint his expression wasn't clear.

"You little fuckers think it's funny? I damn near broke my neck." Crossing the room, he snatched the brushes from our hands. "Think you're a little comedian, Sammy?" He shook the brushes at us and streaked white across our faces. "Fucking hilarious, right?"

Sammy grabbed my hand.

"Fucking things are gonna change around here," Cudge yelled. "I won't put up with this shit."

My left eye stung from paint. "Can we go clean up?"

Snatching me by the sleeve of my t-shirt, Cudge glared and said, "Good idea." In seconds we were in the upstairs bathroom, Cudge fully stripped and standing in the clawfoot tub with the shower on. He threw soaked washcloths at both of us and we wiped our faces.

"You fucking think that's for you? You're gonna clean my ass."

Sammy looked at me. The bathroom was filling with steam. "I ain't wiping your ass," I said.

"Don't fucking use that language. Think me falling is funny? What do you think now? He reached out and pulled me toward him. "Get at it," he yelled. Then he looked at Sammy and spoke without nearly the same fierceness. "You get the front."

I blocked Sammy with my arm, preventing him from moving. "Leave him alone." My heart was a fist punching from the inside, but I couldn't will my body to do more. "I'm telling Mom," was all I could muster through tears.

Cudge shuddered like he'd been doused with cold water. There was a pause, and a sudden clarity in his eyes. "Go downstairs and clean the fuck up," he said. Me and Sammy stood motionless. "I said get the fuck out."

Mom lays down and places her head on my lap, my money-stealing mess of a mother. I run my fingers across her forehead the way she did mine when I was a little boy. It's been nine or ten years since she did that. It was before Sammy and it was always the same. She'd put me to bed and put her fingertips at my hairline, her nails always just long enough. "Michael row your boat ashore," she'd sing as she raked her hand through my hair. It was a time when I felt, intuitively, that there was order and fairness in the world. All children went to sleep this way because that's how it's supposed to be. Mom sang and my parts were the halleluiah refrains until I drifted off.

Sammy is upstairs asleep, and somehow I stop worrying about where the fuck Cudge is. It's me and Mom and a silent house. With her head on my lap I begin to sing our old song. At first, it's just me, but when I get to "meet my mother on the other side," she squeezes my free hand and I know what the gesture means. She is ready to sing the part that used to be mine.

8

Mark isn't at school, which is not like him. At lunch I'm tempted to sneak away and see what's wrong, but I'm chained by the understanding that I can't risk anything out of the ordinary. Invisibility is the word of the day, and this is exactly what I imagine as I sift through the halls amongst teachers who stand totem-like, arms crossed, keeping watch. Except for when Constance McVicker trips me before English, the day hazes until fifth period when Mr. Gurber, who teaches History and Social Studies and says things like "Dyn-O-mite" and "groovy" thinking that it makes him cool in our eyes, pulls out one of the odd little Kentucky histories he's famous for. Good for him. He doesn't know that in three years they'll close this school because it's falling apart and too small, like the rest of Orgull.

"Today," Mr. Gurber begins, drawing out the last syllable, "I'm going to share a little about the ol' Harpe brothers." He twists the end of his artificially brown handlebar moustache and tells us how, back in the day, this clan of Harpes robbed people traveling the Ohio River, stripped them naked and threw them off a bluff. Sometimes they'd cut the person open, fill them with rocks, and sink them in the current. He doesn't know about my father's drowning, so I can't hold it against him, but the detail is enough to make me nauseous. I look to either side of me, the other kids rapt, while all I care about is where the closest trash can is.

Mr. Gurber is practically nonchalant as he relates the detail of Big Harpe smashing his baby daughter's skull against a tree because she was crying. "That's right," he says, as if *this* is what should shock us, "the Harpes had wives." As he speaks, I'm doing my best to hold everything down and I try to concentrate on anything but him. Over his shoulder

I notice the white, skull-sized oval of something he's erased on the blackboard. The longer I focus, the more it becomes Cudge watching me. It's a ghost-face stare from a midnight wall that won't let me turn away even as Mr. Gurber ticks off the ways the Harpes killed dozens of people and how they were brought to justice. This is when he turns to the blackboard and gets an inspiration. With the corner of his eraser on the oval he marks out blank eyes and a frown on what was Cudge's face, draws the outline of a similar form next to this, and marks "Xs" across all four eyes. Beneath these he draws yard long necks, which he informs us represent the stakes on which the severed heads of the captured Harpes were propped for display, roadside.

It's more than I can I stand, as I practically fall out of my seat and run for the door where, just as I open it, I vomit into the hallway. It all happens in seconds. Dizzy, I cling to the doorknob, my other hand gripping the jamb. I pull myself upright, wipe my mouth, and look at Mr. Gurber with apology. "Good gravy," he says just before Jenny Smith croaks "Oh no" and upchucks her lunch onto the desk in front of her, lighting a fuse of screaming and desks rocketing away from the rancid epicenter.

Me and Jenny are sent to the nurse's office, but I don't wait for the poor girl whose school life I've probably ruined. I run-walk down the hall, slip on my coat and toboggan, pull a scarf out of my pocket, and prepare to turn left instead of right. I'm going to see Mark. I don't care. The janitor is rolling a bucket and mop down the hall. He's a stocky, bourbon-faced guy and I read his expression as he passes, *you little fucker.*

The bite of the cold has lessened to the point the sun in the open sky manages some effect, enough that I move the scarf from my face and accept the chilled air into my lungs. It steadies me, and as I calm I understand it wasn't the Harpes that sickened me as much as what I've been holding in. Mark has no idea how far Cudge went. I have to tell someone and it has to be Mark.

The walk, the march, to his house gives me time to think about where I'll start.

Passing the Baptist church, small and cream colored, I notice the paint job begun in the fall didn't make it as far as the weathered spire. The sign out front announces services and includes their saying of the week in block letters, "God inspires when he's your soul's attire." I wonder if this is my problem. We aren't that religious and look at what's happened. Look at the Callihans and how happy they are. I will start going to Mass with them and I'll take Sammy with me. I'll fix all of this.

I couldn't know months ago it would come to this. It was Cudge's presence early on, after all, which allowed my feelings for Mark to finally manifest themselves. I remember the day. At school, Jerry King and a bunch of his goofs stuck a melted ice cream sandwich, still in its wrapper, down my shirt, and then took turns fake congratulating me with slaps on the back. I didn't say anything, just went into the boys bathroom, cleaned up, put my gym shirt on, and pretended like nothing happened. But it was one of those days where I felt a fury inside me that I knew if I ever let out I'd end up in the hospital, so I pushed it all down and went along…as usual. That night, Cudge had a date with Mom. Things with them were going better than I could have hoped for and I was running out of reason to resist. As a joke, he brought Sammy a sack of Swedish Fish, the bulk kind.

"Will you eat *these* on a sandwich?" Cudge asked, smiling beneath that oversized amber moustache of his. Sammy took the sack eagerly and struggled to untie the knot before Cudge undid it. He returned the sack to Sammy who eagerly plunged his little hand into the multicolored candy. "Guess it's raw fish today," Cudge joked. Mom looked at me as if to say *See, he's a great guy.*

I held out my hand toward Sammy to show her I was happily playing along. "I'll take one." His mouth was already bulging with the gummy candy and I could smell the vaguely fruity sweetness

"Hell, no," Cudge said, reaching into his pocket. "Why share?" He pulled out a second bag, mostly the same Swedish Fish, and held it out to me. It rocked in the air between us for a second before I recognized I had no choice but to accept it. There was something besides Swedish Fish in the bag, a box of candy cigarettes, a non-sequitur of an inclusion that made me wonder if Cudge somehow knew I'd taken up smoking.

"Cudge, you're such a sweetie," Mom said.

"You got two good boys there, Betty-doll." He had his arm around her waist, and the two of them were looking at us like we were angels, no, like *they* were angels. Wary, I was honestly trying to give in to the idea we really were suddenly on the verge of some big happy ride. It's hard to admit, but if not necessarily persuaded, I was at least swayed. I hadn't yet opened my candy when Cudge clapped his hands. "Betty-doll, we better hit it. Max's or something else tonight?"

Mom demurred. "You decide."

"I always decide. Guess you like it that way."

"Little man," Mom said, placing her hand on the side of my head, "you and your brother'll be okay tonight?"

"Sure," I said. By this point, she didn't have to bother mentioning dinner or getting Sammy to bed. Even before Cudge. And, now that he was around, I was beginning to like having the house to myself. I could turn off the shit-kicker music and play Duran Duran as loud as I wanted, stay up for Johnny Carson and listen to jokes adults laughed at, and I hoped someday I'd understand. Sometimes Mark snuck over after Sammy went to bed and we watched TV on the couch, awkwardly slung over each other during *The Love Boat* and *Fantasy Island*. I can't quite give it a name, not fondling certainly, maybe learning.

That Swedish Fish night, late, *Ode to Billy Joe* came on. I said something about Robby Benson being good looking and Mark said "yeah, he is," but we were saying something entirely else without having to speak it. Mark was wearing a faded red shirt with its large pagoda-like Atari logo and his heavy bangs dangled just above his eyes like a half-raised curtain. It wasn't like the movies and I don't know if this is how it happens for everyone, but it really was just a smile from Mark, a small one, and the gaze, that told me we were feeling the same thing. He took my hand, pulled me closer toward him. Now we were both smiling, I suppose because this wasn't like outside the funeral home. Neither of us had ever kissed anyone, not like I thought we were about to, and there wasn't any fear. There wasn't anything in the world for me in that moment but Mark; no thoughts of Mom and Cudge coming home nor Sammy upstairs, no worries about having feelings for another boy in a way I knew was wrong. I couldn't know that not much later Cudge would find out about us and hold it over me. It was perfect and simple. Only Mark and Mark and Mark.

He lay stretched out and pulled me fully over the thin, firm plank of him, his body larger than mine, limbs longer. Bobbie Gentry began singing from the TV, and the two of us looked to the screen for a second before coming back to each other. "Okay," he said, as if we were at the edge of a lake about to plunge in hand in hand, or no, as if we were bank robbers about to burst through the door for a first daring heist.

"Okay." I slowly lowered my face until my lips touched his and I felt them gently part.

A block away from the Callihans' I pause in front of the ironworks compound run by Leroy Carter. Peeking above the fenced off courtyard are the kinetic, gleaming metal sculptures he's famous for. Although my world is pretty much as small as Orgull, I have no doubt Mr. Carter is our most celebrated citizen even beyond our borders. Some days he's outside his gate smoking a cigarette in his sooty engineer's cap, and any time I ask he lets me wander around his whirling sculptures as long as his cigarette lasts. There are more than a few white folks in town who resent that a black man has so much status, but when people come to buy his sculptures, they spend money in our town which makes all the difference to Mr. Carter's detractors. "Kid," he once said to me, out of the blue, "I've met assholes every place I've lived. Don't grow up to be one of 'em." With that he smiled, flicked his cigarette into a rusty coffee can on the ground, and gave me the time-to-go sign with a tip of his head. Suddenly, now, I realize I have no idea why I've stopped here except that maybe I'm desperate to be like Mr. Carter, to be a person living for art and kindness rather being than the person I am.

When I arrive at the Callihans' door and knock, I realize I don't have a story. What am I doing out of school? Nobody answers. Through the window I see that the living room is daylight dark and a large green suitcase sits next to the couch. Mr. Callihan has returned, but clearly nobody is home. An envelope and what appears to be an invitation, a quilt of color, sits on the coffee table. It's like looking in a shoebox diorama just before the finishing touches of the family figurines. I've been in this room so often I'd know just where to place everyone: Mr. Callihan in the high back chair next to the floor lamp, Mark sprawled on the couch rereading his dogeared copy of *Rumblefish,* Mrs. Callihan leaning into the room announcing dinner. I try to imagine where I'd place myself, but no, *you'd ruin it for everyone.*

When I get home, Mom is on the porch in Cudge's thick brown coat. She's wearing his toboggan as well, smoking a cigarette. "Bring up the mail," she says, apparently not surprised to see me home early. It's a stack, more than usual, full of the catalogs Cudge requests but never reads. "I'm headed to work in a bit. Half shift," she says as I hand her the mail. "Oh, and school called."

"What'd they say?"

She doesn't look at me, just smokes and sorts through the pile on her lap. "I told 'em I'd bring you in the morning. You're in trouble." She looks up and winks. "With them. But I told 'em what was going on about Cudge gone missing."

"It's hard to just sit there knowing...I mean not knowing."

"What now?" she says, inspecting an envelope with suspicion and then sliding it toward me. "This one's yours."

The envelope is legal size, gray, addressed to me in white letters embossed on the narrow red tape from a hand-held label maker. The entire address is sealed over by clear packing tape. There's no return address, and the fifteen-cent stamp—a pink and blue W.C. Fields portrait, juggling—has been slapped on askew. I open the envelope, but there's no paper, just an assortment of little red strips winking with white lettering, all of which I shake out next to me. "What in Jesus' name?" Mom says, leaning down close as I follow the implied instructions. It doesn't take long. There are just seven pieces, and though I imagine variations, I'm certain I've got it right.

<u>LITTLE MAN I AM COMING BACK 4 YOU FAGOT</u>

I'm so absorbed it takes me a moment to focus on the misspelled word I've just placed in front of my mother. Everything between my heart and brain is a sudden, loud buzz forcing me to shut my eyes. *What's happening?* "Am I crazy, Mom?" I ask, looking at her. She stares at me like I'm some sad, weak creature, a sick puppy that has to be put down. "Did I see him or not? You have to tell me it was you."

"Damn it," she says, tossing her half-smoked cigarette into the frozen yard. She slaps her hand next to the words which disperse into a jumble, *fagot* separated from the rest. *What did Cudge tell her?* "I'm going to give you the benefit of the doubt. Maybe you had some sort of hallucination or a bad dream, but what you asked me just now, that isn't to ever come out of your mouth again."

"But…"

"You think I'm not sitting here wondering what the hell all this is? Think it's sitting easy on me wondering if you've done something really brain-ass stupid? Whether or not a wrong word to the sheriff might get you sent off?"

"I didn't."

She pulls a cigarette from her pocket and lights it with Cudge's shiny Zippo. "I'll tell you, that pile of plastic words right there comes as no small relief. I was beginning to worry for you."

Relief? I look again at *fagot*, the letters milky white on a red background. "This doesn't make it better. Someone's after me."

"What brought all this on? Something happen between you two I don't know about?" *I have no idea what you know.* "Little man?"

Fagot. Fagot. Fagot. "Last Saturday when I came home, he told me to suck his dick."

"Holy Jesus, what? Why would he do that? That's bullshit. You're full of shit."

My head is tilted downward, but I see my mother just below my brows, cigarette between her fingers frozen an inch away from her lips, brown eyes, Sammy's eyes, except intent and hard. "I said, your husband told me to suck his dick." I raise my head. "I told him to fuck off." This isn't the entire truth, but it's all she gets.

She turns away and brings the cigarette to her lips, eyes darting back and forth, but she's not looking at the yard so much as something in her head. "It doesn't make sense. Why the hell would he do something like that?"

"Because," I say, picking up *FAGOT* and holding it out to her between my thumb and forefinger shoving it toward her. I know exactly why I'm doing this now, this way.

"What about it?" I don't move, just keep my hand in the air between us. It takes her a few seconds. "Hell, Conner," she says, finally catching on. "You did *not* tell me that. I don't wanna hear that shit."

"I didn't *say* anything."

"Who is it? That little shit, Mark?" She can't help herself. "That's what I thought. Jesus you've got some half-ass priorities."

I gather the red strips and stand up. To my surprise, my mother flinches. "I wouldn't hurt you. Fuck. Wish you could say the same to me."

I turn to go inside but she takes hold of my wrist. Below her grip, Cudge's message is clenched in my hand. "Where you going?"

"To call the sheriff."

She stares at my fist for a few seconds and then at me. "No way are we giving this to them."

"We have to."

She tugs me down to eye level. "Listen. You don't want to be that kid in this town." *I'm already that kid in town.* "You don't want to put that on your brother either." *Shit, Sammy.* "Remember a few years back, Daryl Hansen, how they wheeled him around town after he got his knees broke? He was in a god damned neighbor's garage getting blown by their son, some college kid piece of trash and the garage door opens. Dad's home. You think anyone blamed the old man for going after Daryl with a tire iron? You think your little friend is going to appreciate it when a pack of kids jump him after school and beat the shit out of him?"

"I won't tell about the fight with Cudge." Years later I will remember my mother's brown glare, the surprising fierceness. I will think about this moment as well as the time she put her head in my lap and listened to me sing. I will think she was undiagnosed.

"You suppose the sheriff's not going to be a little curious about Cudge's choice of words there?" She pointed to my clenched fist. "You think he's not going to start asking questions?" I sag back down to the porch. "There's a whole lot of shit gonna come down on you if you take this road. So here's what you got to get in that head of yours. I didn't raise a homo and Cudge never did a thing to you." She pauses and looks back and forth into each of my eyes to see if I understand. "Get it? I... did not...raise...a faggot."

I should be startled, but I'm not. It's too late for that. I rise slowly and step off the porch. "Mom," I say before I walk away. "You're right. In fact, you didn't raise me at all."

9

I head downtown, hands plunged into my jacket pockets, one of them holding Cudge's threat. Tomorrow Mom will drive me to school and we'll see what kind of punishment I get for ditching. I could apologize and fling the red word strips on the principle's desk, tell her I've had a bad few days, let Mom explain why her spelling-challenged husband is calling me a faggot.

There's something wrong about this, a kid my age having to think "what am I going to do next?" And practically every day since Cudge showed up. I settle for the alcove of an empty store front, the very location where fifteen years from now I'll have my own shop. It's cold, but not so cold I want to go home. I slouch against the door and slide to the ground next to an upside down "Schmidt's" laid out in red and white tile in front of me.

Across the street and down a couple doors in front of the bar, a station wagon pulls up and parks, cream colored with imitation wood siding. The driver is Jodi King, the bar owner's wife. I know her like I know a lot of people, because I live in this tiny shit-ass town, but Mom and Cudge probably know her a lot better. She steps out of the car and pauses when she sees me. She's wearing a black blouse and jeans cinched in by a fat red belt with a shiny oval buckle. When she's satisfied that she recognizes me she goes to the back of the car where she double arms sacks of groceries and takes them into the bar. I have no idea how important this woman will be to me, how one day in the future she will invite me to the apartment above the bar and open a box of secrets. She has no idea that will be a mistake.

In a couple minutes the door opens and Jodi leans out to take another squinting look at me. I raise my hands, asking what she's staring at, which she takes as an invitation to cross the street, pack of cigarettes in her hand.

"You're Betty's kid, aren't you?" she says when she's standing in front of me.

I don't bother getting up. "Yeah."

"She know you're not at school?"

"Yeah," I say.

She crouches and extends the pack of cigarettes. "What kid in this town don't smoke?" she says, laughing. I don't care that she knows nor that apparently this is a game that adults like to play. For this I stand, and she joins me, pulling matches from her front pocket. "Heard about your daddy," she says after my first drag, and she can tell I'm confused because she corrects herself. "Cudge."

I'm trying to think who Mom would be talking to already, and I try to act calm, like on any given day someone I hardly know would say this to me. "What'd you hear?"

"That he's took off on y'all."

"That got around fast," I say, fumbling with the pieces of Cudge's note in my pocket. I've no idea why she's taken an interest in me, except maybe for the gossip.

"Orgull ain't no bigger'n a postage stamp." Lighting a cigarette for herself, she leans against the window. Just over her shoulder is the faintest gold remnant of the word *Notions*. "Your momma okay?"

"Thing is, we don't know if he's taken off or's just pissed off. Guess she's confused."

"They have a fight or something?"

"Not really." She's making me nervous but I use the opportunity, just in case. "We were all gone this weekend. He wasn't too happy we left him alone."

"May be on a bender." She points at the bar over shoulder with her thumb. "The man can throw it back."

"Oh," I say a bit too eagerly, thinking by happenstance I've come around to the answer of what the hell is going on. "Did he come in?"

"Didn't see him, which is unusual." She takes a long drag and laughs out the smoke. "Probably saved us a broken glass or two."

I gently snuff out my cigarette. "For later," I say, slipping it behind my ear. I have my own stash, but it's a way to finish off this conversation. "I should get going."

"How 'bout you?" she asks as if I haven't begged out.

"How about me what?"

"You didn't talk to him or nothing this weekend?"

"Not really," I say, because I'm starting to feel like I've said more than I should. "Me and my brother were at a friend's all weekend."

"That's right," she says as if she's already got an exact fact in her head, and this is when I know to absolutely stop talking.

"Have to get back."

"Yeah," she says. "Me too. Nice talking to ya, and tell your momma Cudge'll turn up. Daddy'll make sure of that one way or another."

"Who?"

She looks genuinely surprised as she hangs a thumb on her belt buckle. "Thought you knew. Sherriff Vale; I'm his daughter."

I don't even bother to say goodbye, just turn and leave. *Mom's going to kill me.* It's like I'm a pinball, shot off without any idea where I'm headed. So I pull my toboggan tight over my ears and walk toward the river where the water is flat and steely, low. I take to the rock-strewn bank and head south. If I had a boat I'd shove out and float all the way to the Mississippi and into the wide open ocean. Just be done with Orgull.

"Hey fag," I hear. I don't have to turn to know the source. It's Gavin James, who almost made it through his junior year of high school. He'll be on his bike with a miniature plastic skull dangling from the handle bars. "I said, hey fag."

I look over my shoulder, confirming another of life's random shits, Gavin with his hard bangs and close-set eyes. He's astride his bike, slouched and wide-stanced, as if sitting on a Harley. I'm not in the mood for his routine. "Fuck off," I say.

He sits up straight because it's the first time I've spoken back to him. "Guess suckin' dick has put some piss in ya'," he says, grabbing his crotch. "Betcha wanna gob my knob."

Now I'm facing him and, and *I'm sick of this shit.* "Finally, Gavin," I say. "All this time I thought you were a fag just like me. I mean, it's kinda obvious but to hear you fucking say it. So yeah, whip it out and let's go for it right now." I walk toward a clearly confused Gavin, a kid who could beat the shit out of me, *has* beaten the shit of me, but he raises his hands almost like I've pulled a gun on him.

"Queerbate," he says, standing on one pedal before jetting off toward town. "Homo." But I barely hear it because beyond him I catch a glimpse of what looks like Mr. Callihan's gray Buick.

***

When I think about the chances I had to prevent what's happening, I sometimes come back to a surprisingly muggy night last fall, late, when Sammy spoke to me in the darkness from his bed across the room. "You awake, Conner?"

"What is it?" He'd been laying on top of the covers in nothing but his underwear trying to get cool, but it wasn't working.

"Do you hear that? What are they doing?"

I knew exactly what it was. I'd been pretending to sleep through the sound of Mom and Cudge having sex. Dad gave me "the talk" early, when I was around Sammy's age, because I'd walked in on him and Mom, but Sammy was still innocent. Earlier that evening, Mom and Cudge were sitting on the couch drinking before they went to bed, laughing at nothing that was actually funny. When I told them goodnight from the foot of the stairs I could smell beer and bourbon. Whatever they were celebrating continued in a muffled form in their bedroom along with intermittent thumping against the wall. "Go back to sleep," I told Sammy.

"But what are they doing?"

"They're just playing. Go back to sleep."

"*What* are they playing?"

Why was I in that position? What was I supposed to tell Sammy? That in the room down the hall his mother was drunk and naked and that Cudge was drunk and naked, too, and fucking her? And then was I supposed to explain to Sammy just what fucking was? *Well you see, little brother, when a mommy and an asshole love each other....*

"Jesus," I said after I couldn't take it anymore. I jumped out of bed. "Stay here." At the end of the hallway I took a breath at Mom and Cudge's bedroom door, half wanting to go back, tell Sammy to get dressed and take him away, get both of us out of there for good. The two of them could have each other. But then, as always, I thought about what Cudge might do.

Something had to happen, so I took another breath and knocked. The room grew silent, and then whispers. "It's Conner, Mom. Sammy can hear you guys." When there was no response, not even more whispering, I went back to our room, thinking maybe they were drunk and embarrassed enough to go to sleep.

"Did they stop playing?" Sammy asked.

"I guess."

He was quiet for a few minutes, but I could just make out his fingers twiddling on his chest, something he did at night when he was thinking something over. I tried to sleep, and I was getting there when he interrupted. "Conner," Sammy said, "what kind of dogs do you like? You like Dalmatians?"

"Go to sleep."

"I can't tell you but I got a secret," he said.

I opened my eyes and half propped myself up. "Oh yeah? What is it?"

"Can't tell. I promised."

"Good," I said, figuring that he was about to tell me anyway. It was likely that one of his little friends, as usual, had extracted the promise over not much. I waited.

"If I tell, will you promise to keep it secret?"

There it is. "Yeah. What is it?"

"I'm getting a puppy."

I sat up. "Did you ask Mom?"

"Not allowed to. It's a secret."

"Jesus, Sammy," I said. "She's allergic. You can't bring a puppy home."

"Can too. Cudge says so."

"You asked *him?*"

"No," Sammy said, clearly upset. "He said...."

"He said what?" I asked this innocent little voice in the dark. As much as the fact I knew there was no way we could have a dog in the house, I also didn't like that Cudge and Sammy were having private conversations. I'd done my best not to let that happen.

"That's the secret part."

"Sammy, what did Cudge say?"

He crossed his arms in front of his chest. "He's getting it for me when it's born."

It's not that I didn't want my little brother to have a puppy. I always wanted a dog myself, but if Mom came within even ten feet of one, her eyes puffed up like they'd been replaced with billiard balls. It figured Cudge didn't know that or didn't care. I plopped back down. "Go to sleep, Sammy," I said. It was no use right then ripping from his arms the puppy he had surely already imagined right down to the wagging tail.

"Don't tell?"

"I won't," I said, though I wasn't sure it was a promise I could keep.

In the blue-black of the evening light, I watched as Sammy reluctantly drifted off, one small, naked leg dangling from the side of the bed. The entire house was silent, and I felt my body slowly relax. I had, in the previous few minutes with Mom and Cudge, with Sammy too, imposed a kind of order, drawn a line, and it felt good. A breeze pushed through the open window, tickled over my shirtless chest. Muggy as it was, there was comfort in those quiet minutes. And then, from down the hall, I heard the door of Mom and Cudge's room open, and footsteps, not hers. The hall light clicked on. I closed my eyes, thinking *oh hell* as I turned my back to the sound. When Cudge stopped at the door, I knew it was him without looking. It was as if I could actually feel his shadow slide over me. I was motionless as he approached and stopped at the edge of my bed. I remained turned away from him, eyes shut, like when I was Sammy's age, convinced some odd silhouette in the room was a monster. If I just kept my eyes closed it would go away. I found out that only works when you're seven.

"Badass," Cudge said. I didn't move. Kept my eyes closed. "Little Man Badass," Cudge repeated.

Reluctantly, I turned, pretended to wake. I could smell Cudge's sweaty body, the odor reminding me of a too-used washcloth. When my eyes fully opened, he was standing near the head of the bed in three-quarter profile, naked, dark except for where light from the hallway outlined his body. He was partially erect, his dick fat and wet looking. "Jesus...," I whispered, not wanting to startle Sammy awake. "What—"

"No." Cudge cut me off. "You don't talk. See this." He pointed to his dick. "Your mother and I were in there having a hot thrill and you fucking almost ruined it."

"Sammy could hear you guys," I whispered firmly.

"I don't care if the fucking Pope heard us. Mind your own." He grabbed his dick and shook it once. A fleck of wetness landed on my chest but I didn't dare move. Cudge turned and walked out of the room. It wouldn't be the last time I saw him naked.

I waited until the hall light was off and heard the bedroom door close. Wiping the wet from my chest with my blanket, I sat up with my face in my hands, my body rocking slightly from the beat of my heart, a Morse code saying, "Get out. Leave. Take your brother. Get out." Some mix of fear, bewilderment, and a misguided belief it was my job to be strong kept me right where I was. If only I'd been brave enough to do something then, I wouldn't be where I am now.

"Sammy," I whispered. There was no reply. He was still asleep, a fact I experienced as part relief, and partly as a sudden sense of being alone. On the wall opposite, near the ceiling, window light cast what looked like a grayish blue kite, the kind I'd built out of newspaper and dowel rods. The form wasn't new to me. It was there

most nights, sometimes as a diamond, sometimes a space ship, and
sometimes merely a black cross on a blue background.

I didn't know what I was going to do, what I could do. It was
a shitty situation, which is what I whispered out loud right there
in the dark, on the bed. Cudge was an ass, dangerous even, but it
was an undeniable irony that some things changed for the better
after he married Mom. For the first time since our father died there
were moments when she was actually happy, or, at the very least,
not depressed. Just that night she'd made us fried chicken and corn
on the cob, smiled as she said, "Eat up," and gave us each two
pieces of chicken instead of our usual allotment of just one. Before
dinner I'd looked out of the living room window and saw her and
Cudge sitting on the porch stairs, sharing a cigarette, her head on
his shoulder, each with a beer and empty shot glasses at their sides.
I tried to convince myself Cudge's volatility was worth it for her, my
mind constantly discovering new levels of contorted logic.

Minutes after Cudge left our room, I heard Sammy turn in bed.
"What's a hot thrill?" he quietly asked.

"You were awake?" He slipped out of bed and sat next to me,
legs hanging off the bed. In the mirror across from us he looked
like a small gray ghost in the shape of a boy. I patted his back. "He
scare you, Sammy?"

"Not too much. I kept my eyes closed." He turned and sat
cross-legged. His eyes were dark and shiny as sewed on beads. "But
what did he mean?"

"Just one of his stupid sayings." I wasn't certain what I should
say, but I didn't want Sammy asking our mother, or worse, Cudge. "I
think we should just go back to bed and forget about it. You'll figure
it out when you're older."

Sammy let out a deep sigh. "I'm tired of people not explaining
stuff." He laid back on my bed and stretched out like a dog on its
back. "Nobody told me about toilet paper."

"What are you talking about?" I was relieved by this unexpected
change of subject. "Are you telling me you need someone to explain

toilet paper to you?"

"Not now," Sammy said, turning on his side. "But one time I just kinda noticed that it comes in squares and so I asked Mom how many I'm supposed to use and she just laughed and didn't even answer me."

I wanted to laugh but I heard the familiar earnestness in Sammy's voice. For some reason, the world had become for him an assembly of things he didn't understand, and he felt as if the key to it all was purposely kept away from him. "How many squares did you decide on?" I asked.

"Eight."

"That's too bad," I said, poking my foot into his rib. "The answer is six."

Sammy giggled, and slid up next to me. "I'm luckier than you," he said.

"Why's that?"

"Because I have you for a big brother."

"Thanks for that," I said. "But I've got you, so I guess we're about even in the luck department." We were quiet after that and in minutes Sammy fell asleep in the crook of my arm. I listened to the house, which had gone mute except for an occasional tick of wood. *We made it through another day*, I thought, forcing myself to imagine that Cudge hadn't just barged into our room. I stared at the ceiling for I don't know how long, but if every night ended like that one, I remember thinking, maybe everything would be okay.

10

I've seen Mr. Callihan's Buick. They'll wonder why I'm not in school but I don't care because now I have a direction, back to the Callihans', and I run, barely noticing the cold air filling my lungs nor the tendrils of feral honeysuckle vine that scratch my face when I get too close to the edge of the road. When I get to the house I see that the front curtains are closed and there's a light on inside. There's an unpleasant question on Mrs. Callihan's face when I knock and she opens the door. And something different. She doesn't invite me in. She's tired-eyed and looks nearly as gray as her sweater. "What are you doing here?" she says sharply, looking beyond me into the cold.

I tell her the half-truth, that I got sick at school and they sent me home. I came by to see if Mark has the same thing. "Can I come in?"

"Go home Conner," she says. Now she's crossing her arms and I sense the smile I'm used to isn't coming. Something's wrong. "What happened to your face," she asks, but then, quickly, "Never mind. Go home."

"Can I see Mark?"

She softens a bit and leans toward me. "Oh, sugar, I'm sorry. You can't. You can't ever see him again."

I feel it once more, that tremor that came when I learned about my father. I look past Mrs. Callihan hoping to find Mark, but except for one lamp, the house is dim and silent. "What happened? Is he okay?"

"Yes," she says. "He will be." She leans against the door and places a hand over one side of her face, shaking her head slightly. "I know what you boys have been up to. I'm so disappointed." I'm certain she detects that I'm a deer caught in the headlights because she doesn't wait for a response. "It just…goes against God and nature."

Two thoughts immediately collide in my mind. Cudge is the only person who knew about me and Mark, and he followed through with a threat before he disappeared. I'm afraid to ask but I have to. "What did Cudge say?" I ask.

Mrs. Callihan looks confused. "Your stepfather? Did he do this?" She reaches into her sweater pocket and produces a piece of paper which she unfolds and hands to me. It's the same embossed red tape, only in one strip and adhered to the sheet.

YOUR SON IS A FAIRY

Mrs. Callihan rubs her arms against the cold and looks at me as if I should know what she's about to say. "We found it this morning right here on our door mat. Mark was all tore up about it. Conner, he told us."

"Please let me talk to him."

Mrs. Callihan looks at me, her head shaking in pity, an expression I've never seen from her. It's almost as if I'm talking to an entirely different woman than the one a day earlier. "Sugar," she says, "we need to get out of this cold. It's time for you to go home."

"But I'll see Mark at school anyway. Why can't I…"

"Mr. Callihan took Mark to his grandmother's. He's staying with her until we move for his job. Sugar, you know I love you, but you've caused a lot of harm to this family. I can't have it. You boys smoking was bad enough." On any other day I'd want to know how long she'd known about Mark's cigarettes. She reaches into a sweater pocket and retrieves a rosary of pink beads, which she considers for a moment before continuing. "My son needs to get right with God and it just hurts my heart to know your mother…" She stops herself, eyes welling, and turns to go inside.

"Wait. What were you going to say?"

The door is half closed but she pauses and looks directly at me, her eyes wet and shining. "It's not your fault. This is what happens to Godless children. I should tell your mother but I think it's just best to keep a distance." She's halting, almost can't continue. "I have to protect my son, Conner. From you. Find God, sugar. It's your only hope. Take this black sin off your heart." She disappears behind the door as it slowly closes and makes a sound like the snip of scissors through string. I'm left staring at the door's pair of inset rectangles near the top, looking like cold, blank eyes as if the house itself has just died. When I turn, I see that it's winter. I see it, the naked dogwoods across the street a flay of spiny grayness jutting into the silence of freezing air.

My chest feels tight, as if the hand of the cold world itself is squeezing the breath out of me. I will find Mark some way. I think of that last glimpse of him yesterday in the rear window of his mother's car when I was about to walk into a house expecting to see my dead stepfather laying frozen in our bathtub. Mark was thinking I was about to face a lot of trouble no matter how well I played it. He loves me. He could have told Mrs. Callihan the truth about Cudge, but he didn't. Now I stand in front of the house he will never again occupy. I am alone and I am Godless.

I take a last look at the house, then run toward home as fast as I can, taking the back way through the woods, the frozen leaves beneath me sounding like the piston-chug of a fast-moving steam train. Mom will be at work. Sammy will be at school. The wild card is Cudge's whereabouts. I run past many of the houses I've broken into in the previous months, past the Chell's whose "silver" mint julip cups went missing, past the Kings and Smiths, who lost worthless candlestick holders, past the Faldwell's whose lawn I mow and leaves I rake and perhaps the only people I regret stealing from. I run until I see the rear of our house and its four windows, each dark and impenetrable as the back side of dominoes.

I don't want to go in but where else is there for me? The one place I felt safest and most loved has rejected me. I am unfit, a black-souled sinner. The deteriorating sandbox Dad built for Sammy sits near the house, one side separated with spilled out sand thick and clotted as the scar left from an old wound. When I'm alongside of the house, I hear voices in the living room. It's Mom and a man. Just before I make the corner, I see the bright red taillight of a sheriff's car. In the days to come, the state trooper will lumber up our drive, and the sheriff will return. He'll talk to my mother, and Sammy, and he'll take a particular interest in me. There will be many more red taillights.

II

11

We are about to get an unwanted visitor.

A couple decades have passed since Cudge disappeared and hardly a day has gone by that I haven't thought about him, thought about the grayish blue corpse in our bathroom that somehow rose, grabbed its wallet and keys, and bolted. My personal *Dawn of the Dead.*

Today, Lamb and I sit on the porch of the home which, except for college, I never left. Our cat, Mrs. Kravitz, sits patiently at the edge of the yard, dark silver tail whipping at the prospect of spring chipmunks in the woodpile. We're blessed that she's a terrible hunter, though occasionally a vole or some such rodent ends up on the welcome mat. More often, she lays at my feet bits of wire, string, or scraps of paper. Never Lamb, only me. After each gift she looks up to me with her intense blue eyes, mews, then walks off demanding nary a scritch. Kitty Hallmark moments we call them.

Lamb and I each hold a Yeungling brought up from Nashville, as we note Mark's birthday, the boy who was snatched away from me by his parents. Gone. He managed one letter. One. A note really, that I like to read on his birthday as a ritual to torture myself with what I recognize as an unsustainable standard of Love. "You know," Lamb says with a laugh, "I'm the only wife in the world that would put up with this." She sets down her beer and returns to the lady's derby hat she's constructing on one her many blocks, each with its own name. She calls this block Julie. The hat itself is a wide brimmed faux straw affair with blue lotus and yellow ostrich feathers, a commission. I've married a milliner and part time CPA, and I know everything about her. She thinks she knows everything about me.

Smooching in her direction I say, "You're the only wife in the world that would put up with *me*. It's your curse." I watch her for a second, admire the dexterity of her narrow fingers and the care she takes in attaching each piece. When she leans close, her straight black hair falls forward creating a kind of proscenium. I imagine the section of the hat directly in front of her as a thrust stage, the flowers becoming set pieces, or no, the actors. Mark's letter, except for once a year, is folded in quarters, worn now at the creases. It's not the three hole punch nor the blue lines of college ruled paper that reminds me how young we were, but Mark's awkward block printing announcing itself as a teenage boy's. Feet up, the oncoming spring in the pin oaks and redbuds, I remind myself I've made a new, better life, but I return to Mark just for the reminder of that old feeling, impossible as it was. Probably not healthy, but it's hard to forget because the letter ends with a promise that I've never forgotten. Having Lamb around when I read it keeps me from getting too maudlin.

"So, what does he say this year?" she asks without looking away from her project.

"He's in Paris having coffee and a cigarette at a cafe. There's a view of the Eiffel Tower from his bedroom."

She blows a wisp of hair away from her face and it obeys as if it's afraid of what might happen if it doesn't. "What movie is that from?"

"What movie isn't it from? He wants me to drop everything and meet him in Belize. There's a check enclosed."

She tosses one side of her hair back and turns to me with a wink. "Go for it. Your imaginary passport is in the house."

"See you in a bit," I say, turning to Mark's letter. Lamb has heard it before, has sat in bed with teary-eyed me as I've read it, listened to my wine driven garish pronunciations about having a lavish funeral for it that we both know will never happen. The letter always survives and this time I read it to myself. My mood will be different on the other side and we both know it.

Man, Conner, this all fucking sucks. I can't call cuz it's

long distance and they'll know. Mom took me to see a priest at grandma's church. Dads barely talking. They're all praying and talking about mortal sin and shit. They made me cut my hair because they suddenly decided it was too much like a girls. Dad got an apartment and I guess you'll see movers at our place pretty soon because we're going to Indy for his new job. My life is all fucked up. Yours too I bet. I asked Mom about you cuz I hoped maybe I'd find out what happened with Cudge. But she won't hear your name. So heres the deal. I don't feel bad about us. I know I should but I don't. I'm scared though. Because WE know but it's different when other people know. I mean, with Dad, suddenly I'm a queer. Actually his "son isn't going to be no queer" is what he said. We're queers. So fine. But we have to be careful. You already know that. And here's what else. I promise I'll come back. I fucking promise. When I get a license. I'm coming back. Maybe we'll take off somewhere. Okay? Mark

I guess he lived his life like I did. Just shut up and shut down, at least outwardly, because inside, that promise kept me going for a year and a half. There weren't any more letters, but I looked forward to Mark's sixteenth birthday because I knew, I knew the next day I'd see him pull into our driveway. When that didn't happen, I reminded myself his birthday fell on Sunday, and after the first few days, of course, he had school. I had a bowling bag jammed with clothes sitting in my closet, waiting to be snatched up. But no Mark that first week after his birthday, nor the following. No Mark in all these years. Nothing on the internet. I'd been a boy desperate for a voice, for the world to understand me. He was a start and I lost him. It sounds silly, but even to this day I find myself thinking, *Damn it, Mark, you promised.*

By now Lamb has the timing down. "About done?" she asks. Mrs. Kravitz is at my feet having deposited an aluminum gum wrapper. Rubbing across my leg, she trots off toward the house, her day's work done.

"Same time next year?" I say to Lamb. I refold the letter and tuck it into its sea green envelope with no return address. The stamp, a stylized eagle in white over a purple background, is pasted at an odd angle in a way that makes the bird look as if it's peering down at my address. I've always imagined Mark deciding to write this letter, then searching his grandmother's house for these materials, snatching a moment in time when he could slap on a stamp and get the envelope into the mailbox. A minor bit of heroism which over the years has become nearly as anchored in my memory as if I'd been there to actually see it.

"What do you think?" Lamb turns the hat around on its block. The combination of feathers and silk blossoms look like a blue-and-yellow fireworks display.

"If that's what somebody ordered, you've hit it on the nose." People pay her plenty of money for these hats. She knows I'm kidding.

"So, about the letter," Lamb says, getting serious. "Can you imagine yourself sitting there reading it at seventy?"

"I hadn't really thought about it."

"You know it doesn't mean squat to me but…"

I look at her as if to say, *I know*, and she understands me well enough that I don't have to explain that I get it. The time is coming, or has already passed by years, for me to move on.

"I've never understood why you gave up on finding him."

I take the last swig of my beer. "Mostly figured whatever reasons he had for staying away must have been good ones. I trusted him. That, and 'No matches found' got to be too depressing."

Lamb leans on the arm of her chair, resting a hand in her palm. "And the fear of rejection."

"Thank you, Mrs. Freud."

"That would make *you* Mr. Freud. Not so sure you're qualified." She beams and her eyes disappear. The way she smiles might be her most reassuring quality. I'm not certain where she got it. Her parents, both Chinese, were attentive but humorless. Even during college they pressured her to marry, something she was distinctly not interested in. Half out of spite, one day she brought me home. The Huang were mainly polite, but visibly unimpressed. "History major," her father said to me casually as he spackled his dinner with fermented cabbage proudly made biweekly in their basement by Lamb's mother, who boasted that her Korean-American bridge partners envied her skill. "Civil rights. Clearly you're a very smart boy." And then, "I believe a bachelor can live on that degree."

I did my best to get through it. After a while, when I didn't whither under the thinly veiled displeasure with their daughter's date, Lamb was won over. "Sigmund?" she says now because I haven't responded. "You in there?"

"I'm sorry, Ma-dam," I offer in a terrible French accent. "We haven't met. Dr. Piaget at your service." I offer my version of a European flutter of the hand.

"Don't know him," Lamb says. "I cut class that day." She looks at the envelope in my palm, gesturing toward it as she stands with her grand hat. "What if I said next year I might skip this whole letter thing?"

I'm not certain why this has come after all this time, but it's clearly on her mind. "I'd respect that."

"Because we're having a baby pretty soon," she says, stepping inside the house, the screen door popping into the frame. I turn, but the angle through the mesh allows only for ovals of her light brown skin, as if she's disassembled and floating on the other side. "Big changes coming. You have to be present in *this* life."

"It's a happy one," I say as her form disappears into the room. No need to add anything. We have a kind of love only we understand. She's made her point. She also knows the reasons I'm sometimes distracted. It's not just Mark's face I'll find across the room at a restaurant or the su-permarket—never really Mark—but for a long time now, Cudge as well. He's shown up in dreams, in a car behind me. Once I caught a glimpse of him on *Law and Order*, a bald old man walking on the street in the background. Another time, when nothing else was on, Lamb and I found ourselves watching a rodeo. We had to switch the channel because I saw Cudge mounting for a bull ride. *You're right, Lamb*, I think, *maybe now it's me who's keeping them around.* What is that? Addiction? Some masochistic fear of abandonment?

"Think maybe you can get to the tree today?" she gently calls from inside. There's no rush on pruning, but Lamb knows a little distraction might be good for me.

"On it." I head to the garage where I stash the letter with the other ephemera from my childhood, most of it stolen, that I don't dare bring into the house, especially the jarred thorn that is Cudge's desiccated finger. It was in this garage Mark brought me to my senses about what I'd been up to, but only after I'd dragged him into it. You know someone loves you when they're willing to join a teenage crime spree. Cudge had it right. I was playing the little badass. Pin some burglaries on him. It was months after he'd married Mom and I'd changed my mind about him in a big way. He didn't belong. In the beginning the stealing was me without Mark. Not really all that difficult to break into the first house. Even now most people in Orgull don't lock their doors because nobody has anything worth taking, a truth I confirmed pretty quickly. From house number one I took a radio that I later discovered didn't work, and over the course of time there was silverware that wasn't silver, drugstore figurines, small things with negligible value. It was a series of burglaries nobody seemed to notice in aggregate because it wasn't something I could accomplish quickly, a frustration that was part of the reason I didn't feel all that guilty about what I was doing. I'd stolen cigarettes and magazines worth more. I also figured that eventually these people would have their things returned. So, I kept on, and without one valuable item, I hoped an accumulation might do the trick, except that it all felt like it was adding up to not much. Who cared? Then Mrs. Faldwell, whose lawn I mowed, paid me to shovel snow from her walkway. From outside her window, I saw an antique crystal pitcher displayed on the mantle, the winter light spraying a patch of diamonds to one side. It was the fanciest thing I'd ever seen and when Mrs. Faldwell told me she and her husband were leaving for the holidays, I knew I'd return.

A few days later I watched the Faldwell's RV headed out of town, tailpipe fogging the cold air. I made a phone call. This time I'd need Mark's help. Maybe that wasn't so. Maybe I just wanted him there. Before dawn, I woke, bundled up, yanked a toboggan on my head and snuck out toward the Faldwell's through the wooded area behind their home where I waited for Mark. Earlier, when I called and asked for his help I half expected him to hang up, but he said he'd meet me before I could explain what I needed, which made it easier. "We're going to steal something," I said.

"What's going on?" he asked, but it sounded like much more. His voice was thin, anxious, as if saying *I need you.*

There was more that I wanted to say, but I simply repeated myself hoping he'd understand. "We have to steal something."

He was quiet but I didn't press. "Okay," he said, finally. "But I can't talk now. Mom's hovering."

When I heard Mark stepping through the woods, my nervousness subsided. "Hey," he whispered. "Why the fucking mystery?" He was swallowed by a bulky, white nylon coat, jeans, and the light blue toboggan he often wore to school. I wished I'd told him to wear dark clothes. There was something else that struck me. I couldn't put my finger on it before because I saw him every day at school, but alone in the woods just then and standing face-to-face, I knew what it was. In the past few months he'd grown a lot. Enough that I sensed that I was looking *up* at his eyes. That was months before I would conjure the words "I love you."

After I explained what we were about to do and why, mostly why, Mark shook his head slowly. I'd left out as much as I could while still doing my best to paint Cudge as the problem he was. Our house had practically gone on lock down. Nobody could come over, not Mark nor any of Sammy's friends. The phone was for adults and emergencies. The thermostat could be changed by just one adult hand. "Ya'll fooled me," drunk Cudge said once, mainly to Mom. "Sweet as pie until you got your hooks in me."

The new rules left me and Mark with school and sneaking out, hardly a moment by ourselves. Taking Mark's chilly, bare hand, I spoke softly now. "Please," I said, "I've got to do this, and I need you." It was true. This wouldn't be like one of the comparatively easy walk-ins I'd already done. The Faldwell house would be locked for sure.

"Why don't you just fucking tell someone how bad it is, Conner?"

"Because if that doesn't work it's only going to get worse." And then I let him in on something. "He knows about us. I don't know how, but he does."

Mark's eyes widened as he began to understand the implications. It seemed somehow easy keeping us secret, but the fact was that we lived in a small town in Kentucky where some people still talked about Hanoi Jane, and where, at school, the custodian never bothered to scrub away the stick figure effigy drawn in a stall of the boys' bathroom. Underneath, in thicker penciling it read, "the only good fag is dead fag." As if in allegiance, next to this, someone else scrawled "69 Rules!" My name was written beneath the figure.

"But," Mark asked, mulling over the break-in, "what if we get caught?"

"I'll take the blame. I promise." I looked at him directly, hoping to find his answer, but his eyes seemed to have grown darker, even in the predawn light, and didn't betray what he was thinking.

"What about you?" Mark asked. "You haven't told me everything. Has he ever actually?"

I gripped his hand instead of saying that I'd felt Cudge's fingers reach into my underwear, that he'd slapped my face with his hard dick and made me stare at him in the eyes. And worse. Reasons to kill him.

Remaining silent, he looked at the ground. "Man, Conner," he said. "I hope it works so we can be normal again."

Over the years I've thought about that conversation a lot, especially hearing the word "normal" from Mark's quiet voice. I've thought about my life with Lamb and how most people I know might say I never found my way back from my father's death, but they're wrong, I've told myself. I understand what I feared most, that life with Cudge became our family's *life*. That's what I was fighting against. Someday, I promised myself, I'd build something new from the ground up, my version of the Callihans.

Me and Mark had stolen a few things together from the store before, magazines, candy, cigarettes, but we'd never done anything like what I had in mind, and even though I didn't like the escalation, I convinced myself there was no choice. Stupid kid. That's why I needed Mark and why I reminded myself this was also for Sammy and Mom. I was doing it for them, too. It was a kind of self-brainwashing, telling myself *I* could handle anything Cudge threw at me, but Sammy was too young and Mom's ability to stand up to her husband fluctuated like the graph line on a heart monitor.

It was cold, maybe more so than I realized because I was so focused on what we were about to do. Me and Mark stood at the tree line defining the border of the Faldwell's back yard. The house itself looked as if it was asleep, a snuggled-in target. Patches of snow dotted the lawn, and a small tree stood near the house, naked, like the bare underwire of a stripped umbrella. The houses on either side were still and unlit, and somewhere in the neighborhood a rooster offered a weak, insomniac crow. "I guess we're going to do this," I said quietly, waving Mark to follow as we snuck along the fence line toward the house, every step on the crisp earth grinding in my ears as if it was decibels louder than it actually was.

When I got to the house I flattened myself to its side and Mark did the same. "This is crazy," he whispered. "We have no idea what kind of shit we're getting into."

I took a breath, thinking about what we were about to do. This one was making me nervous because it was an actual break in, and, well, the Faldwell's were about the nicest people in town. I decided I would only take the crystal pitcher. When they caught Cudge, she would get it back. Beyond that, if it was too heavy, I made up my mind about unacceptable alternatives. Nothing with a photo in it, nothing that might have obvious sentimental value, nothing that looked like it might have been given by a grandchild. "I'm going inside," I said. "You be the lookout."

In his puffy coat Mark looked like a frightened version of the Michelin Man. "You're leaving me out here?"

"Just grabbing the pitcher and dashing."

"What am I supposed to do if someone comes?"

Like so much of what I was doing, this wasn't a question I planned for. "I guess whistle through the window and take off running."

"Can't."

"Everyone can whistle."

"Not me." He made a wheezed attempt to prove his point.

"Then I don't know, yell 'hey' or something." I was done talking. The more we spoke, the less confident I felt.

Placing a gloved hand on the sill of a bedroom window I tried to push it upward but it wouldn't budge. The closest option was the bathroom window, which gave more easily than I anticipated and thudded open. I stopped and looked around. No lights came on in the other houses. Pulling myself in with a foot in Mark's hands, I slid face first into the room, grabbed the edge of the bathtub and allowed my legs to fall in with me. The thump was minimal, but I held still for a moment just to be double sure that I was alone in the house.

The first thing that became immediately clear was that I should have brought a flashlight. The only illumination in the house came from the oncoming lavender sky and a bud of glow from a hallway night-light. Heading toward the sound of a ticking clock at the front of the house, I found the front room a bit more hospitable, its windows serving a large gray waffle on the rug. I wasn't entirely unfamiliar with the house, but a problem made itself immediately apparent. The pitcher was no longer on the mantle. I looked around through the dark, but it wasn't to be seen, nor in the dining room, nor in the kitchen. Mark was outside waiting, so I had to think fast.

Back in the front room nothing struck me as the obvious thing to take that would be even remotely worthwhile, would trump the small mound of odds and ends I'd already stolen. I thought of Cudge. What would make sense for *him* to steal? In the corner was a glass case with Mrs. Faldwell's cherished Hummel collection which she'd shared with me over lemonade after one of my lawn mowing stints. The shadowed figures faced me as if they were curious about my presence, an accusatory hamster-sized army. The mantle over the fireplace was now a jumble of grimly lit holiday knickknacks bracketed by two brass candlesticks. Nothing called out to me as something a burglar would take. Even the television, a fat gray bubble in a wood console, thwarted my purpose.

I'd been in this very room before, but I hadn't planned that there wasn't anything in it worth stealing besides the pitcher. The tick tick tick of the Faldwell's cuckoo clock with its metronome regularity rose in my ears. Then a fuzz of light outside sharpened into distinct beams as a car stopped across the street and idled. I watched as Christmas lights pinned along the eaves of the house switched off and a woman in a gray jumpsuit emerged carrying a lunch pail. Like so many people in town I knew her and didn't know her at the same time. She often waved to me when I mowed the Faldwell's lawn. Walking directly to the car, she paused and looked in my direction. I ducked, and waited to hear the car pull away. It was clear to me right then I should have started earlier. Orgull was waking up, was *already* awake. The ticking of the cuckoo persisted as if it was intentionally trying to tease me, call me out for not being scared off already. I wanted to tear the thing off the wall.

Seconds later I was back at the bathroom window, whispering for Mark as I extended my last-minute theft. "Take this," I said. "It's all I could get."

"Is this what I think it is?"

"Probably," I said, sliding from the widow. "Now run." We sprinted across the back yard, Mark holding onto our prize like a running back tucking a football. The trees in front of us stood tall, the branches above a confusing, wiry tangle of black veins. We continued through the woods all the way to my house where we slipped into the garage.

"Are you kidding me," Mark said, out of breath and leaning on the door. "You stole a cuckoo clock? We went through all that for this?" He held out the clock and set it on a tool chest, a shining red metal behemoth Cudge bought but seldom used. "You think you're going to get him put in jail for that?"

"And the other stuff." I'd partly convinced Mark to help me based on the idea that the pitcher would make up for my trivial haul thus far.

He raised an eyebrow indicating he wasn't impressed.

The air was going out of the balloon, but I was willfully ignoring the hiss, all the while the voice inside me whispering, *You're thirteen. How could you possibly think this plan was going to work?* Years later I'd understand that was precisely why. Through the window I saw that there were no lights on in our house, but that didn't mean much. Cudge had us living almost as if electricity hadn't been invented. "I got scared, so I just grabbed something," I said. "The pitcher wasn't there."

"They're not going to put Cudge in jail for a fucking cuckoo clock." Mark hopped up on a work bench, removed his toboggan and shook his hair out, the effect of it like one of those ladies on T.V. advertising a bobbed home perm.

"I know," I said, joining him. I was in deep, and desperate to salvage the effort. "I have to get something good."

"Do this shit again?" For some reason it struck me that his mother never heard him talk like this. Boys with secrets.

I sighed and leaned against Mark. "Well," I said, "*I* have to." He rested his hand on my shoulder and we sat for a little while staring at the clock.

"Know what I wish?" he asked after a while. "I wish it was maybe two years from now so we'd be big enough to beat the shit out of Cudge."

"Two years for *you*," I said. He was being generous. I was more than aware how much faster he was growing. "More like three for me."

He squeezed my shoulder. "More like four."

We were joking, but I felt his speculated years stretch out before us like a field of land mines with no discernible horizon. My father must have faced a similar moment, imagining a future that seemed to hold nothing but bad options. Maybe he'd looked backward as well and thought he hadn't accomplished enough to feel like he mattered. At thirteen, that might have been what saved me. I didn't have the burden of a failed past, and with Mark sitting next to me, though it's not something I could have put into words, nor even fully understood,

I felt like, landmines and all, a happy future was still possible. Looking out the window at the house, I sighed. "Four years. I don't think I can wait that long."

Mark tapped me on the head to get my attention. His gaze was intent and led an expression which was some mix of anger and sympathy underscored by the freckled crescents of light beneath his eyes. "No, we can't," he said. Not long after, in late winter, he'd be writing me a letter from his grandmother's house. The last I'd hear from him.

12

I'm living, at least as far as anyone can tell, a quiet life in the same town I've pretty much always lived in. Neat lines, though always tentative, as if I've drawn my world with an Etch-a-Sketch. One bump, I fear, and.... I'm thirty-five and some change, have the habit of counting until I reach halfway to the next year, so this day I am clinging to thirty-five and also clinging to the trunk of a tulip tree and sawing limbs. Nobody beats the shit out of me anymore. Not since Cudge disappeared and people started to whisper. Not about me, but about my mother. Proximity to evil has its benefits.

The sound of my tree trimming fills my ears, a fact I notice less than the act of subtraction itself, the crash of falling branches, the kind of diminishing I've never achieved with my memories.

In a few minutes, from high up, I'm watching a stranger, a tall, older man, walk up the street. Normally a pedestrian isn't cause for much notice, except in this case it's immediately clear the man isn't from Orgull, nor from anywhere near. There's not much happening on our street that calls on anyone who doesn't live here to take a stroll. The man's cane-assisted gait is steady but slow, his left foot pointing slightly outward. A bit stooped, he wears what looks like a straw fedora, a grayish sport coat that sags a bit, and most noticeably, a bright red bow tie.

The presence of the man makes me consider a view so familiar I rarely notice it anymore. Later in spring, when the trees fill in, our neighborhood will largely be closed off by a curtain of leaves, but now I observe the lower portion of our road and this stranger. His journey is bordered mainly by shotgun houses, some of them camelbacks. They're simple structures, not much longer or wider than train cars. One of these, the Eubanks', sports a flag jutting from the crown of the pitched roof. The flag is all bright greens and yellows centered by simple lilies and tulips. The houses themselves are mainly dingy white, each with brass or black metal addresses. The man pauses for a moment, draws a piece of paper out of his jacket pocket, checks it and looks in my direction. It's not certain that he notices me, but he seems satisfied, because he tucks the paper back into his pocket and continues.

I return to the work of cutting dead and damaged limbs from the tree, but I'm distracted. Something about the old man. I think he sees me because he's crossed to our side of the road, alternating his attention between our house and the uneven asphalt. A tethered, scrunch-faced dog I don't know, with a tail curled like a passed-out question mark, offers half-hearted barking. Other than that, there is only my sawing and the early dotta-dotta-dotta of a woodpecker.

When he's cut the distance in half, I have to stop sawing and grip the tree more firmly because I can just make out his face. My eyes play tricks on me once again, because even in this old man I recognize a bent version of Cudge. Enough so that I realize it's the first time I've thought that Cudge would be in his late 60's now. I've really never imagined a version of him other than the one that lived in this house. An old panic creeps in, irrational as I know it is, especially since my worst fears about Cudge don't include this hobbled version. I begin furiously sawing another dead limb because I can't just stare at the man. It's not as if I'm inconspicuous in my purple baseball hat and bright blue t-shirt, a bright jiggling fruit as I half stand on a ladder, half on a branch of the tree.

When he reaches our driveway, the man plants his cane and takes off his hat, revealing a thinning pate of bright white hair. He's reached his destination, and although he's old and slow I'm shocked into motionless. If this isn't Cudge come back to life, it's his crumpled twin, a mannerly version. If it weren't for the hair I'd be convinced. I step fully onto the ladder and cautiously come down out of the tree. The man stands as straight as he can, hat and cane at his side, but he doesn't walk onto the property. I descend into the detritus of branches on the ground and pluck up the pole saw half buried beneath them. "Can I help you?" I call.

The distance between us is maybe eighty feet. The man cups his ear and I tentatively say the name I don't want to speak. "Cudge?" His posture doesn't change.

"I'm sorry to intrude," he begins in a well-worn voice as he walks slowly up the drive. He keeps his hand to his ear, until he judges that he can fully make out what I'm saying, though I don't repeat myself. We are about twenty feet apart when he stops and leans on his cane. I grip the pole saw and wait. "I'm looking for Betty Hotter," he says.

"I'm her son," I say stiffly, one knee quivering. It's been years since anyone inquired about my mother. "What do you want with her?"

He pinches at the brim of his hat and clears his throat. "It's about my son," he begins. "You'd likely have known him; he was married to your mother."

Holy shit. Raising my chin, I offer a hard stare. "What's your name?"

"Skee Hotter. And I'm awfully sorry I caught you off guard."

I approach cautiously, walking with the scythe-like pole as a kind of staff. Death as a weekend arborist. "Where is he?"

"My boy?" He centers his cane in front of him and leans on it with both hands. "That's why I'm here. Was hoping your mother might fill me in on that. You're not Cudge's son by any chance?"

The suggestion prompts a scoffing grunt that I'm not at all sorry for. "Betty never mentioned you." It feels odd to speak her name. I rarely do anymore. Not long after Cudge was gone I stopped calling her Mom. She was Betty. I think she understood why.

"He might not have claimed me. Had good reasons not to mention it. But that's neither here nor there. Just looking to learn a little about him and…." He pauses, which is a mistake because it gives me the chance to jump in. I don't want any part of whatever this is.

"Mister," I say, "I don't know where you came from nor how far, but I guarantee you our family doesn't want anything to do with yours. Cudge was enough for a lifetime."

"Of course, but it seems like maybe my son's portion got cut short."

It's a rich assertion and I let him know by flicking up the brim of my cap. My knee is no longer quivering, but I'm starting to heat. "Around here that's an opinion not too many people would share."

"Young man," he says, and I can tell he's trying to remain calm, "you can't think I bought a ticket from L.A. to Louisville, rented a damned car, and drove to your pissant town to rile up your family. A phone call. Your mother might have just called, given me ten, fifteen minutes."

"If she didn't know you existed—"

He cuts me off. "I sent a letter. Letters. A few years back."

I have no idea what he's talking about. There's been nothing and I tell him so, though he clearly doesn't believe me.

"A little of her time and I wouldn't be bothering you right now."

"We gave you all the time Cudge was worth."

He takes a breath, and I'm guessing an argument isn't what he's after because I see him physically let go of the tension. He recalibrates, adjusts the red butterfly that is his bow tie, and takes a quick look at the yard while he calms down. Not much for him to look at. Some daffodils and an upturned bathtub partially buried. "Really. If I can just have a word with your mother," he says, "I can be on my way."

I begin to respond but it's clear he knows he won't like what I have to say because he raises his hand, and I surprise myself by halting.

"You have to understand, I gave up on Cudge when he was a boy. A long while back, I promised his grandfather I'd try to find Cudge. I never did. It's getting awfully late to keep that promise. You know how that works on a father's mind? That the one thing you know about your son's life is that he's vanished from the face of the Earth? And, hell, I don't even know much about that." He taps the ground with his cane as if bringing the moment to order.

My concern flares because he's not just looking for Cudge. He knows his son is an erasure. Present on a Friday, gone by Sunday. "He left us," I say. "Took off. Never heard from him. No offense, but good riddance."

"Right," the old man says with a knowing smile. "Except, it's odd. You'd think he'd light somewhere. Register a car. Get arrested for God's sake. Something. But from what I can tell he just went missing."

"He did," I say with a shrug as if Cudge had merely been a swatted wasp. "I was fourteen when all that went down. I can't tell you anything more than what you can probably find out from the sheriff's or that you don't already know."

"Son," the man says, "I'm an old man trying to set some things right. I just want to hear a little about him of a personal nature. That's the only reason I'm looking to speak with your mother."

My eyebrows draw into furrows and my jaw clenches. "Don't call me son," I say. "But I'll sure tell you a little about Cudge, if that's what you're looking for." I turn toward the house searching for words. I see it every day. Two stories. Charcoal gray with a screened, off-white door presiding over a haphazard porch that isn't quite plumb with the wood slats. Snatching the cap from my head, I'm nearly ferocious as I turn. "Mr. Hotter, your son ruined lives. He was not loved. I'm guessing he died unloved."

"Okay, okay," he says, trying to calm me down. "Seems to me just because a man wasn't liked is no reason to look the other way when he gets killed."

"Who said anything about Cudge being killed?" The man stares at me and I stare back. Seconds pass. I hear the woodpecker again. Dotta dotta dotta. I have an idea. I turn again to the house. "Lamb," I call. "Need you for a sec. Bring the car keys?" Turning back around, I narrow my eyes to size up Skee Hotter, this man who looks so much like a question mark version of his son. "There was an investigation, Mr. Hotter. Nobody looked the other way. Your son up and left, and, frankly, it wasn't soon enough. But fine. I'll take you out to my mother's."

We stand in silence for a moment before Lamb emerges from the house. She's wearing her up-close glasses with thin black frames. In her hands she holds another hat, this one lavender and half sewn around the brim with purple silk roses. She looks at Skee and smiles.

"Surprise package," I say. "Turns out old Stepdad wasn't born in hell after all. This is his father."

The hat drops to Lamb's side. "Oh."

"He thinks Cudge was killed."

Another "Oh."

"Not necessarily, young lady," Skee says. He introduces himself and backtracks. "It's just after so long—"

"I'm Lamb," she interrupts when it dawns on her I haven't formally introduced her.

He extends a thick, veiny hand and the space around our little group contracts. "Lamb. That's unusual."

She laughs. "More unusual than Skee?"

"Lamb," I say, intervening before they get too chummy, "is my wife. Mother of our daughter in a few months. You know, the whole happy family thing. Be nice if we can keep going along without being reminded of Cudge." I look at Lamb, shaking my head, hoping she understands what's happening. "Going to take him out to Betty's."

She brings a hand to her mouth and looks back and forth between me and Skee. "Really?"

"He wants some closure. That right Mr. Hotter?"

"Something like that."

"You poor man," she says. I kiss Lamb on the cheek as she retrieves the keys from her pocket. "You haven't been to your mother's in a while," she whispers. "You sure about this? I can drive him."

"It's okay," I assure her.

He asks to use our restroom and before I can say no way, Lamb says "of course" and leads him toward the house. She takes him inside, then returns to the porch where I wait. "You think that's really Cudge's father?" she asks looking over the top of her glasses. Her tone is surprisingly enthusiastic, as if this is a fascinating development. Maybe for her, but she has no idea of the fireworks going off in my mind, the faces of Cudge and Betty and Sammy and Mark flashing forward, until it's just Cudge, the red moustache, the rough hand that even now I can feel on my abdomen, the rough hand I feel covering my mouth. Over the years I've told Lamb a lot about my childhood, about some of Cudge's lesser abuses, that one day he left us. I didn't tell her everything.

"It's him," I confirm. I don't need verification. I see the resemblance in the old man's face.

"And he shows up after all this time?"

I'm trying to figure out, on the fly, exactly how to handle this. When you've got something to avoid it's difficult to think straight, and when there's more than one thing, it's nearly impossible. I can handle the old man, I'm pretty sure, but how do I do that without explaining my past to the newest people in my life. "Regret can be a powerful motivator," I tell Lamb. "The old man is probably trying to tie up loose ends before he goes." As I say this I wonder if that's how it might be for me in another forty years. If I'll be telling my daughter *years ago a man came to visit Daddy. He was asking questions I didn't want to answer but I'm going to tell* you. I shrug to feign the insignificance of Skee's visit, but it isn't what I'm feeling. His unwelcome arrival shakes my sense that I've created a safe world for me and my new family. It's as if once again Cudge has revived and roamed.

In minutes Skee and I are on our way. "Lovely," he says, hat in his lap, as we pass Lamb in the driveway. She waves, and I recognize her sympathetic expression, though in the moment I'm not certain which of us it's meant for. "I'm not here to cause trouble," Skee says. "Look at me. Just a broken-down old man. Harmless as a fly."

"Conner," I say. "My name."

"Yes," Skee says. "Somehow we never got around to that."

I'm stoned faced as I point. "Last name's on the mailbox." Our address appears in black lettering on a gold background, each adhesive tile applied slightly askew from the next. Below the numbering is a smaller set of letters more aligned—GRAYSON, covering the shadow of HOTTER. Or maybe it's just that I know that name used to be there.

"Well, Mr. *Grayson*," Skee says, "I truly am sorry to have troubled you. Can't blame you for the shock. But I did try. I did write those letters. I'm just not good with these kinds of things. I suppose who is?" He laughs. "You know I had the idea if I walked up to your place instead of driving in it'd seem a speck friendlier. That rental they gave me looks like something from the FBI."

He has a car. Even better. "It wouldn't have made much difference if you showed up in an ice cream truck."

Removing a large pretzel rod from his jacket pocket, he asks with a look if I mind, then explaining it isn't so much a snack as a replacement for a forty-year tobacco habit. Tells me he still smokes in his dreams.

"Good pretzels you got out here. Plenty of salt."

"Grippo, I bet." Not that I care, but it invites a segue.

He takes a bite, then pinches the remainder between his fingers as if he's holding a cigar. "I think that's right."

"Speaking of your rental," I say, "no offense, but maybe I'll have you follow me. So we can just part after."

He thinks for a second, deciding if he can trust me, I'm guessing. But what choice does he have? "Should we call ahead?"

"Not necessary."

"Okay, then," he says, mulling and staring past the windshield where Orgull's main street is a tightly packed block of old store fronts that has every reason to give up but isn't quite ready. The red and black sign for Max's Tavern hangs over the uneven sidewalk and nearly across the street is my own shop, antiques, closed on Fridays until Spring sets in just a bit more. "No too fast, huh?" Skee requests as he swings the passenger side door open. He's slow getting into his car and getting it started, the winking brake lights fooling me until I realize he's hitting them as he gets adjusted.

Finally, we're on the road, and I can't believe I'm going through with this. Skee has rented a dark blue Lincoln that fills my rearview mirror as I lead him outside of town to an intermittently paved road. Asphalt. Then gravel. More asphalt. It takes some effort to reach my mother, and I've little incentive anyway. On the right side, an open meadow is speckled with yellow flowers and centered by a collapsed building, a wreck of gray wood and tin roofing. It wasn't in much better shape when I was a kid. On the left is a hillside that stretches ahead of us. A curve in the road follows its border. This hill is dotted with cabin-sized houses, each with a rutted driveway, and Betty's is just beyond that. Then I'll be done with Skee.

Slow as we're going, rocking with each bump and pothole, I've time to think. There's no doubt in my mind after this, Skee will want to get out of Orgull as quickly as he can. His solitary walk up the street, an old man dropping by unannounced, recalls the visits I got from Sheriff Vale, even years after Cudge's disappearance, and then years beyond his retirement.

After Cudge was gone, people expected Betty to pack the bags and take her children as far away from Orgull as possible, but she stayed, was the caretaker of what became a kind of mausoleum for our secrets. I knew the rumors about Old Betty Hotter, which is what people called her even before she got old, maybe because by the time we were done with Cudge and all the aftermath, she was a hull, withered. She was too young for the nickname, but it stuck. Some speculated she had hired a hit man or that she snuck back to Orgull and did in Cudge herself. They said she killed him for life insurance. She said *they* watched too many crime shows.

Be a kid at school when your stepfather has disappeared and all the parents have been gossiping that your mother did him in. You don't necessarily disagree, but you know you have to keep your mouth shut. Initially, it's obvious the other kids are looking but not saying anything. Nobody can say anything until that first asshole cracks a joke. In me and Sammy's case the initial thing that went around was kids randomly coming up to us, waving their hands, and saying "Abracadabra, Poof!" It didn't last because either they figured out it wasn't that clever, or because Sammy and me just stared, refused to react. I'll say one thing. The conversation about me certainly changed. I got a little dark and for whatever reason, after not-too-long, I wasn't that skinny gay kid everyone picked on anymore.

There were those few in town who saw us as a family abandoned. Betty did everything she could to encourage it, producing tears practically on cue, and sometimes I recognized the brand she'd shed after my father's death. There were enough that felt sorry for us. They raised money, even fixed up the house a bit, but the price was biting our tongue against what we knew was being said behind closed doors.

I begged her to move a number of times, to take me and Sammy where no one would know we were the brothers with the killer mother. "If we move," Betty told me not long after Cudge's disappearance, "they'll think I did something for sure."

"They think you killed him anyway," I told her.

"Not Vale," she reminded me. Then she put her hand on the side of my face and tilted her head in a motherly gesture rare for her. On her head was the blue paisley bandana she'd taken to wearing instead of fixing her hair. "You and I know the truth, little man," she said. That's when I began to have my own reasons to remain with the house, when I started to think that even if I went away, eventually, I would be back.

There were lots of truths then, but none of them seemed to matter to most people. The sheriff was different though. Vale didn't take to any of the theories about Betty killing Cudge. I remember him telling her so. I was standing next to her when he pushed his hat up off his distinctly pink forehead. "There'll be talk, Betty," he said. "But I know you didn't do your husband in." It was a temporary comfort because he had another suspect I'd come to find out, me. Fourteen-year-old me.

The lazy crunch of the road reminds me we're moving awfully slow, enough so that I feel my hands shaking on the steering wheel, and not because of a bumpy ride. I'm out of practice. Before the bend ahead, half way up the hill stands a portion of a house where Betty and Larry lived for a short while, most of it charred. The ragged edges remind me of an unfinished jigsaw puzzle. Slowing to one side of the road, I wave for Skee to pull up next to me and unroll his window. "Since we're out here," I say, pointing up the hill, "thought you'd be interested. That was Betty's place once." It's been a while since I've visited, but for the longest time, when I passed this burned out house it spoke to me in a way that finally convinced me to just stop making the drive at all. On what remains of the roof stands an aerial antenna but it's anybody's guess how long that will last. That was me not so long ago. Not even thirty and I felt like that. Obsolete hardware on its last legs. I had to make a change.

We are stopped on the road. Cudge's father is feet away. He's gotten out of the car and looks at Betty's ruin of a house longer than it deserves. A surge fills me. Not adrenaline quite. Not fear. Confidence. *I can go through with this. Fuck Cudge.* "Come on," I say. "It's just around the way."

Skee rubs the back of his neck. "Sure doesn't look like much to live in when it was standing," he says. "Hope your mom is better situated now."

"She is." I give him all the time he needs to resituate himself in his car before I take my foot off the brake and allow mine to crawl forward. Past the bend I check the rearview mirror to see if Skee understands the curve ball I've thrown, but he seems focused on the back of my car and the hillside which has run out of houses and instead towers with kudzu laden trees. But we have arrived at our destination, the narrow gate of a cemetery surrounded by a low stone wall.

I pull the car into the weeds and wait for Skee to catch on. The cemetery isn't large but there are an impressive number of headstones. The uneven rows of leaning monuments stare at me like an undisciplined army. It's not difficult to imagine that someday this patch of land and its tenants will be forgotten, buried under vegetation, become a ruin. A thousand years from now archeologists might dig this up the way we plow for pharaohs. No respect for the interred. Crack open the coffins and sift around in the bones like its nothing.

Skee's door opens, his white hair leading into the sunlight almost like a dandelion afloat. I allow him a moment, watch him survey Betty's final home. He places his hat on his head and nods slowly before walking to my car where I meet him, cross-armed. "So, yeah," I say, "there lies the only person I know who could tell you anything about your son."

"Kind of a dirty trick. Don't you think?" Skee raises his cane and gestures across the cemetery. "Dragging me all the way out here, for God's sake."

I should feel bad, but I don't. I want this man to know there's nothing for him here. I lean back on the car, take a deep breath, and wait until he's had his fill. The fact is I don't come out here. It's been years since I've been across that stone wall. Lamb thinks it's a mistake, but she doesn't push because she was with me the last time when I barely made it through. No interest. None.

"Well," Skee says as if he's done. I turn to get in my car but he continues. "Haven't been this close to a cemetery since Myrna's funeral. That's my wife. Can't bring myself to visit her grave. Got a grief counselor says it's okay for now. Says there'll come a day when the need to be near Myrna will be greater than the pain I feel." He looks at me directly with what I see now are gray-green eyes. "Good for you, young man, for making my heart hurt."

"I was…" I start, but it comes out as a near squeak so I begin again. "Was making a point. There's nothing left of Cudge here. Betty was it."

I'm not certain he's listening because he's turned and walked to the cemetery wall that comes up to about his knees. He stands for a moment, almost like someone looking over their garden. "Myrna is buried on a hillside at Forest Lawn. Heard of it? At first I didn't want our plot there. So many markers planted in the ground. Too anonymous. Whole lives reduced to two feet of stone. 'But the view,' she said. I laughed and told her she'd have a much better view where she was headed."

"Cute."

"Sure. I was a son-of-bitch before I met her. Crops ups now and then since she died." He waits for a moment, then turns. "Okay, then. Let's go." I reach for the door handle but he stops me. "No, young man," he says, and I when come back around, his cane points toward the cemetery. "I mean, let's go see your mother."

13

"Would you ever be sad enough?" Sammy asked me. This is the question on my mind as me and Skee walk across the cemetery.

"Sad enough to what?" I'd asked. We were standing on the Clark Memorial Bridge, at its center, the Ohio a slathery green flow beneath us. It's the bridge our father leapt from.

Sammy put his chin on the railing, hair tickling in the breeze. "To jump."

I wasn't sure how to respond. He wasn't stabbing dead wildlife any longer, but in the three years after Cudge's disappearance the purpose of Sammy's questions became increasingly more pointed and unpredictable. Early on, repeating something he heard at school, he asked me if Betty was bad luck for her husbands, and despite my consistent refusal, he repeatedly asked exactly what Cudge looked like when I came home that day to ask about the knife. Not what his mood was or if he appeared ready to race out the door, but what he looked like, as if he suspected something. In the days leading up to our visit on the bridge he had been similarly obsessed with getting me to take him to the place where Dad jumped.

"Sammy," I replied, "I couldn't ever be that sad."

The two of us stood side by side, looking down river, a gentle wind in our face. It really didn't seem all that dangerous, I remember thinking, judging the distance between us and the water. And the river is slow there in early summer, held up by the locks and the McAlpine dam. It seemed to me as if our father would have had to make an effort to drown.

Sammy threw his arm up and pointed. "What kind of bird is that?"

"Are you serious?" I said. The object of his attention had glided from beneath the bridge low across the water and away from us. "You don't know a seagull?"

"Oh," he said. "On TV I guess." He squinted as he tracked the downriver progress of the gray and white bird. "What's it doing here?"

"I don't know," I said. "I guess he's searching for food or a mate or something."

"In Louisville?"

"Geez, Sammy. Maybe he started out way down at the ocean and he didn't find what he was looking for and he just kept going." The gull caught a gust and lifted up and over the distant tree-lined bank and it was gone.

"It'll be sad if he doesn't find it."

"If he doesn't, he'll go back to his family," I said.

"What if his family is what he's looking for?" His expression registered a genuine concern that surprised me. It was just bird, after all. But the question itself still haunts me, because what happens if you don't find your family, and how do you know when you have?

I patted him on the shoulder. "Hey," I said. "Trust me. He'll be okay."

Sammy watched for a few seconds, to see, I guessed, if the seagull would reappear. When it didn't, he turned to me. "You ever hear about depression?" he asked.

It was an innocent question, tendered with the same casualness as if he wanted to know if I'd gotten word of a new flavor of ice cream. "Where did you hear that word?"

"Maybe sometimes depression can get passed to the kids. I read it."

I had no idea what he'd been reading, but it made me feel terrible that a boy his age was thinking about such things. "Are *you* depressed?"

"Sometimes I think so, but then I laugh and stuff. And I guess sad is different than depressed."

I put my arm around him. "We've had a lot to be sad about," I said, "but the reason I don't get depressed is because I have you."

"And Mom?"

"Sure," I said, squeezing Sammy's shoulder, "and her." But even as

I said it, I knew it wasn't true. By then I'd given up on Betty. We lived together, and she brought food home, but I had no use for her. I'd gotten a job sacking groceries after school and on weekends not so much to bring money into the house as that I wanted to be independent from that place. I wasn't yet resigned to the fact I'd never be rid of it.

"Conner, you take good care of us." Despite all that happened, Sammy maintained a sweetness in his voice, a bright-eyed expression that showed more optimism than perhaps what he was actually feeling.

I paused and took a deep breath. I hoped what he said was true; at least I tried, but why had that become my responsibility? Before our father killed himself, had he even a single thought about who would care for his family? If things were so bad, wouldn't he be leaving behind even worse? Hadn't he? Just blocks south from where Sammy and I stood, Thomas Merton had his great insight during the late 1950's. We read about it in school. He was at the corner of Fourth and Walnut when he had the epiphany that he loved all the people, all the strangers around him. He loved being one of them, a member of the human race, no better or worse. What granted Merton, I remember thinking, such an intervention? What god, two decades later, didn't have time to look to the right and see my father standing on the bridge, contemplating leaving behind the people Merton loved? Or worse, what god saw and ignored?

"Know why I wanted you to bring me?" Sammy asked. "Because I was little when Daddy died and you guys wouldn't tell me anything. One minute everything was all sunny and the next all dark, and there was no one telling me when the lights would turn back on."

I leaned into the railing close to him. "I haven't thought of it like that."

"I wanted to see the place where the switch turned off."

"So, is it light now?"

Sammy stood up straight and looked around as if to take the question literally. To our left were the modest high-rises of downtown Louisville backed by a hazy blue sky. Behind us on the bridge, steady traffic buzzed like a swarm of bees. "If I was here by myself," Sammy said, turning to walk back to the car, "maybe not."

I was unsure if it had been the right thing to do, bringing Sammy to the bridge. But my brother was right; he had been shielded from most of the details about our father's death, and then Cudge's disappearance. Maybe it was worse having left so much for Sammy to imagine, and that seeded by the things he heard on the playground at school. But Betty insisted. One day in the car, when Sammy asked if it was true that Cudge had jumped off a bridge as well, she gasped and pulled over. First, she looked at me as if I knew what to do, but then she turned to Sammy in the back seat. "Sweetums," she said, "when somebody dies, we don't talk about them. We let them rest. Like Daddy. Anybody who's saying what you heard about Cudge is making a sin. In our house we don't repeat sins." Betty looked again at me, and I understood, though I couldn't recall if she'd ever before invoked the concept of sin.

"That's right," I said. "When I hear that stuff I just shut my ears."

"But…" Sammy began before Betty cut him off, raising a finger.

"The only butts I care about," Mom said, "come from cigarette's and pork." It was a joke I knew he'd recognize as Dad's. Sammy was right. We'd kept a lot from him, and it was clear our drive to the bridge hadn't entirely satisfied. "I might," he said as we got in the car and closed the doors.

"Might what?" I looked at him, but he was staring straight forward.

"Someday. Be sad enough to jump."

14

"God damn it," Skee grumbles, pretzel rod hanging from the corner of his mouth. "Most people spend so much time running away from death and here I am chasing it down."

We walk to the section of the cemetery where nearly all the headstones are set flat into the ground. They are bunched much closer together than the older markers. Some of these are studded by bouquets of faded silk flowers and tattered American flags. The tip of Skee's cane taps in front of each stone as if he's checking off boxes. It takes a few minutes to find Betty's marker. A person would think a son might know where his mother is buried. The stone is a brown granite rectangle with her name next to Dad's, birthdate listed, followed by a dash, but then nothing. I never bothered to have it completed.

A breeze lightly rakes through the trees at the border of the cemetery. Skee secures his hat and looks around as if the moving air is delivering a memory. "Myrna and I went down to Mexico," he says. "Drove across the border to Tijuana. Best Chinese food we ever had. We kept going all the way past Rosarito. Slept in the car near a rocky beach. That's what I'm hearing right now, waves shifting stones."

"Never been to the ocean," I say.

"You're hearing it." He tilts his head in the direction of the trees and listens again, smiling. I'm doing everything I can not to lose it, to keep my throat from entirely closing up from grief, and not because of Skee's story. It's because, two graves down, is the name I can't bear to look at, gray on black, Samuel James Grayson. My brother didn't make it to twenty-one. Skee nods at a thought and his expression turns somber. "It turns a man's thoughts, being out here. Doesn't it? Myrna and I planned to travel the country after we retired from the shop. But it was when the boys were all dying off of the AIDS. Our young friend Robert got ill. Poor kid. Came to us from Idaho. Then he was in and out of the hospital 'til he didn't have anywhere to go and Myrna insisted he come live with us. I remember her saying she didn't understand. If she'd had a child just disappeared into the world she'd hunt day and night for him. I never told her about Cudge."

"Ever?"

"For a lot of years after Robert passed, Myrna was in and out of the hospital, too. Ended up being her retirement. As you might imagine, what she said weighs on me because I just let Cudge and his mother go."

"Sad," I say weakly, half embarrassed that I'm mostly thinking about how Robert might have died. I remember at first barely having heard of AIDS as a kid, thought it was a faraway city disease. And then it sunk in that people like me were dying. Skee is lost in his own thoughts. He tells me about his wife in the hospital, part of her hair shaved away. Dry, peeling lips that he dabbed with a wet cloth. He talks about bed sores and staph, his wife practically rotting away right in front of him. But it's not his wife I'm thinking of. "Robert," I ask. "Was that AIDS?"

Skee darts me a look as if checking for accusation, but his expression relaxes. "It was a bad time for those boys. Reagan didn't give a damn."

"I had a friend I worried about when all that was happening," I say. "We lost touch." Every time some new statistic came on the news or video of a protest, Mark immediately came to mind. I had this story in my head that he would have moved to California or New York. "It was stupid, but I felt pretty safe here."

Skee eyes me for a second as if I've said something disrespectful. "Unless you were double-gated back then, you didn't have anything to worry about." The silence that follows is awkward. "Okay then," he says, "we got a little off topic. A bit morbid even. Out here at your mother's grave and we're talking about other people dying. He looks past me and points with his cane to Sammy's stone. "Any relation?"

"That…" I begin, barely able to speak, "…was my brother."

Skee nods sympathetically. "He was young. I'm sorry."

A sudden weight falls on me. I'm not ready for Sammy. "He was," I say, one hand grasping my scalp. "But that's not what we came for. My mother is dead. You see that. I'm sorry, but anything the sheriff doesn't know died with Betty." I turn, still holding my head. "You'll have to find your own way back," I say as I start for my car.

In the driver's seat I'm shaking so badly I can't get the key in the ignition. Skee remains where I left him, watching in my direction as a cardinal flits across the cemetery. It lands on the wall nearest me, pip-pip-ping for a couple seconds before fluttering off among the headstones. So many shared last names. There are families here, including mine. Generations. This is why I don't visit, because as hard as I've tried to build a family of my own, here, I feel alone. It's a word I've been told isn't true. Doesn't apply. But, hell, I'm the last man standing. I am related to nobody. I think of Sammy and my head drops to the steering wheel. *Sammy...Mark...Fuck.*

15

I sit in the car at home. If Skee returns from the cemetery, I'll take my cue from Betty. Anything more to be said on the subject of Cudge will go with me to my own grave. *Except for maybe* that, I think, looking at the white garage standing at the rear of the property, a neatly painted structure, small and trimmed in blue. Lamb suggested someday we can turn it into a playhouse. But that isn't possible. I want to give our daughter the world and everything in it; the garage is mine, was when I was a boy, and it has to stay that way. It's where I keep Sammy alive. It's where, amongst the baby food jars filled with nuts and bolt and nails, screwed to the wall, I keep the grim memento that is Cudge's finger.

Lamb thinks I'm selfish on the point of keeping the garage off limits, that my tools and half-finished projects are enough to claim it for our daughter. It's storage, my storage, simple as that. My vault.

I'm still trying to hold everything together, have my way because that awful, early life of mine gives me permission. It's what gave me courage to drag Skee off to my mother's gravesite thinking he was going to have a talk with her. I did something terrible but necessary in misleading him. So many of the old feelings flooded through me when he announced who he was. Mostly, I was afraid. It had worked for so long to say as little as possible and that's what I retreated to.

Fate. Had he come a day earlier or a day later he wouldn't have found me in the yard nor even at home.

I'm startled by a knock on the car's trunk. It's Lamb. Checking myself in the mirror I see that my eyes are red. She'll know I've been crying. "It was a little tough," I say, stepping out of the car. "I can't take seeing Sammy out there."

She puts her hand on my shoulder as we walk to the house. "I kept my mouth shut," she says, "but I was surprised you'd take that poor old man out there." Her dark brown eyes are friendly but unusually intent.

"You're going to hate me, but I kind of let him think we were going to see Betty…alive."

"That's what I realized after you left." She gives me a mother's disapproving look. "Oh, Conner."

"I wanted him to understand that the answers to questions about his son are buried out there with Betty." This isn't entirely true and I hate doing this to Lamb, but as far as I'm concerned, I don't owe any favors to Cudge nor any of his family that might come out of the woodwork. Suddenly I'm imagining a swarm. I look out at the street as if there'll be a convoy, or even Skee returning in his car. "I hope this turns out alright," I say, mainly to myself.

Lamb doesn't respond, but I sense her eyes on me. And then I see Mrs. Kravitz sitting in the front window eyeing suspiciously, something I know better than to think. She's a cat, but she has known me about as long as Lamb. There are things I want to explain that Lamb has every right to know, but I can't. This is the great tension of my life, the need to speak honestly about Cudge to the people I love and at the same time the feeling that it's an impossibility. I have a life, a growing family, which is a happier situation than anything I had a right to expect twenty years ago. Somehow things have turned out, while not perfect, calm. At first it took a lot of effort. I'd been responsible for propping up the family after Cudge's disappearance. Sammy was too young to have helped out and Betty was useless. But the weight has lifted. Good things have come to pass and I hope Skee's sudden appearance won't change that. I built this.

"It's all very strange and disappointing," Lamb says. She gathers her long black hair over her shoulder to inspect the ends, something she does when she's trying to work out a problem in her head.

I sigh. "Feels like even though he's gone, Cudge found a way to stalk me."

"There's a Chinese superstition….." Lamb stops herself clearly thinking the moment isn't right. Her expression of concern is endearing.

In fact, it's just what I need.

"It's okay," I say. "I can handle superstitions. Long lost fathers, not so much."

Lamb removes her glasses and holds them at the corner of her mouth before she breaks into a big goofy smile. "Something stupid like if you cut your toenails after dark they'll turn into a ghost. Is that what you've done, Conner? Let me look at your feet."

"Very funny," I say.

"My grandmother told me that one."

"That's one cheery granny."

Lamb smiles. She is trying to let me off the hook, lighten the moment, which I appreciate, but as much as I want to, I can't quite muster the goods to join her. I continue: "And there's more than one way to be haunted." We know each other well enough to end the conversation there. She tells me she loves me as she heads inside, and I kiss the air in her direction.

"Oh," she says, turning. "Mrs. Kravitz left us a baby garter snake. How do you take yours? Medium rare?"

"And scaled, please."

"And I called James. Left a message about...." She waves her hand in the air as if to collect everything that's important to me.

"Thank you." James won't get in until late tonight, but the mention of his name calms me. As usual, Lamb knows exactly what to say. Life has gotten good, finally. There are two people in my life I care about more than anything in the world, Lamb and James. If not for them, I might have ended up as some broody loner on the last stool of the bar, occasionally popping off about how unlovable I am. But here they are, Lamb and James, rare gifts from a world that has taken so much from me. Although, this is where things are complicated.

As Lamb disappears into the house I think of that last vision of Skee standing at the cemetery, an old man wearing a red bow tie. An old man wearing a red bow tie and looking for his son. I am about to be a father myself. Wouldn't I drive to the ends of the world for my daughter? Didn't I do that for Sammy? I think now I should have treated Skee differently, but it's done with.

I look out at the greening yard and feel the house at my back. Not long before I started college, Sammy told me something odd. I'd mentioned to him that there were acceptances from schools outside Kentucky, but in the end I just didn't think I could leave. "Probably end up in this house forever," I said.

He shook his head. He was starting to lose his baby fat, and I could see that sometime in the not-too-distance future he'd be tall and thin like Dad. "If you stay here," he said, "Cudge is your lizard's tail. It may fall off, but it's always going to grow back."

It was a strange thing to say, though I suspected he was right. Even so, there were reasons I had to stay that would never make sense to him. Even when I went to college, I was home by late evening the first two years. If Betty hadn't eaten dinner, which happened often until Larry came back, I'd make her something and send her off to bed. I could usually tell when Sammy had cooked by the dishes in the sink and whatever open can sat at the top of the trashcan. Eventually, through different methods, the two of them would leave the house for good and I would stay.

These days it's not the house that remains on my mind. It's the garage. In the rear is a large double-doored cupboard about three feet deep and attached at the ceiling, a measurement which is only true externally. Inside from the front to the back panel the space is nearly six inches shallower, a hidey-hole clearly by design. Not long after Betty and Cudge married, I'd been looking to stash a *Playboy* swiped from the liquor store. I discovered that one side of the garage cupboard's rear panels are pegged, rather than nailed, and it's no trouble to slip it away. The extra space was stuffed with mildewy, crinkled newspapers from the 60's and three women's panties. This space is where I hid the magazine, Cudge's finger, and, later, the random hoard of a failed plan against him. And letters, Mark's, Sammy's last. And there the cache remains.

16

    Sheriff Vale always met me on the stairs of the house. Over the years this ritual was largely the same, Vale arriving with new questions about Cudge, obviously testing theories he wasn't willing to outright state. My mother put a stop to it when I was a sophomore in college, and then I spent two nervous years living in Louisville. When I returned, there was Vale, hoping that a more adult Conner would have a different story to tell.

    Vale's final visit was different because he was no longer a sheriff. He was an old man recovering from a heart attack, sitting on my steps without invitation, secure enough to believe he didn't need one. His face was deeply lined. The upper lids of his eyes sagged over his lashes, and he had the antiseptic smell of aftershave. Gone was a sheriff's hat in favor of the shock and swoop of salt-and-pepper hair which he'd let grow long in the back. His forehead had darkened to match his face. As was his way, he motioned for me to have a seat next to him. It had been quite some time since we'd had one of these talks, and I was pleased, but not surprised, that I was no longer nervous. I'd gotten my degree in History, and maybe the most important thing I learned is that most of the time, nothing much happens. Nearly all the time, actually. History with a capital "H," I'd come to believe by then, is the collection of anomalies that occasionally creep into our otherwise unremarkable lives. So, at that point, it felt almost as if I was sitting down with a longtime friend, or maybe a tough old Pawpaw. My confidence might also have been boosted by the fact Vale and I had switched positions. Now I was the upright, even-shouldered one, though he was still an imposing figure, if even just for the fixed expression that always seemed to have a question behind it; but the ratio had changed.

Vale planted his boots one step below us. "First time I was out to the house…." His voice trailed off into thin gravely clicks as if he was considering the accuracy of what he was about to say. "Was just after your stepdaddy went missing."

I pointed to the corner of the yard where our old tub was half buried in the ground, a concrete statue of the Virgin Mary in its recess with orange and yellow leaves gathered at her feet almost as if she'd called them forward. "Strange time that was. We aren't even Catholic." It was an idea my mother borrowed from a half dozen houses around town, but for me it was a monument to what I had to learn to unsee. She knew exactly the irony of installing such a grotto in our yard.

Vale contemplated Mary and the bathtub, then laughed. "Guess I knew that. Guess I know a lot of things by now."

It was a different tone than our early conversations, I noticed, reflective, not at all accusatory. "Lot of responsibility in knowing things," I said.

"I ever tell you I seen a man killed right in front of me?" Vale continued to look out into the yard but didn't seem to focus on anything in particular. It was the time of year when the air is full of the sound of shedding. "Fella was beatin' on his wife so I come out just in time to find 'em standing in the yard." He pointed toward two places on the driveway as if he was seeing the couple at that moment. "There she was with a gun on him and the jackass rushes her and bam. Dead as a piglet in a pond."

"I think you told me that story when I was a kid."

"I expect I did." Vale shook his head, placing his elbows on his knees as he leaned forward. "I don't guess I said this part. Couldn't blame the old gal. She was beat all to hell and it wasn't the first time. I come out there one time when she was buck naked." He gestured to his groin. "She was just all tore up, down to everywhere."

"I suppose there are situations," I said. It wasn't lost on me what Vale was getting at, but I didn't mind. In fact, I did something I'd never done before. I asked if he'd have a bourbon with me.

He lightly smacked his lips as if to work up the taste. "If you promise you won't tell Jodi," he said. That made me smile because he sounded like a schoolboy eager to get away with something. Jodi was Vale's daughter, the same woman who found me skipping school that day I was slouched across from the bar she ran with her husband. In his later years, Vale lived in the apartment above.

"I can keep a secret," I said, standing.

"Ain't that the truth."

When I returned with our glasses, I paused at the screen. Vale was walking in the yard with hands behind his back. He'd been in my life so long it was as natural a scene as if it were Sammy. "See something interesting?"

"I reckon it's all interesting," he said, returning to the steps. I handed him his bourbon.

Vale put his nose to the glass. "Someone taught you right, boy," he said, and I understood that he was referring to the drop of water I'd dapped in the liquor. He took a sip and smacked his lips again before getting around to what he came for. "Now, I was saying I don't blame the old gal for what she done." He looked right at me, but there wasn't any evident malice as he asked the question more directly and with more assumption than he ever had before. "Give an old man some satisfaction. Will ya?"

Leaning back, I let the sun fall across my body, thinking of a time when Cudge hit Betty, and worse. I still had shreds of care. "Let me ask you this, Vale," I said, taking a sip of bourbon, the aroma of charred oak arriving before the taste. "Did that woman get sent to prison?"

"She did. For a bit."

"And was that right?" I sat up. "I mean, if you really think there was some justification for killing her husband."

He squinted and brought a crooked finger to his lips. "In my line of work, I met a lot of people'd be better off dead. And for a lot less than killing a man. But that's why we have the law. 'Cause if everyone starts making a list.... Well, sooner or later we're *all* bound to end up in someone's comeuppance bucket. Can't have folks knocking off other folks like cans off a fence rail."

"True enough," I said. "But, you don't think there are exceptions?"

Vale knocked a heel on the back of the step like he was shaking off dirt. "It's one thing to understand why something was done, like that woman I told you about. 'Nother thing altogether to say there shouldn't be consequences." He locked in on me again with those familiar blue eyes. "Did ya do it boy? Did ya do in your stepdaddy?" He was close enough that I smelled the bourbon on his breath.

I knocked back my glass and waited for the heat, only briefly losing eye contact with Vale. I'd seen his face this close countless times, but there was something new. The intensity of the past was gone, replaced with what I took as a form of understanding, almost camaraderie. As a boy, the early insinuation that I'd killed Cudge was met by my angry and outsized denials. Because of Mrs. Callihan, he knew about the knife and that was enough. Betty inserted herself on my behalf, but it was also clear she didn't mind that the spotlight was off of her. The truth is I also found a kind of power in being a suspect. A reason to be defiant was exactly what I needed, was something to curate. After all the questions had been asked and re-asked, I arrived at a response that froze everything in place, was for a lot of years a source of strength, and that was to say nothing at all. Sitting there with Vale, bourbon in hand, I felt like he understood me, and so in reply to his question, I said nothing.

His eyes darted back and forth between mine. "Well," he said with a smirk, and finishing his drink, "least your story's consistent."

"That it is," I said, watching Vale rise slowly and step off the stairs.

"Guess I come out here to say this, Conner. Thought about you a lot over the years. Maybe too much. And your family." He squeezed one hand with the other like he was working pain out of the joints. "There are all kinds of consequences. Some come quick." He snapped his fingers. "Others...they kind of gnaw at you over time. Be a day when you'll want to say something. Always is. Maybe it'll be 'cause the right person with the right ear comes along. When that time arrives, speak what'll heal your heart, son."

I patted the area of my chest where my heart would be. "Rock solid here," I said. It was a lie and Vale knew it. I saw it in his doubtful expression.

"You know I took some extra interest in your stepdaddy's case over the years."

"I do, and I've wondered. I mean, it's not like he was an abducted child. JonBenet Ramsey."

"No," Vale said, "not that poor little girl. That's the thing, young man. You never gave me credit where Cudge is concerned. *Knew* the man, to an extent."

I thought Vale was going to continue but he stopped. He didn't say goodbye either, just walked to the end of our long drive and into the half shade of the maple where the dappled light glittered over his white hair. Then he gave a single nod and offered a farewell sweep of his hand as if wishing me luck.

That visit on the stairs turned out to be the last time Vale and I spoke, though in the months following, in town, we acknowledged one another with a short wave. Vale was right, as it turned out. More and more often there are times when I've felt like I can't hold it in any longer. Something happened in my house that I can't explain. Was Skee's arrival the moment Vale told me would come? There had been something forgiving in that final conversation, and now I wish Vale was alive to hear everything I know, think I know, about Cudge's disappearance, that it would be he and not this stranger trying to pry open the coffin of my past.

17

It's early evening of the day Skee showed up. Lamb and I are sitting on lawn chairs in front of a fire, each with a beer. With the baby on the way, she allows herself just one. Mrs. Kravitz is sprawled across the length of one of my thighs as if it's a great outcropping in a Disney movie. The air is spring cool, and we appreciate these days knowing that in a month or so the humidity and mosquitos will mock our desire to be outdoors. Not far off is the pile of limbs removed from the tulip poplar. I'm wary—when in my life haven't I been?—but Skee didn't return from the cemetery, so after a couple of beers, some of the tension has fallen away though the memories are stirred. I am thinking about me at fourteen and Bobby Franks. I ask Lamb if she'd ever heard of him. She searches her memory briefly and takes a sip of her beer. "Nothing," she says.

"Chicago. Leopold and Loeb?" Her expression remains blank. "Crime of the Century?"

She rolls her eyes and chuckles. "Can't keep track of all those."

"1924. Kid about the same age as me when Cudge was around."

"This isn't going to be one of *those* stories is it?"

I put a hand out to the fire. I know what she means, but it doesn't matter. It's on my mind. I tell her how Franks was walking on the street when Nathan Leopold and Richard Loeb lured him into a car for a ransom kidnapping. "But the thing is," I say. "They pretty much killed the kid right away. I mean, these guys were like eighteen and nineteen, and they were wealthy. It was about the sport of it."

"Ahh, spring," Lamb exhales, adding no small amount of sarcasm. "Tulips, dogwoods, and homicide."

"Point taken," I say, though I'm not deterred. "So, these two do this to prove they can get away with the perfect crime." I tell her how, before they tossed the boy's body in a culvert, they poured acid on him and stopped for a hot dog. "Then at the trial, Clarence Darrow comes along…"

"The Monkey Trial guy?"

I nod. "…and it's genius. Darrow blames it on Nietzsche and their college education. The judge buys it and instead of death, gives Leopold and Loeb Life plus 99 years on the reasoning that they're minors."

Lamb shoots her palm over her head as if to say she has no idea where my story is going. "Okay," I say. "Something else. I once saw a two-headed calf. Lived for three hours."

"*Muuuch* better," Lamb says, looking at the tree limbs. "If it wasn't so close to the house, we could have a bonfire."

"Maybe that's the reason we *should* have a bonfire." I hold out my bottle as if I'd just made a toast but Lamb doesn't return the gesture. She is looking up the street at approaching headlights. We're so used to the habits of our neighbors, it's an automatic reflex to think, *who could that be?* In seconds, Skee's car rolls up and parks lengthwise across the end of the driveway. *Shit.* I make out the silhouette of him in his hat. Then the car's overhead light blinks on, though he doesn't immediately step out of the car nor appear to be looking in our direction. "Guess that *was* pretty dickish of me to take him out there."

"Ya think?" Lamb says. "Was hoping to hear that come out of your mouth."

"I've made better decisions, I know." Together we watch Skee make it up the driveway on foot, cane in hand. "You could have driven in," I say when he's close. Mrs. Kravitz stares at the stranger for a few seconds, tenses as he continues to approach, then jabs me with her back claws as she jumps away. She has the right idea.

Skee waves off the suggestion of driving in. "I was jotting some notes. Not so good at backing up the rental." His voice sounds calm and friendly, as if I haven't slighted him a bit.

Lamb extends a beer. "If it's all the same to you," Skee says, "I best not partake." He reveals a handful of pretzel rods. "I'm best to make do with these. I *will* take a seat if you're offering." He removes his hat and makes a quick bow in my wife's direction. "Lamb, it was?"

"Mother of my little girl," I say, patting her belly, then quickly snapping my hand back. Of all the inconveniences of being an expectant mother, it's the liberties people take in touching Lamb's belly that gets on her nerves the most. "I'm not Buddha," she'd recently grumbled at an unfortunate grocery store cashier.

She half stands but Skee shakes his head and smiles against the formality. He sits, leaning his cane against his thigh and placing a pretzel between his lips like a cigarette. "Never had kids with my Myrna. Wanted 'em, but it never came to pass." If it weren't for the circumstances and he was just some stranger I saw walking on the street, except for the fact there's so much of Cudge in him, he would pass for a kindly old man.

"Sorry to hear that," Lamb says. "This will be my first. Five months and counting. Truth is, if you'd asked two years ago if I was going to have children I would have said no, but then I got the bug."

"Lamb," I say, "I'm sure Mr. Hotter didn't come here to get a pediatric history."

Skee shifts in his chair and takes the cue.

"Got a lot done there," he says, looking at the tree limbs. "Damned productive day."

I continue to be surprised. The old man seems as calm as earlier. It's difficult to imagine that he is any kind of true relation to Cudge. "Needed to be done," I say. "Poor tree's on its last legs."

"Last *roots*," Lamb offers.

"Right," I say after an awkward pause because this is all dumb. We're all just beating around the bush.

"My day wasn't as fruitful, as you know," Skee says.

I finish off my beer. "About that…."

Skee holds up a hand and licks in the last of his pretzel like a frog consuming the tail end of a dragonfly. "No, no, young man. I put you in an awkward position, showing up unannounced, asking to meet your departed mother. Asking questions about a time I'm damned sure you'd like to forget." He reaches into his pocket and produces another pretzel, holding it between his thumb and forefinger. "Thought about it on the drive back. I might have done a better job of introducing myself."

"Same goes here," I say, raising my empty bottle. He tells Lamb that he hasn't been to a cemetery since his wife died and the Mexico story about how they'd driven down from Los Angeles in his Falcon Futura and slept at the beach with the top down. "So maybe the memory was worth the trip," he says. "And for my part, I should say, I'm not here to cause any trouble. I made a promise to myself I'm trying to keep is all. It'd be a real gift if I could make good on that by getting back to L.A. with a better idea of who my son was and what happened to him."

Nothing Skee says is unreasonable. But I know what even reasonable questions can lead to, and I also know Lamb won't put up with me continuing to be unkind. I think quickly about what I can and will not say, how I might sound generous with what I know, despite my interrupted apology. My own father, a man with two sons, seemed finally not to care enough about us at all when he jumped off the bridge. What is it about Skee that sent him across the United States to find out about a son he hasn't spoken to in decades? What if Dad had cared this much? My entire life would have been different, including the fact of this moment. "About Cudge," I say, "I can offer what I know my mother told Sherriff Vale and the little bit I know myself."

"That would be of great help," Skee says.

"I confess I'm reluctant to tell you about life with Cudge. I doubt it's the kind of stuff a father wants to hear." I gnaw at a splinter on the side of my thumb, but Lamb reaches out and brings my hand back down.

Shifting in his chair, hat in his lap, each of Skee's eyes contain a light blue star. "I'll tell you what," he says. "If the situation was reversed and it was Cudge asking after his dead father, I guess I'd want folks to fill him in warts and all."

"Alright," I say. "I'll trust you to sort it all out."

"That's all I ask." Skee pauses for a second and leans forward eagerly. "You two ever been out to L.A.?" It isn't the question I was expecting. "Been to a television program? I mean right where they film it?"

Lamb laughs. "Conner, leave Orgull?"

"I went to college," I say. Lamb rolls her eyes because I graduated practically up the road in Louisville.

"If you get a chance," Skee continues, "you really ought to go. Myrna and I went to the Carol Burnett program. She even got to ask Carol to do her Tarzan yell. They didn't show it on TV but she did it for us. Real nice lady. Funny program."

I look briefly at Lamb to see if she has any idea why we were suddenly talking about an old television show, but she is watching Skee as if she's actually interested in what he's saying. "Mr. Hotter...," I begin.

"Skee."

"Skee. I appreciate that you came all this way, and I truly am sorry I took you out to the cemetery. It was wrong of me. I'm certain I can't help you much, but like I said, I'll tell you what I can." I start with something positive, telling Skee how my mother had been in a funk after Dad killed himself and Cudge came along and at first made things better for her. It isn't really a story I can stretch very far before getting to the one that even Lamb hasn't heard. Cudge was fired from the Colgate plant not long before he disappeared. "Beat up a coworker he suspected was having an affair with Betty."

"You're kidding," Lamb interjects, leaning toward me. "You never told me that. Were they?" Between the two of them I feel like the most interesting and the most dangerous person in the world.

I stand and poke around in the fire with stick. If this is going to take any length of time, we need another piece of wood. "Not really. Larry was just nice to us and Cudge blew it way out of proportion." Half of which was a lie, because I knew what Mom and Larry were up to, and when I was done with college Betty moved in with him. For Skee, I'm trying to give an impression about Cudge without talking about the harder stuff.

Skee removes a notepad and pencil from his jacket pocket and pops in another pretzel.

"What's with that?" I point to his note taking, suddenly thrown back to those days when men in uniforms were asking me questions and doing just this same thing.

Skee taps his forehead. "Just memory. Coming up on eighty, after all."

"You're kidding," Lamb says. "Eighty? And you're out here doing this?" Her dark hair is streaked with yellow refraction from the fire.

"Not exactly about to expire tomorrow," Skee laughs. "But I guess I look it."

Lamb demurs. "Not at all. It's just I'd think you'd be enjoying retirement instead."

"Guess this is making *use* of my retirement, or at least it'll have to do." He turns to me. "I don't doubt Cudge was an S.O.B. Was when he was a boy before I gave him up. But I was hoping to find out he'd changed. I mean, isn't there some honor in fighting to keep another man away from your wife?"

"Yeah," Lamb says, sounding as if she's working to keep the moment as light as possible. She winks. "Wouldn't you fight for me?" It isn't a question I need to answer. There's not anything in the world I wouldn't do for her. When she wanted to cut back and work part time as a CPA so she could devote more time to derby hats, I was all for it. When her parents nearly convinced her not to marry me, I practically walked around on my knees for days until she said yes. "What if," she'd asked the day before we married, "you meet a guy and want to marry him." I laughed. "In Kentucky? Never gonna happen."

"I don't want to sound rude, Skee," I say now, making an effort to use his first name. "But to be honest, 'honor' isn't the word I'd associate with your son."

"What's a word you'd use, out of curiosity?" He puts his pen to pad in preparation, making me aware I'm filling space, as if transferring the contents from one storage locker to another.

I pause. This is where I have to be careful. All I want is to give the old guy some information about his son, satisfy as best I can whatever journey he's on in his own life. There's nothing but downside for me in giving up more than that. "Look," I say, backtracking, "that's the best I can do. After my father died, Betty was in a real bad place, and when Cudge came along, it's true, things brightened up for a while. I won't deny that. And it didn't feel like every time that the mail came we were going to get kicked out of our house."

"That's something at least," Skee says.

"But if you want to know the truth...." The fire offers an unexpected pop and we all turn. There remains the smallest of flames rising from what looks like a pile of glowing orange vertebrae.

Skee returns to the conversation. "I would," he says. "I'd like the truth." He places his hands on the arms of his chair, one side of his face gray-blue as a half moon.

"Cudge could be downright scary. That house was a prison after a while and Cudge was the warden. We were looking to escape. We were looking for someone to rescue us. Maybe Betty thought Larry could be that person. I tried to be for my brother." Nothing I'm saying is wholly true. But it's true enough, and I watch Skee and Lamb closely to make sure it's going over.

"I see," Skee says, shaking his head. "It's not as bad as you built up, but I did hope better for the boy. He sounds a lot like his mother. Apple doesn't fall far from the tree. Course I didn't do him any favors by giving up on him." He offers me a look of sympathy. "And for that, young man, I apologize to you."

I'm caught off guard. I can't remember anyone apologizing to me for what Cudge did to our family. Not even sure that's something my heart has been looking for. I can't find words, so here I am finding myself with a sudden and unexpected well of tears. It's all I can do to hold them back. The closest my mother ever came to an apology was an afternoon when we were hanging laundry. Cudge had been gone six months to the day, a fact I knew because I marked off the time, and I told Betty as much. She stopped midway through hanging a pillowcase. "It's just you and me, and Sammy from now on," she said. "I want you to know that. We'll have peace. You earned it, little man."

Nothing followed and she continued with the laundry, but the certainty in her voice convinced me that she meant it. She never again called me by my nickname after that.

"I didn't—" I began but she stopped me, spoke from behind a linen scrim.

"I don't care what you did or didn't do, Conner. We're just a quiet little family now. Church mice."

I thought maybe once Cudge was gone, we'd get our mother back, damaged as she already was, but she remained stuck in some sort of fantasy world. When a few families in town held two weeks' worth of fundraisers to pay off the house, she played the twice abandoned wife role so well I was almost convinced she cared. She thought I'd earned her a commuted sentence, of sorts, and my reward?

So, I'm sitting with Lamb and Skee, after years of being silent. There's something dangerous and almost cathartic about the moment. "Larry. His last name was Gaines," I say. "The Sheriff talked to him, to all of us. Couldn't come up with anything more than Cudge skipped town." I unleash every fact I can think of, sprinkling in some hard truths, that Cudge started drinking harder after he got fired, got in more fights. And then there was the series of petty break-ins. Yeah, that.

Lamb interrupts, "Whoever was breaking in, might have done something to Cudge?"

"It was a theory," I say, taking a swig from another beer. "But I've always thought," and here I look at Skee, "with no disrespect, Cudge just pissed someone off for the last time."

"By doing what?" Skee asked.

"I said it's just what I think. If I treated other people the way he treated us, I wouldn't doubt it. No sir." I squeeze Lamb's hand in preparation for what I'm about to say next. "Skee," I say, "this next part might be a little difficult to hear."

"I want to know it all," he says. He offers the slow nodding people do when they want to assure you of their need.

"Your son was dangerous," I say. A herd of stories thunder through my mind, images of Cudge hovering over me so close I can almost feel the sweaty weight of him, but I say "It was all I could do to keep him from touching my brother. Honestly, I wanted him dead." I stop abruptly, reconsidering the choice. Lamb and Skee are silent, clearly unsure of what to say.

"Cudge was a child molester?" Lamb is stunned. If she only knew the proportions of what I've told and what I haven't.

I backtrack. "Betty was no help, but I was there. I don't think he ever got to Sammy. He came at me naked and drunk one time but I…stopped him." Skee is rigid and intent. "Look," I say, "you deserve to know the son you're trying to recover. Maybe it's not worth it?"

He shakes his head slowly and pinches the bridge of his nose. "A man wonders what he could have done differently."

I understand the sentiment more than I can express. What percentage of my own life have I asked this same question?

"Don't even think about blaming yourself for something like that," Lamb says. She shoots me a look of reprimand that morphs into a concerned shrug as if to ask what she can do for me and what we should do with Skee, this suddenly defeated looking old man we don't know and who still hasn't looked up.

"Jesus," I say. "It was stupid of me to tell you."

"No," Skee says, "I needed to hear it. I should hear everything. A boy experiencing something like that." He sits up straight and closes one eye as if he's considering something. "Don't take this the wrong way," he says. "I wonder. Is there any satisfaction in it?"

"In what?"

"You said that when you were a boy you wanted Cudge dead. Looks like maybe you got your wish."

There's the thing I can't say here, what I was told I didn't see. When I found Cudge in the bathroom the sight had shocked me. Grim is a word I didn't own then, but it fits. Cudge was nearly submerged in the frozen bathwater, still as a mannequin and almost as artificial looking. Even then, for a second, I feared him as if he might reanimate, pop up out of the tub and lunge at me. Skee has asked how satisfied I am that Cudge disappeared. I pick up my beer, see that it's empty, and set it down. "Did I get any satisfaction out of Cudge's vanishing into thin air?" I say. "Relief, maybe. A sense of justice. But satisfaction? It was too late for that."

"Justice?" Skee raises an eyebrow. "Awful as the boy might have been, I'm not one to subscribe to the idea that what happened to him was any kind of justice."

"But they don't know what happened to him," Lamb says.

Skee leans in with a very serious expression directed entirely at me. "But your mother had him declared dead."

"What are you talking about?" This is news to me, and I'm wondering if it's something Skee knew when he arrived, part of his own game. If I was ever in control of our conversation, I know I've lost it. I've put myself on the side of condemning a dead man and I'm more than a little uncomfortable about where this is going.

Lamb reads the surprise on my face. "Are you sure that's right?" she asks.

"First thing I looked into." Skee keeps his eyes on me. "Strange that you wouldn't know a thing like that."

Just like Betty. Shit. "We weren't exactly close, Betty and me."

"You might understand, what with you playing that little trick on me today, it seems to me there's something not right."

I'm the only one sitting here who knows anything even close to the truth, and now I have to lie in front of Lamb, and *to* her. "I'm guessing she wanted to be finished with him. No need to bring Sammy and me into it." Now I'm convinced that my best defense is to press my point. "Forgive me," I say, "but you didn't live with Cudge." I look back toward the house and find an image in my mind of Sammy standing on the front steps. "What I was saying before. Maybe Betty was getting some justice."

"Sorry about my damned foggy brain," Skee says. "But I'm a little unclear young man. Are you saying my boy deserves to be dead for something actual or something you thought he was going to do? Or in your mind is it all the same?"

I stiffen bolt upright ready to shoot back but Lamb intervenes. "Maybe that's enough for tonight," she says, reaching across my chest as if we're coming to a quick stop in a car.

I'm too out of my head to listen. "I was fourteen years old and I was terrified every second I stood in this house after your son moved in. I was terrified for me, for Sammy, and for our mother. She married him and then she couldn't shake him. She wanted him gone."

Skee doesn't respond and Lamb is silent as well. The problem here is that I'm more familiar with the circumstances than they are. In Lamb's case, it's my fault and intentional. Except for the barest of details, I have refrained from recounting the circumstances of that life. I've sought a new definition of family, consciously, and that doesn't include being defined by the first. "Betty was an abused wife. She wanted Cudge out of the house, and she didn't conceal that fact when she was questioned."

"Okay," Lamb says, raising her hands in surrender. "I don't think I can handle any more tonight. Really."

Skee looks at both of us but doesn't speak. He reaches into his pocket and pulls out a pretzel rod, giving an unsatisfied look before returning it. "Probably right," he says, shaking his head. "My son treated you terribly and you've both been very good about all this." He smiles and jots down a few notes. "Except for, you know, how we got off on the wrong foot this morning." He begins to stand, reconsiders, and sits back down. "Your brother out there, if you don't mind my asking. How did *he* die?"

"He was killed in the Marines." This is another lie I've told so many times it's second nature. Sammy left home for the Marines but he was not killed. Like my father, he took his own life. It's easier, I learned early, to keep up the lie than to have to worry about the sympathetic queries that invariably follow.

"I see," Skee says with a hint of skepticism in his expression. "It's hard no matter how they go. Haven't gotten over Myrna."

I find myself drawing circles with my finger in the palm of my hand. "Then you understand," I say, "why we're kind of done here."

"Just one more thing, really." Skee says. "It just came to me. I'm so sorry. It's a longshot, I know. Your mother had Cudge declared dead. Out at the cemetery, think she gave him a stone?"

"It *is* a long shot," I say. "About as long a shot as you can imagine."

His eyes go teary but he doesn't cry. "Guess that's it then," he says. "It's all a damned dead end." He looks at the ground and shakes his head. "Can't even visit his grave." It's an unpleasant reminder of the walled off parts of me. Until today, I've refused to go the cemetery. Not for Dad,

Betty, nor even Sammy. I avoided updating Betty's stone after I buried her. Then, when time passed, what was the point? "Of course," Skee continues, "might just be the reason to poke around a bit more."

"You know who Skee should talk to?" Lamb says, and I recognize her tone of sympathy. I shoot her a look but she's already speaking directly to him. "Jodi. She owns Max's."

Skee writes down the name.

I sigh. "She isn't likely to know much," I say, calmly. "But Cudge was a regular and her father was the Sherriff. He talked to just about everyone who knew Cudge. Smart old man, so who knows?" Vale may have been the only person who ever truly understood me.

"We'll take you," Lamb says. "Right now."

"A minute ago you'd had enough," I say.

"Conner," Lamb commands. "All this is about as new to me as it is to him. If there's a chance this poor man can get some answers about his son…. Look, you can stay here, but I'm taking him to meet Jodi."

I assumed all this time she'd be on my side, which apparently isn't the case. I have to go, if only to intervene. Skee looks hopeful. I reply by nodding, choosing to focus on the warmth of Lamb's hand. One good thing, I think, is that the daughter she carries is missing this episode. She's the only one of my family untainted by Cudge and I want to keep it that way. I thought I'd tied all that off, but the knot apparently wasn't tight enough. Skee's arrival proves I haven't quite done the job, but maybe now, I think.

"Last thing I want to do is cause trouble between you two."

Too late. Maybe it's me, but I get the sense trouble is precisely what Skee is up to. I've got to get ahead of it. "But it's Friday night. I doubt Jodi will have time."

"No, no," Lamb says. "It's fine. We're fine." She squeezes my hand. "We'll call James. He should be there too." It's the last thing I want, James getting in on this, but now it's inevitable.

"James?" Skee asks.

"That's a road I don't want to go down," I say, shaking my head at Lamb.

"Fact is, it's a bit late for me. How about three tomorrow?" Skee asks. "Got some things to check on in the morning. Maybe I'll look into a marker for the boy."

"Perfect," Lamb says, getting ahead of me.

Skee begins to stand but he's having a problem with the chair giving him enough support, so Lamb offers him her hands, which he takes. "Long day," he says.

Slow getting down the driveway, Skee stops at one point and takes a deep breath before continuing.

"I hope this'll be over tomorrow," I sigh as Skee drops into his car.

"It *can't* be," Lamb says. "That poor old man has a bucket full of fresh history. Sounds really messy, Conner." I know she's disappointed in me and more than concerned. "How come you never told me all that about Cudge?"

"I have. Some of it, anyway. It's behind me. And I swear I didn't know about that declared dead business."

"I'm your wife, Conner. Your best friend." I look at her, suddenly overcome, but I fight it back, clenching my jaw as if that will keep everything in. It's true, she's been my closest friend almost from that first day we met in college. "More importantly," Lamb says, "I'm the mother of your daughter." I take one of her hands and she looks at me briefly, porch light painting a crescent along one cheek. In any other life she'd be right; she should be someone I can turn to always, but there are just some things I don't want to speak and other things I can't and this moment, holding Lamb's hand, is the aching proof.

"You're certainly going out of your way for him," I say.

"I had to offer, Conner. We'll see if he shows up." Her voice cracks with disappointment. "How much have you told *James* about Cudge?" And this is when my heart falls.

It's going to get worse. A lot of bodies have piled up during my lifetime. I can't know it yet, but Skee's arrival means there's going to be one more.

18

I haven't figured out exactly what I want James to know, and what I need to hold back…. And Lamb…. I've spent twenty years wrapping myself in half-truths and fictions. I'm discovering that all I've done is mummify fourteen-year-old Conner. If the gauze is being removed anyway, how much more for James? Is it too late to say "Oh, by the way…?"

Lamb and I were already calling each other husband and wife when we met James. I was twenty-nine and he was thirty-eight. Not a giant difference, but enough that I remember thinking of him as an interesting older man. At a dinner not long ago, I reminded him what I first thought about him and he said, "Conny, you're getting up there too, but you'll *never* be as interesting as me." He was smiling, but also, it's true.

The night we met I was with Lamb up in Louisville at The Connection, a gay club bigger than I had ever imagined. Bigger than New York big: huge dance floor, five or six separate bars, a full-sized stage with cabaret seating. Who knew Louisville could have something like this? James wasn't shy, and he kind of sidled up next to me and Lamb. Before I knew it, the three of us were dancing. Here was this tall, handsome man, and out of everyone he'd taken an interest in me. That had never happened before, not this way.

At the end of the evening, when we were standing outside, I was both exhausted and maybe hopped-up on adrenaline because this really great-looking guy had latched onto me and I hadn't yet exhibited the million-and-one irritating habits that drove men away. Of course, I learned that's what I wanted, reasons not to be liked.

I stood outside the club with Lamb, waiting for James to ask me out as we said our goodbyes, but it didn't seem to be coming. "Lamb," he said, "you tarted up deary, it's been great." Back then, she would wear anything, and that night she was in the last phase of *I'm young-enough-to-get-away-with-this*. She sported a zebra striped mini-skirt, fishnets with a black t-shirt, and wore a generous helping of white lipstick that she purchased almost entirely because it was called "Danger Angel."

"You're an amazing dancer," she said to James, squeezing his bicep. He was worked out, not lean, but he was pretty hot in jeans and a tight black t-shirt. The two of them looked as if they'd coordinated outfits. I was unfortunate. Jeans and a red long sleeve button up. I stood, waiting for them to get their love fest out of the way, still hoping he would get around to asking me out.

"So, Lamb," he said, "wondering if I might get your number."

"Oh," she said, looking at me, "um...." I couldn't believe it; and I don't know exactly how far my jaw fell open but I'm sure it mirrored hers. "Well, but Conner—"

"Because," James interrupted, "if this one doesn't ask me out tonight I'd like a way to get ahold of him." He turned to me and offered a wink and a sly smile.

"Jesus," I said, "You ass." But I was smiling too.

Lamb laughed and feigned heartbreak. "Is it the lipstick? I can change."

"Deary," he said, pointing to me, "unless you can change into him, it's no use." Who wouldn't fall for a guy with an opening act like that?

Now I lie in bed wondering if Skee will return tomorrow and how this will all play out. I am thinking, too, of Sammy as I stare at the ceiling. Lamb had more questions after Skee drove away, but I only replied with tears held back as long as I could, enough that she knew not to press further, enough that she got in touch with James. She didn't make me talk to him, told him I was asleep.

I finished two more beers in silence, and then we went to our separate bedrooms, an arrangement we agreed to even before the first day of our marriage. I lie in the same room me and Sammy shared as boys. Back then, before Cudge, we talked about such things as turtles crossing the road, or something someone said at school, anything to prolong falling asleep. Sometimes Dad popped his head in and lightly scolded us for the chatter. On our better nights we might get him to sit at the end of one our beds and talk about the Cincinnati Reds or UK basketball. It was easy to want to stay awake in the world I *thought* we lived in.

All these years later, and in that same room, I am unable to sleep. *Cudge* is *dead.* Those three words cycle and recycle through my thoughts as if my mind is a velodrome. I don't know why a death certificate makes it feel true, finally, but it does. And I don't understand why Betty would dot that "i" and not tell me. She created the haunt, knew he wasn't returning but pretended otherwise. Except, in a way, he has. Skee. It wouldn't surprise me if Betty knew that a day would arrive years off when someone would come around asking questions. She was smart enough to die first.

Maybe it was around the time Betty filed the paperwork, or she felt it coming on, the heart attack, because a few weeks before that she called me to the house she shared with Larry. By then she was a wreck, never without a cigarette, smoke tinged hair, deep lines scoring her face. She'd been drinking, which is maybe why she broke her silence, the only time since Cudge disappeared. I sat across from her in a plaid chair that smelled of soured beer. "I know you don't have much use for me," she said. "Think I was a terrible mother." As if a genie emerging from a lamp, a thin stream of white smoke rose from the ashtray next to her.

"No, Betty," I said. "You were a *selfish* mother."

She shook her head as if to pity my remark. "What a mother won't do for her children. You don't know the sacrifices."

"What's that supposed to mean?"

"The knife," she said, veering, and then, with a hint of sudden foggy-eyed glee, "We never talked much about that."

It was true, she and I never had, and the way she said it made me feel as if this moment was half accusation, half shared secret. "Cudge took off with it." I said. "That's the story, right?"

She dragged on her cigarette, the lines of her face gathering. "Selfish mother? I got rid of the damned thing for you."

"When did—"

She shook her head, put her hand up, held it there, her cigarette a nubbed wand. "Just want you to remember momma's little favor after I'm gone." She picked up the empty glass next to her, inspected it, then set it down, looking around her for the remedy.

"Favor? Jesus, you're fucking nuts, Betty. That little detail's what kept Vale coming back."

"I was protecting you."

I stood, ready to leave. "You were protecting *you.*"

"You shit. Remember them little plastics? The puncher tape message in the envelope? Larry and me was scaring the shit out of you so you'd keep your mouth shut."

Five embossed white letters on a red background flashed in my mind like a single burst of firework. FAGOT. I sat back down. "So I'd keep my mouth shut," I said, "or so I'd go nuts?"

Betty looked at me almost maternally, almost. "I'm not saying it wasn't a rough thing to put on a boy, but you did right by our family."

Then it hit me. "You did it to Mark, too."

She shrugged me off and lit another cigarette. "That there was a freebie," she said with a blast of smoke from the first puff. "Wasn't about to let you go down that road, and anyway, Larry figured—"

My voice rose over hers. "Mark was the only friend I had. They sent him away." Years fall away. I'm a boy watching a boy in the back seat of a car, driven off. "You killed us."

"Oh, come off it. I had a responsibility, and that was about keeping you away from any part of the kind of friend he was turning out to be. It's another thing you ought to be thanking me for."

"Right. I forgot. What a mother won't do for her son. Lucky me."

It was a standoff, but Betty did something unexpected. She smiled and snuffed her smoked-out cigarette. "Right down to the end is it? Okay, then. Go." She shooed me with her hand. "But some day, Conner, when you got a wife, and kids playing out front of that house I give you...." She paused, then jabbed. "*If* you got a wife and kids...you'll know I done the right thing."

I asked directly. "Betty. What did you do with the body?"

"Fuck you," she said and her eyes snapped out of their glaze as she raked her fingers through her stringy gray hair. "Saved your little murdering ass and this is what I get?"

"What," I repeated, "did you do with Cudge's body?"

Betty shot up from the chair, lost her balance for a second, then composed herself. "You," she said, pointing at me and holding the gesture as she spoke. "I never give you up in all these years. Hell, I couldn't say it, but I was damn proud we were rid of that son-of-a-bitch." She lowered her hand and slowly approached, a wrecked figure in a tattered robe. Anything but a mother. "But when you come at me with this foolishness about me having done something with Cudge's body, that's playing the game unfair."

Now she was directly in front of me, shorter, but eye-to-eye. "Alright," I said. "I didn't kill him. You didn't hide him. It was the Tooth Fairy, moonlighting. Thank you for this touching moment."

The next time I'd see her would be in a rented casket.

Without James here in bed with me, I do something unusual, slip into Lamb's room and climb in next to her, hold her as I did in college when she was distraught over some break-up or a bad-for-her-but-not-for-most-students grade. Only now, the gesture is meant to comfort *me*. I am reassured by this fractionally larger version of her with our daughter. Happiness to come. But there's something else. Side by side with Lamb, I'm surprised by an unexpected gulf, a distance Skee's appearance has not so much created, but exposed. It keeps circulating within me, all that I cannot tell this person who, along with Sammy, and now James, I've loved most.

I lie silent, trace a thin shadow on the ceiling to the dark corner where it terminates. Outside, a quiet rain becomes a shooshing underplay. Lamb wakes and turns on her side toward me, groggy. "Can't sleep?"

"Brain won't turn off."

She yawns and rubs her eyes. "We got kind of a shock today," she says, propping herself up on her elbow.

Kind of? It's certainly an understatement. "I wish my mind was a dry erase board so I could wipe it all away."

"Careful," Lamb says, tapping me gently on the head. "There's people written in there who love you."

"Oh, I'd draw a circle around those and write 'save.'" The ceiling fan above us is still and black as the fat X of a treasure map. "Do you remember early on when I asked if you really wanted to do this?"

"I remember exactly. I didn't hesitate. It's not what I would have predicted for myself, but…." She throws her hands into the darkness as if to say, *and here I am.*

"I have to admit you surprised me."

"I guess in the end it was the infrastructure. I wanted a child and I wanted to choose a family for him or her. I chose you."

"And James."

"Of course…and James. Wouldn't have if you two could get married."

"In Kentucky? Never happen."

"Such the pessimist."

"California, maybe. New York, but here? No way."

"Lucky me," she says, returning her head to the pillow. "Oh, and something weird. Before I fell asleep I was thinking. You're actually kind of related."

"To James?"

"Skee, dummy. I don't know how it works, but technically, isn't he your grandfather?"

"Jesus," I say, "We're trying to turn my brain *off*, remember?"

She apologizes and we're quiet for a while. Then she turns to me again and runs her fingers through my hair front to back. Exactly what Betty used to do when I was a very young child and she cared. "Remember this?"

"I do." In college, when I was stressed about something, an exam or paper, another phone call with Sammy in which he sounded even more remote than the previous time, I could go to Lamb's, put my head in her

lap and she calmed me just the same way she is now. I'd let it slip that
Betty used to do this, and before she understood how I felt about my
mother, Lamb took up the gesture herself. What could I say? "College
seems like a long time ago," I say.

She laughs, offering exaggerated version of her mother's Chinese
accent. "Guess Mom was wrong. 'That boy, he not good for you.'"

"Your parents are definitely not my number one fans."

"Hey," Lamb says, "I got married like they wanted, and we're giving
them a grandchild. They can suck it."

"Not *exactly* like they wanted," I laugh.

"Beggars can't be choosers. Besides, they think you're a good boy.
Just not the right boy. But, since I don't need any boy, you'll do." Lamb
yawns and kisses me on the forehead. "Brain off?"

"Brain off," I say, which isn't entirely true, but it's as close as I'm
going to get. In minutes she's asleep. Sleep, a condition that feels like
a faraway destination for me. I listen to her soft breathing for a while
and think about the people we'd been when we first met, that very odd
pairing. Her parents had good reason to doubt that I am a match for
a daughter who can use both sides of her brain, who would end up
being a CPA *and* a hat designer. A "milliner," as Lamb reminds me. She
met my mother exactly twice, and Sammy a few more times. But the
house was so sad back then it was unbearable to bring her to Orgull. By
comparison, Lamb's parents were a romp.

The first time Lamb and Betty met, my mother tried. She cleaned up,
set her hair like she used to, and put some beer in the fridge. I think she
was just glad, hopeful, that after all, I wasn't gay. She didn't allow Lamb
to get away, however, without telling her how difficult it was to get over
losing two husbands. It was all I could do not to ask if she remembered
how difficult it is to get *rid* of one husband.

"Sorry about that," I said to Lamb on the drive back to Louisville.
"She gets that way."

"You warned me. Guess we're even."

"Not fair," I said, "you have *two* parents."

"Well, hey," she laughed. "You can add. Your mom and my parents equal what?"

In reply, I sang "Three is a Magic Number." I'd heard it on TV so many times when I was kid the lyrics were tattooed on my brain. There's a part of the song that goes "a man and a woman had a little baby, yes they did. They had three in the family, and that's a magic number." I never expected the song would ever apply to me, but tonight I smile because it occurs to me that it doesn't. My math is wrong. James. There'll be four of us. It's a family I wish I could have shared with Sammy.

These thoughts tumble through my mind, Skee's return tomorrow competing with Sammy until my brother wins out and he's all I'm thinking about. It's certain I won't be getting any sleep. Gently rising, I go to the window. The yard bulges with darkness except for random porch lights playing peekaboo through the trees. The garage is a dim glow, an alien space craft at the back of the yard. I put on a pair of shorts and quietly head outside barefoot and shirtless. The rain-cooled air is light on my skin, the driveway's gravel under my feet, reptilian. In my hand is Mark's letter, which I plan to exchange for another.

At the garage, I enter quickly and fumble for the small flashlight hanging near the door. I know the path so well I could probably make my way even without light. Navigating through piles of clutter, I reach the cupboards. It's a trip I make purposely infrequent. Finding my way, led by the thin beam of light, I push aside electric clippers that haven't worked in years, a coffee can full of nails, and a boxed pup tent. Behind these is the pegged cupboard backing which I slide just far enough to deposit Mark's final letter and retrieve another, the typed letter from Sammy, sent when he lived in California.

Within the folds of the paper is something I inserted myself, a hand cropped photo of Sammy, a close up of his face, the end of his nose pink from sunburn, eyes squinting against the bright Southern California sun. Behind him is the gray-green landscape of what he said was Camp Pendleton. How would I know the difference? But the feature I always focus on is Sammy's tight-lipped smile, which seems at times a gesture of toughness, and at others, practiced neutrality.

Other stashed items blink in the moving light, things I stole as a boy, a boombox, a small gilded painting of a race horse, the cuckoo clock, table ware. None of these items matter to me. It's only the letter I'm after, this twin relic to Mark's. I read it many times before I hid it and many times since, but even after all that, seeing Sammy's message still causes a kind of thud in my chest. At the same time, it's a way to keep him near, and so, with my narrow light on the paper, once again, I follow Sammy's words to their conclusion.

> *My Brother,*
>
> *Today I am in Oceanside. A good day away from Pendleton. I'm sorry it has been so long since we've spoken. In our last talk you seemed worried. I didn't mean to alarm you. We are always training and it always feels as if we are training for something big. There is much good but it feels small compared to what we might face. Not to be dramatic, but Death has his own army in the world and no opposing force can ever be trained for that.*
>
> *This is a reality I can only be honest about with you, but it also shouldn't be cause for worry. And why I write this is, as always, to say I love you and thank you for being my armor when I was a boy. My brothers at my side here are my armor now. I am theirs. And every day their actions remind me of your own bravery. You held us together when it seemed impossible. I didn't understand then, but I see it now.*
>
> *I know I must be delicate on this next point, and I hope you can make sense of it. But what I want to say is that what I've learned here is that there are no right reasons to kill another human being, but there are moral ones. War is a license to kill, but there are other plausible brands. All of them leave a certain blackness on the heart, some of them you can live with, but that's the best you can hope for. There are alternate wars one wages, and I only wish I had the capacity to talk to you about mine. If I lose, please know I hold close that you have always been in my corner.*
>
> *I love you for living with this different kind of war as I am day to day. You are the Brother of brothers.*
>
> *Your Sammy*

I click off the flashlight. The garage's small window holds the color of unpolished silver. Maybe my brother went to his grave thinking I killed Cudge; not Betty, but me. He convicted me and commuted the sentence all at once within the fiction of military service. Very little in my life is wholly real, it seems.

Over the years Sammy and I had a number of conversations about death and mortality, with Sammy always sounding like he was on some sort of precipice, as if he'd just gotten news of a terminal disease. Once, when I told him this, he came back to me a day later with a word he looked up. "Yes," he said, "you're right. The word is 'morose.'" Enlisting in the Marines had been his idea to see if he could drive those feelings away by learning how to use death as a tool, to manipulate it rather than being manipulated by it. "But Sammy," I'd said to him, "eventually we all go."

"For me it constantly feels like it's happening now." The kid needed help, and until it was too late, I thought I was enough.

We learned that he'd never gone into the Marines. He went to California and pretended. There were no "brothers." The photo was taken somewhere in Southern California, but not at Camp Pendleton. Unlike our father, he left a final note, but it amounted to the same measure of absence. I never understood if he thought he was doing me a favor by staying away, by sending notice of a newly empowered life that wasn't actual. "Maybe he just wanted to give you the space to live your life," Lamb once said to me. She didn't know about the letter, but she knew about how Sammy's life ended and for my sake, she played along with the version I concocted to make a hero out of him. It's a wonder she didn't ask if there were other fictions. Maybe she was focused on the fact I couldn't be consoled. What did he think would happen after he was gone and I found out the truth? Every time I came around to that thought, I reminded myself who had been his role models.

I run my finger across Sammy's message, the paper almost blue in the light, trying to detect even the faintest presence of a single raised letter. Instead, I have the sensation that there is almost nothing there, as if Sammy himself fades with each sentence. I'd written him back and told him I loved him, asked him to call me. Two weeks after writing me,

Sammy took his own life, drowned himself in the Pacific. I've never understood this purposeful act of finality, why he chose the drama of following our father's path into the water. What Dad's suicide started years earlier in Sammy's heart, my brother finished off.

I refold the letter with Sammy's photo and put it away. There are still times when I want to give over to the fiction, pretend that my brother is a Marine, a broody but renewed man. Just say it was true and believe it. The irony is that I can't have that because I killed him off overseas. Powerful fellow, his brother, me, shooting him down overseas, protecting him from Cudge. Sitting in the garage, for the millionth time I think about his suicide and what had happened decades earlier. If I couldn't save Sammy a second time, I hadn't really saved him the first.

A light goes on outside; it's the house. In seconds our screen door pops shut and Lamb calls for me. I respond from the door of the garage and walk to the porch where she is a pajamaed silhouette in front of the screen. "Brain on," I say, standing in front of her.

"No kidding." She puts her hands on my shoulders and makes me look at her directly in the eyes, each shaded by a butterfly wing. "This Skee thing has really got you shaken up."

"I was thinking about Sammy."

"I should have made you talk to James."

That was the last thing I wanted to do because he would have insisted on *talking*. Lamb can let things go. James is a prober. I'd counted myself lucky he was on the road. "No," I say. "I'll be fine. Tomorrow we'll go to the farmer's market. I'll go to work. Skee won't show up. You'll see; I'll be normal by morning."

"It *is* morning," Lamb says. She points to the east and at the hint of dawn beyond the trees. I'm just now grasping how long I'd been in the garage. "Feeling normal?"

19

"But you told me he took off on you," James says, speaking of Cudge. Lamb and I are acting like it's a normal Saturday following through with this once a week ritual, the drive up to Louisville where James has his practice, breakfast at the Twig and Leaf, then a walk through the farmer's market, before heading back down so I can open the shop in Orgull. This is me living my fantasy of normal. In hour, a man from my past will appear and shed a better light on me… at first.

That doesn't detract from the fact that today there is one major chore, meeting up with Skee this afternoon. Our yolky plates are empty, the coffee low, and Lamb has brought us around to the conversation I've been trying to avoid. "So, he's dead?" James asks.

"Presumption of death is the term," Lamb says. I query her specificity with a raised eyebrow. "What?" she says. "I looked it up. You have to wait seven years."

"And he molested your brother." James is incredulous. "I'm just now finding out about that?" Grey at the temples, and wide shouldered, as usual he exudes authority and concern all at once. He reaches across the table and briefly clutches my wrist. "What about you?"

"Whoa." Again, I look at Lamb because clearly they've had a conversation in advance. "I didn't say that. What I said was…" I'm trying to think of exactly what I did say. "…I was afraid something bad could happen because Cudge was so volatile." Even though I'm pretty sure Lamb has already filled him in, I tell him about Skee's visit. When I get to the part about the cemetery he stops me.

"Play nice, Conny," he says, giving the "shame on you" fingers.

"I'm introducing him to Jodi, aren't I?" Neither of them understands how afraid I am that I'm about to lose everyone I love.

Lamb swipes a last fat corner of toast across her yellowed plate and pops it in her mouth, offering something unintelligible. "Yie ingited chngs."

"Deary," James says. "Neither of us speaks Chinese."

She swallows and sticks out her tongue. "I invited James."

"Not a good idea." I snap. "Besides, he has work."

"Come on, Conny," James says. "I only have five patients this morning."

"I'm on your side, Conner," Lamb says, "but since Skee showed up you haven't been thinking straight." James opens his mouth to make a crack but Lamb stops him with a *not-the-right-time* look.

"We're here to support you, Conny. From what I understand, helping the old guy out isn't your strong suit. Besides, it's something different. Like Scooby Doo and we're all climbing into The Mystery Machine."

Lamb is shaking her head, half smiling, half knowing this isn't at all what I want to hear, but James has one more thing to add. "I'm Daphne, of course."

"Jesus," I say, alternating my attention between them, "it's Saturday morning but this is *not* a cartoon." Now I focus on Lamb. "Skee held back yesterday. He didn't lead with Cudge being declared dead. This is not some sweet old man who's just hobbled into town." There's a fence between us, a dangerous border they can't detect and that I absolutely cannot cross. What they experience as recalcitrance, maybe even paranoia, is really fear that something bad is going to come of this. I've felt this before more than once, a family slipping away from me.

I've got a weak hand in this conversation, which continues through to the farmer's market where James likes to buy grass fed beef. "I just don't want you two involved. Let me take Skee to Jodi by myself," I say.

Lamb isn't having it. "I think I should be there."

"You guys have no idea how bad it was," I say, looking to James for relief and finding none. "*Bad*," I continue. "That's why I don't talk about it." We're under the tent of the Mennonite family we like to do business with, partly because they are polite and efficient all at once. James insists they are German Baptist. He and I pick over a pile of small potatoes, red and white orbs whose freshness doesn't seem distinguishable, but our hands pretend as if they are.

Lamb hands the young man a group of potatoes and admires the straw hat she recognizes as new. "Thank you, Ma'm," he says shyly, taking her money. She begins to say something to me but waits until the three of us exit the tent. Her dark eyes narrow. "Skee's son is missing and declared dead. Don't you think he has the right?"

"The right to what? Remind me of being terrorized by that psycho? No, I don't. It's not like I'm trying to be a hard ass, but you heard Skee. He didn't even know Cudge." Lamb drops her arms and looks to James for help, the sack of potatoes dangling at her side. His expression lets me know he thinks I am being more than insensitive. I feel like I'm eight.

A slap on my back. "Conner?" I don't have to ask who it is as I turn. "Little dude!" The voice is older with more gravel, but I know before I see his face that it's Mr. Carter who moved his iron works up closer to downtown Louisville ten years earlier. "God damn but you shot up and filled out." Thank God, I think. Someone who knew me as something other than a fucked up kid. Exhibit A for the defense.

I introduce him to James and Lamb and tell him about our shop, but when I say Lamb is my wife, Mr. Carter can't stifle a laugh. "Wife? Come on now with that bullshit."

James gives me the eye. Lamb shakes her head. Nobody is on my side.

"It's complicated," I say to Mr. Carter. "James is my partner."

Mr. Carter tips his dingy engineer cap up over his forehead—I swear it's the same one he's worn since I was a kid. After giving James the once over he turns to me in approval. "All right then. That's more what I expected." Catching himself, he refocuses his attention. "No offense, Miss Lamb, but this little dude haunted my shop about twice a week even when there wasn't anything new to look at. He mostly checked in on this piece called 'Drill.'" It's true. He describes the stainless steel sculpture animated by wind that looks as if it's a drill bit boring into a limestone block. It was my favorite. "Hardly nobody gave a shit about it except Conner. All the rest wanted the fancy whirly gigs. Shoulda given it to him."

There's an awkward silence, because what is this? I reach. "Orgull sure misses you."

Mr. Carter scoffs. "You mean they miss my money." He reaches into his pocket and takes out a pair of glasses, apparently so that he can truly see us. "Well, now," he says. "Look at us. You're up from Orgull. I'm up from the West End. My daughter lives here now. She's got me to quit smoking…when she's looking. And we come here to pay for five-dollar tomatoes and three-dollar coffee." He looks around. "But my baby is delayed. Wish you could meet her. Moved back from North Carolina to be close to me."

After Mr. Carter explains he's teaching teenagers how to make their own art at his iron works, Lamb interrupts. "I love that idea. I'm a Millner. Never thought of teaching."

"She's also a CPA," I say as if being a hat maker isn't enough.

Lamb looks at me, indicating my intervention isn't necessary.

"Well," Mr. Carter says. "A black artist, an Asian hatmaker, and a gay couple at the farmers market, a Highlands wet dream."

James laughs and taps his nose.

This is clearly the coda. Mr. Carter touches the brim of his cap and pulls out a business card. "Good to see you, young man. Check my booth at St. James this year. Looks like maybe you can finally afford my work." He hands me the card, then nods to James and Lamb. Then he pauses, looking at me. "Never found your step-daddy?"

"Never did."

"Good. That's what I prayed for. You were too good a kid to be around that ass much longer. Every time you come by I could see in your eyes what a wreck you were, like you aged twenty years in six months." It's all I can do not to check Lamb and James' expressions to see if this comment has landed. Mr. Carter looks at them directly. "I told this boy not to grow to be an asshole. How's he doing?"

"Jury's still out," James laughs.

Lamb playfully shakes her head. "B+," she says.

"All right then." Mr. Carter nods, laughing. "I'd have lost a bet. I mean, considering...." He looks at me, knowing I could finish the sentence.

"They've been learning a lot about my childhood in the past few days. Thanks for earning me a little sympathy."

Mr. Carter sizes up the three of us. "Young man. I'm not some angel set down to iron out whatever you got going on here." He taps the card still held in my fingers, and winks. "You were a kid. Now be a customer." With that, we watch as he walks away into the crowd and stopped by a couple who are clearly fans of his art.

James chuckles. "The Wet Dream Team," he declares. "Boy, you *used* to have an interesting life."

"That's for sure," Lamb says. "What is it you're not telling us Conner?" She sets our potatoes down, then brings a strand of her black hair in front of her, inspects it, and pulls it all back in a ponytail, a move I interpret as trying to soften accusation. When I don't respond she crosses her arms and purses her lips. "Well?"

It strikes me all-of-the-sudden, standing in the center of this crowd of people all wandering from stand to stand, gathered here with the presumption of safety, but we have no idea who each other is, not really. I'm with my odd little family that some of these people might find to be, if they knew us, a threatening development, a sign of cultural decline. They don't know my secrets and I don't know theirs. Maybe that's what makes all this work, is why society manages, for the most part, to move along peacefully, all of us silently agreeing not to let on how damaged and dangerous we are. I am no Thomas Merton.

"Look," I say, "this is not really the kind of conversation I want to have in the middle of a farmer's market." I've taken the levity out of Mr. Carter's intervention. More than anyone else in my life, even James, Lamb has the ability to intercede like this. It's part of her protective streak. A professor in our sophomore year speculated that Alexander the Great was gay, and after class, one of the other students was snickering in the hall. "Guess old Alexander took it up the poop shoot when he was a kid."

"What are you talking about?" his friend asked. Lamb and I were walking behind them.

"That's what turns you gay," the first guy said, flapping his wrist.

Lamb sped up and tapped him on the shoulder. "With that kind of logic," she spat, "I guess your mother must have sat on your face when you were younger." The surprise on the guy's face didn't register if he understood her point, but I admired her all the same.

I pick up the bag of potatoes next to Lamb but she doesn't budge, and James seems to be waiting out the impasse. Is there a fraction of something I might say that will be enough for them to understand why I wanted to leave everything about Cudge in the past? "Okay," I say, "I'm going to tell you something and when I do, I don't want to have a conversation about it. I just want you to understand. "Back then, I had Mark and Sammy and they were my whole world. Betty was lost to Cudge, but if I didn't have her around, there would be no Sammy and Mark. So when Cudge took off…disappeared, and the sheriff questioned me…." I stop and take a breath, look away before coming back to Lamb's face which is full of instant concern. James, as usual, is listening calmly. "The thing is, I'm pretty sure Betty wanted me to kill Cudge."

They look at each other and then at me. James puts his fingers to my chest. "Conny, your mother told you to murder her husband?"

"Not in so many words."

"What would make you think a thing like that?" Lamb asks.

"It's hard to explain. She gave me a hunting knife not too long before Cudge was gone. Talked about me being the man of the house."

Now James chimes in. "And you didn't tell that to the sheriff?"

There's a lot of things I didn't tell Vale. "I'm trying to tell you that back then I was afraid if I said anything at all my whole world would be ruined. But you have to know that what I did tell the sheriff was true."

"Good," Lamb says.

"And now I have this new world with you and James and our little girl." I look at Lamb's belly and smile. "I don't want Skee coming around, no matter how innocent you think he is. Not worth the risk."

Lamb shakes her head sympathetically, but she narrows her eyes again as if her body language and her mind aren't in full agreement. "A lot of worlds orbiting you in that story, Conner. Which means we're standing next to the sun. You have to promise me we're not going to get burned."

"Too clever by half," I say.

She offers a reluctant smile. "Only half?" she says, taking the potatoes from me, then pointing to the three of us. "This only works if we're 100% honest with each other."

"Do I hear 90?" I say but neither of them reacts.

I turn to James to see if there's a chance he will stay out of all this, but he's looking at Lamb. We're standing in the center of the market, people with produce-laden bags grazing us on either side, the eggy scent of fresh omelets wafting the air. It's a strange life. In one of my hands hangs a cotton tote bag filled with heirloom tomatoes and bell peppers. Across from us, people mull choices of artisan cheeses and grass-fed bison. And here *we* are talking about a dead man. But as it sits with me, I realize I've said very little, reminding me how reflexive it is to keep my mouth shut when it comes to anything to do with my past.

"But, Conny, you're a man now, not a frightened kid. It was understandable back then. If you know something that could make a difference, you have to go to…I don't know, but some authority." He shrugs his shoulders as if to apologize.

"I think so, too," Lamb says.

I take a breath. She doesn't know it, but she's saying I'm my own worst enemy. There *are* two versions of me, that younger version who'd finally lashed out at Cudge, and this adult version that's trying not so much to protect itself, as protect the boy that I was. That boy who was beat on at school practically every week, who was fucked by his stepfather. This new threat is something I don't know how to defend against.

20

On the way back to Orgull to meet up with Skee, I give in just a little, tell Lamb and James about how it didn't take long for Cudge to assert himself. They've really no idea. Whoever that "nice" Cudge was quickly faded away. We weren't allowed to turn on any lights before twilight and he took the window unit air conditioner from the living room and installed it in his and Betty's bedroom.

Air conditioners and control. That's as much as I want to offer at first by way of example, but even I know this isn't enough, doesn't come close to making Lamb and James feel like they understand any better. So, I go all in, offer what I should not tell because afterward I'll just be a damaged kid to them. Sometimes it was a simple command from out of the blue. Once, he thought we were making too much noise in our bedroom and yelled at us from his, probably enjoying he air conditioning. Recognizing the signal in his tone, what was coming, I quickly led Sammy out, but when we were at top of the stairs I heard, "Hey, little man, hold up."

I urged Sammy away. "Go down to the kitchen." Turning, I stared at naked Cudge directly in the eyes. He was standing in his bedroom doorway, erection growing. I'd seen this tall, pale body before, and I would again. "No," I said, as if that mattered.

"You remember, little man," Cudge said, wiping the corner of his mouth. "Remember our deal."

I went to him, and he closed the bedroom door. His eyes were glassy, but not the drunken glassy I was used to. He pushed me in front of the vanity mirror and took my hand, telling me to hold my index finger and thumb together, but I didn't understand. So, he positioned them himself, taking a tube of Betty's lipstick and drawing a pink ring around the aperture—a mouth. Above that he dotted two dead eyes, then slicked Vaseline in hollow of my palm. Now his penis was completely hard, thick and white. Laughing, he took my hand and rested it atop his wide mushroom head that was almost the same pink as Betty's lipstick. "Now you're fucking Señor Wences," he said. "Go." I had no idea what he was talking about. "Go, damn it!" he growled, forcing my hand around him. For a moment I was frozen, terrified by whatever this new thing was, but maybe out of some deep down sense of self-preservation, I suddenly got it, recalled what I'd already learned, that it would be over quick if I didn't fight whatever new perversion Cudge had come up with.

In a few minutes I was downstairs where Sammy had a chair pushed up to the kitchen sink and was scrubbing his face for some reason. "I didn't mean to make him mad," he said when I came up next to him, trying to hide the ghost of lipstick I'd tried to wash off upstairs. I hoped he couldn't tell that I was shaking.

"It wasn't you, Sammy," I said. "He gets that way." I took his washcloth and wiped a smudge off his cheek. "He's up there and we're down here, aren't we? So, it's fine."

"I guess," Sammy said, jumping down off the chair.

I finished my own face and listened upstairs. Cudge was showering. "Listen," I said, bending down so that I was directly eye-to-eye with Sammy. "Whenever Cudge gets mad, you come find me first thing."

By the time I finish telling this story we're nearly into town, almost home. James is in the front seat next to Lamb, who's driving. It hurts that in the telling I grew to understand this revelation is tactical. I need Lamb and James on my side. It's simpler than that. I need Lamb and James. They've both been silent the entire time, but when I have nothing more to say James lets out a long breath. "Oh, Conny," he says. He's in the front seat next to Lamb, who's driving. "That is fucking outrageous. Why would you keep all that bottled up. You poor kid. I'm guessing that wasn't the only time."

"You don't know the half of it."

Lamb is silent, but I see in the rearview mirror that she's dividing her attention between me and the tree-lined road.

"I guess you see it now, why I'm not so anxious to help Skee."

"But you're going to," Lamb insists, her tone so clearly unsympathetic that James queries her with a look.

"It's not healthy," James says, "keeping all that inside."

"I agree," Lamb says. "You have to get it out. Skee showing up might turn out to be the best thing. And I think James and I deserve a few more cards on the table."

In a few hours I'll know how much James and Lamb love me. If they *can* love me. There's no getting around that Vale's deepest suspicions all pointed to me. Hopefully these aren't part of Jodi's inheritance.

I hold a very bad hand. I've known Jodi a long time. She's sweet. Always ready to help. I fear it might become her worst quality.

21

Lamb and I stand in front of Max's looking at James across the street in the window of our shop, a puppy left behind. Jodi can't possibly have anything to add about Cudge gone missing or I'd know. That's what I tell myself, and I hope that Skee won't show up. It's a perfect spring early afternoon, a busy Saturday for Orgull. Business has been good. People seeking out quaintness or authenticity, or maybe it's like a day at the zoo. The street is lined with cars, and the air carries the sweetness of smoked pork coming from the diner around the corner.

"This place can be pretty okay," Lamb says, face full of sun as she squints, her lashes two black hyphens. "Which doesn't mean you haven't gotten me really confused, Conner. I thought we trusted each other." Before I respond she looks past me and I don't have to turn around to understand what she's noticed. "There he is," she says. "Be nice."

Skee is a block away and he raises a hand to signal that he sees us. He's wearing the same outfit as yesterday, except the bow tie is yellow and he doesn't have his hat. His hair is a glare of white. He's tall to be sure, but with his cane and slow gait I'm not certain it's possible to look more benign. "Can't believe I'm all screwed up over *that*," I say.

"A day ago I'd have agreed, but all this drip, drip, drip."

All I can think is that it feels like there's about to be a flood. I look across the street where James continues to stand in the window. He shakes his head at me as if he expected something more than the frailty walking toward us. I shrug and turn back to Lamb. "Look," I say, "about what Cudge did to me; that's none of Skee's business."

"It would certainly give him an idea of why you've been so rude to him." She pauses, her brown eyes filled with concern. "But okay."

Skee arrives at our side. "Wasn't sure you'd be here," he says, extending his hand.

I accept the gesture. "Wasn't so sure myself." He shakes Lamb's hand as well and the three of us turn almost in unison. The door to Max's is a wide black panel, thickly painted, with a sign warning minors to stay out.

Skee takes a deep breath. "Can't tell if I'm nervous about meeting this woman or going into a bar. Haven't done it for years." He looks at us shyly. "Back when, I'd go in the day and come out surprised it was night."

I try. "We don't have to do this."

"No, I've come all this way," Skee says and he's the first of us to go in.

"Well," Jodi says from behind the far end of the bar. "Hello there." She's just a voice because my eyes haven't adjusted to the dim light, but I know it's her. I squint and confirm that we're the only customers. Max's smells of spilled beer and cigarette smoke, decades of it, which is part of the comfort. It's a room of dark red light except for the fluorescent tubes above a pool table and the silent rainbow flicker of sports on a very small television nestled between bourbons. Skee surprises us by ordering a whisky neat before we take a seat across from the bar fronted by black vinyl stools. *Am I going to have to babysit this old man?*

Jodi has short black hair, dyed now. Her face, a good one, belies that she's old enough to have a little gray. She has an easy smile, and uses it. Around her eyes, wrinkles spray out in the pattern of wheat, and even in the red lighting, these eyes find a way to spark blue. Despite the years, I still see that woman who crossed the street, sweet as anything, and offered me a cigarette. Talked to me about Cudge and tripped me up a bit. We come to Max's now and then, but I've always been a little wary. Lamb says we'll introduce Jodi when she comes over, but Skee raises his hand. "Not just yet."

In a minute Jodi places a shot in front of Skee and apologizes. She's poured bourbon instead. "You're in Kentucky, darlin'." When Lamb and I order beer, she looks at us with a raised eyebrow. Pointing at Lamb's belly.

"I let myself have just one," Lamb says.

Jodi gives a sideways nod as if she's convinced. "Guess it's an improvement over my day," she says, walking back to the bar.

Staring into his glass, Skee looks as intent as if he's just picked up a dance partner. "I remember a time when this drink would be gone already," he says. "Breaking a promise to Myrna. 'I don't care if you drink,' she told me one foggy morning." He stops and taps on his head to emphasize he's not referring to weather. "'Never again in a bar' she told me, but she let me keep the cigarettes. Now that's gone to pretzels." He smells the bourbon and takes a sip, testing it on his lips before throwing it back.

Jodi brings us our beer and looks at Skee with an attentive smile. "'Nother darlin'?" Her voice is low and sandy.

"Not quite yet, but I've earned that one."

"Well, smoke 'em if you got 'em." She holds up a black ashtray. "Everything's non-smokin' in two months."

"Haven't smoked in years."

"Wife make you quit?"

"How'd you guess?" That is how it begins, though it's just small talk. It's as if Lamb and I are watching a play.

Jodi stands behind the unoccupied chair at our table. "Because, darlin', that wedding ring is too tight for your finger." She points.

"Never been off once." He smiles and looks at the ring. "Well now, that's not true. Handed it to Myrna before the damned bypass. So just that once." He looks up at Jodi, and I know the expression. Maybe it's the bourbon too, but he's smitten. He's not exactly ogling, but he's aware. Jodi is wearing a black knit blouse and black jeans. She's cinched in tight with a brass horsehead buckle. "Still like a good cigar now and then." He checks his jacket pocket for, what? A cigar or pretzels? Nothing.

"When the wife's not looking?"

"Recently widowed."

Jodi's eyes soften. "Aww, darlin', I'm sorry." She touches his shoulder briefly. "That drink's on the house."

He waves her off. "Don't want take advantage."

Laughing, her face takes on a pleasant new shine. "Oh, I'll be fine. I *am* the house."

"Okay, well," I say, trying to break up the coziness, but Lamb pre-empts my blunt introduction.

"You'll never guess who this is," Lamb says, overeager. "Jodi, meet Skee Hotter."

Jodi extends her hand and I see the pop of surprise in her face when she begins to catch on. "Relation to Cudge?" she asks as Skee shakes her hand.

"His father," I say.

Standing back and taking Skee in for a second, Jodi gives a nod. "I see it," she says. She takes the seat next to Skee but looks at me, confused. "Don't tell me you got news of Cudge? You look him up Conner?"

Lamb places her hand on my knee under the table as if to say *I've got this*. "Mr. Hotter surprised us. He's out here from California hoping to get some information about his son."

Jodi's look of surprise is a comfort. Perhaps this is going to be a shorter conversation than I thought. "Guess they told you Daddy was sheriff," she says.

"That's why we're here," Skee says. "If you know anything about the boy going missing, it'd be much appreciated."

"Guess I got a few thoughts," Jodi says. She looks at me as if I'm about to be nailed. Or maybe she just looks at me, but she's interrupted by a swing of light at the front door, a customer.

"In for a quick cold one," the man half growls, half sighs. He's short with slung back shoulders and a dark unshaven face which comes into relief when the light from outside disappears. Rolly Porter, whom I've seen around since I was a kid, Larry's brother-in-law. Betty didn't much care for him, which is saying something.

"Tell you what, darlin'," Jodi says to Skee. "I got some things of Daddy's upstairs might be of use to you. Soon as my niece comes in for her shift, we'll take a gander." She excuses herself and the three of us, Lamb, Skee, and me return to each other. All I want is to leave, but I force myself to stay calm. I want my face to read "just another day." But what could Jodi possibly have upstairs?

"Thank you," Skee says to Lamb. "It's a start."

When Jodi pulls Rolly's beer and sets it in front of him, I see her whisper something and he turns around to look at us, raises his eyebrows, then turns back to Jodi and they begin to quietly talk, the television gurgling behind them just enough that I can't make out what they're saying. Lamb takes the opportunity to fill Skee in. The bar's namesake, Max, is Jodi's late husband. He took over the bar from his grandfather and changed the name. He and Jodi lived in Orgull all their lives, high school sweethearts. The bar wasn't necessarily his dream as much as an inevitability, and now it's hers. I'm constantly surprised by how much Lamb knows about Orgull.

It's not five minutes before Rolly is out the door and Jodi is back at our table with a lighter and a pack of cigarettes under her palm. "They just told me you're a widow," Skee says. "Sorry for that."

"Five years," Jodi says in a way that lets us know she's more than moved on.

This time it's Lamb that brings us around to the business at hand. "So, about Cudge," she says to Jodi. "What's upstairs?"

Jodi looks as if she's forgotten, inspects the burned down cigarette she left in the ashtray, and then it comes to her. "Oh, Daddy's boxes. There's this 'n' that. Bound to be something on Cudge." She shoots me an indecipherable look. "He took a particular interest. Ain't that right, Conner?"

All eyes turn to me. "That's a fact," I say, trying to sound easy and relaxed. I force a laugh, unsure how it comes off. "In fact, Vale was asking me questions clear after he retired."

"I know he did," Jodi laughs. She lights another cigarette and takes a thoughtful drag in a way that makes me feel that she's summoning her father's memory.

I float a test. "Skee tells us my mother had Cudge declared dead. First I heard of it."

She raises her eyebrows as if this news is as big a surprise to her as it is to me. "Wasn't no body found or nothing like that?" she asks, and as I shake my head she quickly turns to Skee. "Aww, darlin', I'm sorry." Skee picks up his glass, realizes it's empty and puts it back down. "I guess I oughten say what I was going to."

"What's that?" Skee says. "I don't think it can get much worse."

Jodi looks to me and Lamb for permission and I brace myself. "No offense," she says, "but I was surprised he wasn't done in before he run off. There toward the end, your son could be an outright S.O.B." I nod, not in agreement of this generally held opinion, but in a way to show I'm listening and not overly eager. "Look there, darlin'," Jodi continues, pointing to the far wall, cigarette smoke trailing her trajectory. Underneath a lighted St. Pauli Girl sign is a gold frame surrounding what looks like a dent, but which is actually a legendary hole. "Fellas thought it was funny. That's exactly the size of your son's head."

"Fight?" Skee asks.

"A knock-down, drag-out. Folks played pool on blood stains for half a year before Max did something about it."

"You pray they grow out of it," Skee says. "Hell, I don't pray. Maybe that's the problem. He was a handful as a boy." Jodi gives him the story, a version of which I've heard. Betty was playing pool with a number of people. Cudge rushed in and attacked a man he thought she was there with. "Truth is," Jodi says, "we all thought something was going on there. Name was Larry. That was his brother-in-law just in here."

Skee is looking at the framed dent in the wall. "Well, what kind of man *wouldn't* fight for his wife?"

"The kind that doesn't have a single friend in the bar," I say, tapping my temple with an index finger. "Got to pick your spots."

"Sometimes the spots pick you," he says.

Jodi points again at the wall. "Whoever picked it, darlin', that one didn't work out so well." All of this is confusing me. A minute ago it sounded like she had a box of handcuffs in my size.

"Looks like it," Lamb says.

Jodi turns sympathetic. She tells Skee she figures he's come to Orgull for better news. She also says he looks like a man who wants the truth. When he confirms the observation she says, "That son of yours was a piece of work. I bet there wasn't one tear shed in this town when it come out he took off on Conner's momma. I don't doubt there was a time he was a good boy with you and your wife but…."

"No," Skee corrects, "she wasn't his mother. I was married before."

"I mean to say," Jodi continues, "I'm not suggesting he was always the way he was."

"Believe me," Skee says, "I wish I could tell you different. Still, before Myrna passed, I promised her I'd learn some about my son."

"You know," Jodi says, putting her hand on her hip, "until now I never thought about Cudge having a Pa. Thing was, he was hard to figure out. First couple of times, he'd come in here and play pool back with the fellas and things were okay. Betty'd be here too." She points to the table near the hole. It sits next to a silent, blinking juke box. "One day he lost and the way he acted you'd thought someone had taken his wallet and was playing a game of keep away with it. Got all red-faced and took up a cue stick. Betty couldn't get him to calm down, and my husband, bless his heart, was a smidge of a thing. And then what-do-ya-know? Cudge just comes out of it smooth as a hot air balloon liftin' above the clouds. Just sets the stick down and walks out of the bar. Left Betty with the mess and the bill."

"The more I hear about that boy…."

"Putting you through a trial, I don't doubt."

I lean back in my chair. This is turning out far different than I expected. Lamb looks at me shakes her head slightly to let me know I'm a bit too Cheshire.

"I feel like I owe it to him," Skee says. "I don't know that I did right by the boy. Searched my mind over and over and I haven't come up with what it was that turned him, so I'm hoping maybe I'll come out of here with a better idea of what happened to him. Tidy it all up."

"When can we go upstairs?" Lamb interrupts. "You really think your father had anything that could help out Mr. Hotter?"

Jodi is sitting across the table, looking directly at me, even though she's responding to Lamb. Her blue eyes are bright and open wide. "Darlin', I'm not sure what we'll find. Daddy only talked to me about Cudge now and then. You know, ideas he had. There was certain people but...." She looks now at Skee. "Whatever's tucked away is likely to show Daddy was damn frustrated. It wasn't for a lack of trying. There was a bunch of folks questioned had an alibi."

"Was one of the suspects Betty Hotter?" Skee asks. "I hate to be so direct," he says to me, "but there's no other way." I extend my hand to Jodi, giving him permission to continue.

"Of course." Jodi almost laughs. "Who would have blamed her?"

"We're talking about my son," Skee says, trying to sound as friendly as possible.

"Oh, darlin'. Shame on me."

"No harm," he says. "So, Conner's mother?"

She changes the direction of the conversation. "Don't you think, Hun," Jodi says, "if some harm come to Cudge, Betty and those boys were lucky they weren't at home?" It's a fair point. "And maybe it's just coincidental Cudge was at the wrong place at the wrong time." She's covered all the bases, and her logic makes me feel like I'm wrong-tree barking. "I'm not pretending to be no expert on any of this. Some folks pointed to all the burglaries right around then and maybe it got too hot to stay if he was the one, but Daddy said he figured Cudge more'n likely wore out his welcome with somebody." A strange little flame of pride lights inside me. *That stupid break-in plan of mine almost took.*

Skee leans back, holding his palms just above the table for a second like they are coming in for a soft landing. He sighs and both hands come to rest. "What I can't figure with you people is how you're just fine with my son being dead."

Lamb puts her hand on Skee's and he doesn't pull away. "I don't think that's it."

"Sounds like it's a shame when a good man is killed. But it's a wash when it's a bad man?"

"Hey," I interrupt a little too loudly. Suddenly six pair of eyes are on me, six glowing headlights in the dim bar. "You just went from 'dead' to 'killed.' That's quite a leap."

The front door swings open, and suddenly there's a brick of light filled by a broad-shouldered man wearing a baseball cap, and when the glare wears off I recognize Jake. Jodi stands to return to the bar and winks at Skee. "You stick around. We'll get around to that box here shortly. My girl's shift is coming up." She pauses, touching her chin in thought. "And you should know something else. Conner and his brother was good kids."

Skee looks struck as he turns to Lamb. "Does it sound like I want to pin a murder on two little boys? I came to ask some questions. Seems like I owe Cudge that much. Guess I have to get that picture out my head." He places a forefinger on his brow and shakes his head.

It's annoying. Lamb looks genuinely concerned.

"You have to remember," Skee says, turning to me, "we aren't watching the same channel. You see a grown man. I remember a pale-faced tomato head."

"No shit," Jake calls from the bar, "you're really Cudge's old man?" He has the voice of a tractor trailer. "Rolly said so but I had to come see for myself." Jake's another one I know vaguely from those days of Cudge and Betty. He's in his late sixties now, still large in blue overalls, his name stitched in red over a white patch on his chest.

Skee salutes him with his empty glass.

"Well I never met a bigger son-of-a-bitch in all my life."

From behind the bar Jodi offers and apologetic shrug.

"That's what I hear," Skee says.

Jake grabs his beer and takes the seat Jodi previously occupied. He barely acknowledges Lamb and me but she's not having it. "I don't think Mr. Hotter is feeling up to—" she begins, but Jake plows on, introducing himself and extracting a reluctant handshake from Skee.

"Sure old Larry'd love to know you're in town. He's over to Indiana side permanent now."

"Mom's boyfriend after Cudge," I clarify.

"A damn site better'n that son of yours."

Jodi knocks on the bar. "Jake, leave the man alone. He don't need to hear your bad mouthing."

"Fair enough," Jake says. "I can tell you something to be proud of. That son-of-a-bitch could shoot an arrow like nobody's business.

Fucking Robin Hood."

"Is that so?" Skee says, and he genuinely looks a little brighter for the news.

"Hell yeah. One time at the half-ass fair we have here he set up a target. One of them Styrofoam bucks. And bam, bam, bam. Hit the mark every time."

"I remember that," Jodi says, leaning on the bar. "See there, darlin'. That's something."

"'Course, though," Jake says, "don't change my opinion of him." I'd like to leave it there so I keep quiet. Any response will only encourage Jake to continue. It makes little difference. He changes the subject. "They never did catch who done it." Jake says.

Skee freezes. We all do. "Done what?" Skee asks.

Jake seems a little tripped up, takes turns looking at me, Lamb, and Skee. "I know he disappeared," he finally says, "but it don't take a genius, you know." I look him straight in the eyes as he recovers. There's a moment of silence before he leans back, flopping an arm over the back of his seat and ticking the rim of his cap with his finger. It's as solemn a gesture as laying his hand on a Bible. "If you ask me, I think Conner's old lady paid one of *them* to come down out of Louisville and haul him off."

Jodi stops her work. "Jacob Burroughs," she scolds. Her hands are balled at her waist.

"Them," Jake repeats. "They're thick as thieves up there." He grins. "Literally."

"Don't pay him no nevermind," Jodi says. "Jake, finish that beer and take your white trash ass out of here."

He pushes himself up from the table, mocking Jodi with a tip of his hat. Then he sucks down his beer and plops the bottle hard on the table. "Telling ya. Fella you ought to talk to is that old Tom Turkey Betty run around with. Like I said, he's still kicking around across the river. Might see Larry today. I'll tell him you're in town." Jake stands, then at the door he turns and stares back at us with a roll of his tongue inside his cheek. "Blacks, mister. I bet it was one a them got paid to do it." He shoots Jodi a look and steps out into a glare of daylight as if he's been swallowed.

Jodi shakes her head. "He's a holdout from the old days. The whole damn family for that matter. Acting like Louisville cops; the lot of them. Course, he didn't say the N-word, which is an improvement. Better'n they used to be, I guess. Hope we all are." She presents Skee with another bourbon.

"Has to be the last," he says. "Used to have a hollow leg, but not anymore. Think I could hunt up this Larry?"

Sitting down next to Skee, Jodi squeezes his hand. Her touch is kind but not intimate. "Last I saw of him he was a bitter old wreck."

"That's about right," I say. "Even your dad didn't want much to do with him."

"Still," Skee begins, shaking his head, "if he's listed I might ring him up tonight."

"I suppose it couldn't hurt," Jodi says looking at me. "And I guess there's one thing Jake said might be worth thinking about."

"What's that?"

"Darlin'," she says to Skee, "the truth is, Jake isn't the first one thought Betty put someone up to disappearing Cudge."

22

In less than twenty-four hours Jodi will have vanished just like Cudge. Gone. Car gone too. Her delivery guy will knock on the back door of Max's with no response. Her niece will show up for her shift only to find two agitated regulars smoking out front, cussing that the place isn't open. This niece will get in her car and drive out to Jodi's where she'll find the front door closed but unlocked. In the kitchen, on the floor, will be the smeared contents of a partially eaten Benedictine sandwich, an over-turned chair and an unopened bottle of Bud Light. People disappear.

But for now. "Promised I had something to show you," Jodi says, looking around the bar. "Guess the place'll take care of itself for a spell." She unhooks a small bell, which sways and jingles in front of the door as she returns to us. "Someone comes in, we'll hear 'em." Then she puts a hand to Skee's shoulder and leads the three of us to the rear of the bar where she unlocks a door that opens into a stairwell. "Daddy lived up here after he retired," she says, flicking on a light. "We've never done much with it except for storage."

Upstairs, there are cases of liquor, bourbons mostly, gin, too. But mainly the apartment looks every bit the home of an old man. The colors seem designed to complement beige, the avocado green couch, a painting of a jockey in yellow silks astride a bay horse, all of it not so much dusty as dulled by time. Against the wall is a small desk scattered with papers, some of them held down by a snow globe centered by a lone palm tree. Beyond the living room is a kitchen large enough to include a gray Formica table with aluminum legs and four matching chairs.

"Daddy pretty much holed up in here when he wasn't out working on his hobby." Jodi exits into what I assume is a bedroom.

"And what was that?" Skee calls.

"Private investigating," Jodi calls from the other room. "We was real proud of him. Went and got his license from the state. A man his age." She's sliding things around, and lifting, it turns out, because she re-enters the room holding a cardboard box large enough that it takes both arms to carry. My heart is racing because I hear Vale's voice coming out of the box. *Did ya do it boy? Did you do in your stepdaddy?*

Lamb startles me with an elbow to the side, chastises me for not offering to help, so I apologize. "P'shaw," Jodi says. "I'm pretty sure this is it." She sets the box in front of the couch, signaling for Skee to take a place next to her as she sits. Lamb and I sit across from them, she in a blue wool recliner and I on its similar companion. "I call it a hobby because Daddy didn't really make money at it," Jodi says with not a little bit of anticipation in her voice. "A lot of favors, mostly. Went to all that trouble for the license and couldn't bring himself to charge folks. Mostly it was a reason for him to traipse around in his old Buick."

The top of the box is well worn, held together by a makeshift latch made of duct tape and twine and a large paperclip. Jodi's hands are sunspotted, her nails short, but perfectly manicured with pale blue polish tipped in white. "How pretty," Lamb says as Jodi unties the twine.

"What? Oh," she says, holding out her hands. "My niece insists. Got tired of seeing my old, red bar hands. Now it's paraffin and a manicure whether I want it or not." She flips through manila folders in the box which are lined up back to back as if in a filing cabinet. "This is what's left. Daddy was a tenacious old coot even after he stopped sheriffing. Anything in here related to Cudge is yours." She taps a folder with her finger. "Finally caught up with this one over in Shively. Hit and run. Woman damn near killed a little girl on her bike not fifty feet from our front door." I can't make out the words on the tabs as Jodi continues, but there's a shock in my chest when her hands stop and it's clear she's found what we've come for. "Here it is." She pauses and looks at me "Grayson, Conner."

I'm not surprised Vale has a file with my name on it, but I shrug and go a little wide-eyed as if I am. "He asked Betty and me a lot of questions," I say. There can't be anything in the file I don't already know about. But just as quickly as I think that, another thought pushes forward; what if there is?

Jodi nods in Skee's direction sympathetically. "Darlin', at the very least you'll have the comfort of knowing things were looked into."

At first the folder doesn't appear too thick but it's bulging when it's removed from the box. On Skee's lap it has little weight; the information that might be in the folder, that's the actual weight. "What was your father's interest in old cases?" I ask.

Jodi turns to me with a look that shows she's either confused or suspicious about what's happening. "You're the one that brought him in," she says. *Do your worst.*

She explains that when Vale retired, there were some cases he couldn't let go of, whether they were resolved or not, so he photocopied what he could and kept going. "Lucky me," I say, which is followed by Lamb slapping my knee to shut me up. Jodi reels off a couple of examples of Vale's cases: five decapitated deer found laid out in a circle in the woods, why a woman named Marla James drove to the river and shot her husband in the back of the head before taking her own life.

"They certainly don't sound like a bunch of good-natured folk," Lamb says.

"You actually just used the word folk," I say.

She rolls her eyes. "Something in the water."

Skee and Jodi stare at us, confused by the tableaux. Some of her father's cases, Jodi continues, held his interest because of the personalities involved. Others because of the crime itself. Cudge's case interested her father in both ways. "You'll want to know that Daddy didn't hold to the idea that it was okay for some people to get knocked off and others not."

"I appreciate hearing that," Skee says, rubbing the back of his neck to conjure a thought. "It's like that eye for an eye, or something like that. By my way of thinking, if that's the standard, most of us would deserve a peeper or two poked out."

"Well, go ahead, see what's in there," Jodi says, flipping open the folder. Immediately on top is a short stack of index cards tied with string, and then newspaper clippings, all of them seeming, at a glance and upside down, to contain the general reporting about Cudge. The last rectangle of paper, I can tell, doesn't offer details the same as the others. It's Cudge's obituary. I've never seen it.

Clearly affected, Skee stares at the paper for a few seconds, though it's not clear he's reading until he nods slowly and turns it over, revealing a scrap of newspaper taped to the back. He looks at me, narrows one eye, then hands me the obituary which I read out loud:

> *Hotter, Marion Cudgel "Cudge," 37, passed away, Sunday, February 22, 1982. Cudge was a line operator at Colgate, served four years in the U.S. Army and was a member of St. Leonard Parish. He will be remembered by all who knew him for his loving personality, being a friend to everyone he met and for his unending devotion to his family. He is survived by his wife, Betty, his son, Christian, and step-sons, Conner and Samuel. A private memorial service will be held at Cave Hill Cemetery.*

The date taped on the back is from the newspaper header, though it doesn't show from what newspaper. "She was a fucking piece of work," I say to Lamb. "May 14, 1990. Betty's birthday. I don't know how she got away with this."

She doesn't have to ask. "Your mother," she says, then turning to Jodi and Skee. "And February 22nd is *Conner's* birthday."

I point to the date on the back. "And this is hers."

"Why didn't you tell me about the service," Skee asks, requesting the obituary by holding out his deeply lined hand. "That might have been enough."

"I doubt there was one," I say. "I certainly didn't know about it if there was. Besides, our birthdays? I'm pretty sure it's a giant 'fuck you, Cudge.'"

Skee isn't having it. "No," he says. "People don't do that. People don't go to the trouble like that."

"*People* don't," I say. "Betty is another matter."

"Oh, Darlin'," Jodi says, again touching Skee's shoulder. "Don't you see? That thing's just a wad of spite."

"Cave Hill is a fancy cemetery up in Louisville," I say. "You've seen where Betty lived at the end. She couldn't afford something like that."

"You're just sick," Skee says, turning red. He stands, and at first it looks like he's going to go after me, but he snatches up his cane and thumps out of the room and down the stairs, Jodi close behind. Lamb looks at me, the window behind her flaring light around her, but her expression asks what the hell? I'm not certain, but then I hear the jingle of bells and a second following. "Let's go," I say, hopping up from my chair, and then quickly Lamb is ahead of me and out the door. On the coffee table sit the tied index cards and yellowed newspaper clippings. I know precisely what I have to do.

23

There was a day when Cudge's end became inevitable. When I was a kid I found a spot in the woods near the river I claimed as my own, a place where two mature oaks leaned in on each other like drunken pals. Not even Mark knew about it. The space was all canopy and underbrush, except for a pad of limestone wide and flat enough for a kid my size to lie on and think about the world or think about nothing at all. The river wasn't so close as to be heard, but on the warmest days, its musty odor permeated the woods.

It was on a fall day just months after Betty and Cudge married that I went to my hideout. I was staying away from the house as much as possible. He hadn't raped me yet, but by then what Cudge was doing to us made it clear the less I was around the better, or he'd find an excuse to make life really bad for me. I almost preferred getting beat up at school. I needed the time away, even from Sammy. Under my arm was an old *Playboy* lifted from the barber shop, and in my pocket a pack of cigarettes swiped from a woman's convertible in town. The leaves hadn't begun to fall yet, but the season was fast bleaching away the green and there was more of a bite to the sound of each step I made. As I drew closer to my destination I did what I always did, changed my entry point, fearing if I came in the same way too often I'd create a track like a deer run that anyone might happen on and follow.

I settled myself on the limestone, letting the magazine fall to my side as I leaned back with both arms. The air, warm and still, held me. It was a feeling I never got at home after Dad died, even before Cudge, though that made it worse. I liked these moments for their simplicity. I had plans to bring Mark there. I wanted it to become *our* spot, not just mine.

Which first, a cigarette or the magazine? The cover of the *Playboy* featured a hot-pink background with Dolly Parton in a tight black Bunny outfit complete with Bunny ears atop her mushroom cloud of platinum hair. I wasn't attracted to her, nor any of the women in those magazines, but I was thirteen, and sometimes there were naked men.

"Whatcha got there?" The voice came from the underbrush. It was Cudge. I sat bolt upright. "I said, whatcha got there?" The sound of each word was smoke-bit, raspy. I searched for the face to go with it, but nothing, and if felt to me more like Cudge was invisible than concealed.

"Leave me the fuck alone, Cudge." Then I heard a rustle, saw patches of him rise up from ground level. He'd been lying there, waiting, like a hunter in a deer blind. How did he know about this place? He stood and his form took a more complete shape as he pushed through the brush toward me. He wore a green plaid flannel shirt tucked, as usual, into jeans that were cinched into his waist by a thick brown belt with a Kentucky shaped brass buckle. I didn't move as he stood almost directly over me, arms crossed, leather work boots set wide.

"Think I don't know your every move?" Cudge said, smiling out of one side of his mouth. He'd trimmed his moustache, revealing a pair of thin lips that somehow also concealed his teeth as if he possessed the mouth of a catfish. "Shit," Cudge continued, "I know your game and what you're up to before you even think it." He plucked a low hanging leaf and held it to the light. "Sure. You go down to the store and pinch a magazine, maybe cigarettes…." He paused and looked away from the leaf and down at me. "Might want to hide your shit somewhere other than under your mattress. Your Mom and all. At first I wouldn't have took you for looking at girlie magazines." He returned to the leaf, flattened it to his palm and traced its lines with his finger. "Dolly ain't naked in that one, so if you come out here to choke your chicken over her, you'll be disappointed." He squatted, stared at me until I felt interrogation even in the silence. "Let's have a cigarette." He held out a hand, revealing the leaf, now crushed. "Cigarette."

I reached into my pocket and produced the pack.

"What the fuck?" Cudge laughed. "Virginia Slims?" He took the pack and ripped off the cellophane, tapped out a cigarette an inch and extended the box toward me. "Go ahead, break the cherry."

"I don't want one."

"Too bad. Take one anyway."

I wasn't sure what he was up to, but it showed all the signs of being the start of another one of those times where his sole purpose seemed only to terrorize me. I took the cigarette as Cudge reached into his pocket and pulled out his chrome lighter. I'd endured multiple tellings about how he'd won it in a drinking game that left the loser passed out on the bar.

"Right there's my motto," Cudge said, pointing at the engraving. I didn't have to look. I knew what it said. *The world is your oyster. So eat it!* Cudge popped the lighter open and offered the flame. When the cigarette was lit he took one for himself. "Not bad for lady shit," he said after a drag, standing again and walking a few paces away so that his back was to me.

"So, *can* you, little man?"

"Can I what?"

"Damn," Cudge said, half laughing. "Choke your chicken?"

What could my mother possibly see in him, I wondered. This was before it got really bad. "You're a fucking weirdo."

Cudge exhaled a cloud of smoke, turned back and approached me, stopping when he reached my outstretched legs, the toe of his boot touching the sole of my shoe. "Didn't think so. A little fucker like you probably got a pussy instead of a dick." He gently placed his boot on my ankle, pressed slightly harder when I tried to pull away. I wanted to run but felt anchored to the rock beneath me. "See," Cudge continued, unbuckling his belt. "You got to have one of these."

"Better not hit me."

Cudge laughed and let the ends of the belt flap apart. "Hit you? I wouldn't do that little man. I'm teaching you." His expression was filled with mock care. "Like I said, you want to whack off you got to have one of these."

I was shaking, uncertain what Cudge was going to do with his belt, but he didn't pull it from its loops. Instead, he undid the rivets of his jeans and pulled his dick and testicles through the opening in his boxers. They hung on this plaid background pink and bat-like, were thatched with orange hair. I turned away, trying to block out Cudge's wheezy laugh. Then there was what felt like spit on my cheek, and I spun back around to yell at him only to find my face the target of Cudge's full stream of piss. I pulled away but Cudge pressed hard on my ankle so that I could almost feel bone to rock. "Just sit right there you little shit," he growled.

I pulled away but he pressed even harder on my ankle. "Stop it," I shouted, squirming, the warm liquid splashing my neck, soaking my t-shirt. And as quickly as it started, it stopped. Cudge pulled the weight off my ankle. "What the fuck was that?" I yelled, popping to my feet and backing away from him. I pulled the soaked shirt over my head and threw it to the ground, and I was breathing hard, my face hot. Yet another time I didn't run, maybe it was because Cudge had stopped, looked like a man less dangerous than like someone who'd just ridden a roller coaster.

"That, little man," he said, "was one fucking ice cold thrill."

"You think my mother's going to let you do that to me? I should have said something when you pulled that other shit."

"She will," Cudge said, buckling his pants. "Cuz she ain't gonna know." His voice was calm, confident. He reached into his back pocket and pulled out my pack of cigarettes, took one and threw the pack at my feet. "See, little man, I know you ain't gonna go home to Mommy and talk about how it is you're covered in piss. You ain't because you're a pussy. Or maybe it's because you don't want anyone to know you've been stealing titty magazines and cigarettes."

I stood my ground, tried to be as imposing as I could even though Cudge was at least two feet taller. "That doesn't scare me."

"Or maybe…" He paused, looked at the end of his cigarette, then at me, moving his eyes but not his head. "Maybe it's because you don't want me telling your Mom she's got a little faggot on her hands."

I tried to stay calm. "That's bullshit."

"I could tell her and the whole town about you and that little friend of yours."

I half-lunged a step forward. "You leave Mark alone," I shouted.

Cudge lifted an index finger. "Yeah," he said, tapping the end of his nose, "right there. Thought so. I been tryin' to tell you, little man, I see everything." He took a final, long drag from his cigarette. "If you care about, what's-his-name, Mark and, for that matter, that little brother of yours, you'll shut the fuck up."

The threat struck me still. I couldn't speak at first, then managed, almost in a whisper. "Leave Sammy alone."

"That's up to you," Cudge said, tossing the cigarette to the ground and smashing it with his boot. "See you at the house." He turned and walked through the brush. I watched his plaid back until he disappeared into the woods and then I flopped to the ground, shirtless and smelling of urine. I grabbed the soaked *Playboy* and heaved it, the flapping pages sounding like a startled bird. I'd never felt so helpless. What was I going to do, I asked myself. It wasn't Mark's fault Betty married Cudge and what would Cudge do to Sammy? I didn't want to be responsible for giving him an excuse to answer that question. At the same time, everything was telling me it was only going to get worse, and that's the moment I decided Cudge had to be gotten rid of and I was going to figure out a way to make that happen.

24

Jodi is hunting around for her keys behind the bar and Lamb is already out the door. Neither have noticed that I didn't immediately follow. "Amen," Jodi calls as her niece walks in, nearly plowed over by my pretend eagerness to get outside. "Darlin', you have to watch the place while I put out a fire," she says, tossing her niece a bar rag. She is oddly invested in Skee, pushes past me as I adjust my eyes to the sunlight. I see Lamb at Skee's car, then Jodi scrambling around to the passenger side where she lets herself in. I'm not fast nor interested enough to make it before the car takes off. "What happened?" I ask Lamb.

"I should have left well enough alone is what happened." Both of us look down the block where James is standing outside the shop, fists on his hips. Behind him, a woman with a heavy black purse tucked to her side walks away, looking back at him as if he's some sort of menace.

Lamb takes my hand and we jog toward him. "Think he's upset?"

"Of course. He feels excluded."

When we're almost to him, James begins to speak but I put my hand up. "The old man freaked out," I say.

Lamb sighs. "Conner, it was more than that and you know it."

"It's worse?" James asks. I'm right. His mood changes fast now. He looks around on the street as if he's joined a cabal.

"Look," I say, pausing, because what am I going to say, that this isn't a game we're playing? This isn't *Clue*. And by the way, later, I'm sneaking behind Max's so I can retrieve the folder I dropped out the window. What I come up with is "Let's go inside and we can tell you about the giant middle finger Betty left behind."

"What happened to quiet, little, domestic Conner?" he asks.

"Let's remember," I say, gesturing to Lamb, "I didn't want anything to do with Skee."

Lamb scrunches the hair on the back of her head in exasperation. "Exactly. All that pain you've been carrying around and, until now, not a word to the people you love."

"You matter to me, Conny," James says, placing a soft hand behind my neck. "All of you."

"Only damaged people hold it all in," Lamb says.

Gently squeezing the back of my neck, James leans in and kisses my forehead. "Talk to us."

"Tonight," I say. "I'm kind of rattled." It's true, and I need the time. There are things I cannot say no matter what, but I owe them. Here's the difference. Right now they are thinking of me, but what's running through *my* head is a vision of Skee and Jodi speeding down the road to where? That, and retrieving Vale's file from in back of Max's.

We turn for the shop but James pauses, seems satisfied. "I never noticed," he says with a hand at his bottom lip. Leaning next to the door against the window is our folded sandwich board that reads *HanDesigned Derby Hats by Lamb*.

"What?" Lamb asks.

"It makes it sound like you're Chinese."

I'm looking but I don't see.

"Oh," Lamb says, getting it. "Han." She shrugs. "Well, in Kentucky I'm Chinese, or Korean, or Japanese or Vietnamese."

"If you please."

"*Lady and the Tramp*?" Lamb guesses correctly.

I love these two. I wish I was better.

25

I've made a decision. It's the evening of Skee's fleeing. I run upstairs at home and plop down on the bed next to Lamb who's on the phone. She silences me with a finger to her lips, and it doesn't take long to figure out that she and her mother are still arguing over Lamb's refusal to attend a second-cousin's funeral. They've been going at it for an hour which is the last time I checked in on her. Knowing my dear wife, this is her way of showing respect. She's giving her mother the satisfaction of telling Lamb what a selfish daughter she is. We've agreed, for my sake, at least for the night, to put the day's events behind us, but I'm going to share with her and James the folder I've retrieved from behind Max's. Boneheaded move, but there it is. Maybe that's the best way to have it all out, for us to read together what came of Vale's investigation. I know my name is written on those index cards—more than once. Jodi will assume I have the file, so I expect a phone call. That, or maybe she and Skee will pull into our driveway any minute. I wish Lamb and James could be my sentinels. Maybe I *have* been going about this all wrong, keeping them at arm's length.

Lamb pops off the bed and walks back and forth, giving me the nag nag nag hand sign just as we hear James come home with dinner. Phone cradled between her neck and shoulder, Lamb raises her arms as if to say "just in time."

I head downstairs and into the kitchen where James has already put plates on the table. He's unpacking a bag of groceries when he sees me, an activity he halts in favor of a head gesture telling me to come closer so that he can give me a kiss, which he does. I like his priorities but the two of them seem oddly calm. "It was either Pizza or Thai," James says pointing at the table and the evidence of his choice.

"There's no Thai place around here."

He boops my nose. "Exactly."

"Jesus," Lamb says, entering the kitchen and plopping down at the table. "Listening to Mom, you'd think I was refusing to attend the funeral of my conjoined twin."

I give James the gist of the conversation, while exasperated Lamb shakes her head and lifts the lid of the pizza box with a fingernail just enough to see in.

When she wrinkles her nose, James flips the lid all the way open. "Give me some credit." The pie is half pineapple, which we love and she detests, and half ham, which I hate and she loves.

We all pull a slice, and I take a breath. "Okay," I say, "I have something to show you. Remember, in the interest of disclosure?" James is leaning on the kitchen counter, and Lamb sits with me at the table. "I've done something not so good." I exit to retrieve Vale's file, and when I return Lamb and James are sitting next to each other at the table like parents waiting for a son who's been out too late. They even look nervous, as if they're one step ahead of me.

"What the hell?" Lamb says as I set the file on the table and take a seat across from them.

James is confused. "Is that what Jodi showed you today?"

"Wait," Lamb says, "you took this? That's where you went earlier?"

My palms rest on the full belly of the file. Like so much I don't think through, maybe this isn't such a good idea. "Not exactly."

Exasperated, Lamb pinches the bridge of her nose and closes her eyes. "Conner," she begins, but now it's James' turn to interrupt.

"Kids," he says, raising his hands as if between two prize fighters. "Conny, I love you, but this is turning into some kind of all out weird. Help us out here. I thought we had a moment earlier."

"We did."

"Look," Lamb says, "when you went out today, James and I had a talk." They turn to each other as if to ask *is this the moment?* James nods. "We love you and we want you to know we're both devastated by what

Cudge did to you."

James takes one of my hands. "To be honest, even without knowing all that, I've thought you were a bit fragile. Both of us have. Maybe we're even a little addicted to that, to protecting you."

A large moth flutters on the outside of the window, trying to get in, then as if it senses the room, quickly flies away. It's all I can do to stay in the moment. I've no idea what's been discussed without me, nor what's coming. James, kind and straight-jawed, smiles and squeezes my hand, and Lamb rests a cheek in her palm, shaking her head. "What now?" she says. I begin to explain the impulse of tossing the file out the window but she interrupts me. "No. The three of us, Conner. What's going to happen to *us?*"

"Nothing. It's all going to be okay."

"Because," James says, "this arrangement; it's already more than unusual."

"There are lots of crazy relationships. We've done alright," I say.

"Is alright enough?" Lamb sits up in her CPA posture. "James and I had a realization today. We're not just playing house, Conner. James is your partner. You and he are my closest friends. You are the father of my daughter. You have to protect us too, or this can't work. We won't stay."

Silence. I look back and forth at the two of them. They're serious. *I was* trying *to protect you.*

"Conny, my heart is aching right now because for the first time since we met I feel like there's this huge part of you I don't know." James pauses. "No, I don't *feel* like that. It's just true."

Lamb sighs. "It's like we've just walked out of play into real life."

I raise my hand because I can't take it anymore and I can't lose them. "I get it. Okay." I say that maybe this happened for a reason. It's a way for them to finally understand how fucked up things got when I was a kid, and I point out that the file tab sitting in front of us doesn't read "Hotter, Cudge." It's my name. For better or worse let's have it all out. "It was stupid to take it. I know that. We can give it back tomorrow, but…." I push the file toward them, the pregnant curve its own invitation. "This will help tell you maybe not who I am, but who I was." The only thing I have going for me here is that I know it won't say *Conner did it*.

Lamb looks at the file from the corner of her eyes. "Did you see the rest?"

"I waited."

The moment softens, and James doesn't hesitate opening the folder. On top are the tied index cards, and almost as if he's saving something for dessert, he pushes them to the side, revealing Betty's joke of an obituary, a little grass-stained, which he already knows about. "I tell you, Conny," he says, "your mother had some low hangers." He delicately spreads the clippings with the fingertips of both hands as if preparing for a session of Ouija. Satisfied with the array, he mumble-summarizes the other clippings, yellowed news accounts that offer little I haven't already learned or don't already know. What they should say, but can't, is that Cudge was found dead by Conner Grayson in partially frozen bathwater. Then not found.

One of the clippings includes an odd little peninsula cut around an advertisement for beekeeping equipment. It's circled in pencil, and I don't like the feeling it gives me. Vale is present. He held this. He was reading about the investigation, probably a good portion of the information supplied by him. He sat down with a pencil in his hand, hopeful, I imagine. Maybe I'm thinking about this all wrong because Vale wasn't so consumed that he didn't have time to circle that ad and cut it out along with the article as if it were just as important. Maybe it was. There's a lesson there.

As if on cue, Lamb and I reach into the flattened piñata that is my past. There are photocopies of handwritten notes and the tied stack of index cards written on by hand which Lamb impatiently snatches. Among the photocopies is a sheriff's report, a rectangle of densely packed block letters that look as if the writer was conscious of space. I take up the document and tilt it for better light. Conner, victim's stepson, reported the missing was headed up for a bath when he left with his brother to stay at a family friend's home for the weekend. The stepson reported no sign of the missing upon his return to the home. Betty Hotter, the missing's wife, returned home shortly after. That's the sum total of all they asked us that first meeting and still Vale wasn't convinced. The other photocopies are similar reports written in the same hand. Thankfully, I was consistent.

One thing that's immediately clear about the entire file is how little there is of Betty and Sammy. After he retired, Jodi's father didn't take much interest in them. But me, clearly I was another story.

I tap James on the shoulder and point at Lamb who's staring at the index cards the batch of which is nearly an inch thick and held together like one might tie a bow on a small package. "Working on your X-ray vision?" James asks.

Frowning with concession, Lamb sets the cards down. "It just occurred to me. Don't you think it's weird Jodi hasn't called or come up here? I mean, it wouldn't take much to figure out who took this stuff." She shame-squints her eyes at me but it doesn't work. "Should we be looking at this without her?"

"Wonder yourself," James says. "It's time we meet Pandora." He unties the cards and fans them like a hand of playing cards. I move my chair closer for a better look. The cards are sequentially numbered, some written in pencil, others in several colors of ink, the handwriting in the later cards is thinner, and condensed. The letters squash into barely readable threads. Vale wrote these over a long period of time.

The first card contains one sentence in emphatic black lettering. *It was the boy,* and it's clear Lamb and James take note of this detail because they both look up at me. "Don't act surprised," I say because I understand this is the weightiest "it" they've ever read. In four syllables Vale implies that Cudge more than disappeared. At some point soon after Cudge was gone, Vale began writing on these cards, and the first thing he wrote, his first suspicion was that he thought I killed Cudge. What gave him such certainty? I shake my head. "Item 1. That's a big part of what I've lived with and who I am. A suspect. But remember, I'm here, not in jail."

"Such a comfort," Lamb says, patting her belly. "Daddy is only a *suspect.*"

"Was," James says almost hopefully.

My past as piñata. I can only hope the contents don't pour out.

The next card is filled front and back. *Confirmed Betty and boys were away (if dead, how many days?). Betty displayed expected emotion at husband's disappearance—at first. The boy nervous, too consistent. Missing deceased's wallet and hunting knife owned by boy.* "Wait," I say, snatching the card from James a bit too urgently. "That's new."

"You had a hunting knife, Butch?" James is genuinely surprised. "You can't even slice a tomato."

I'm not sure what to say. I never said a word about the knife to Vale. Fucking Betty. "Yeah, I had a knife. Before she died Betty told me she got rid of it to protect me, which is bullshit." I point to the sheriff's report. When I tell them who gave it to me and why, they stare in disbelief. Or is it fear of what might be coming next?

"That can't be right," James says. "A mother wouldn't do that."

"Lamb," I say, "you met Betty. Remind him about the second time."

"Oh," James says as if he's put two and two together. "I've heard that story. Once is enough."

I was still in college up in Louisville, and I brought Lamb down with me to check on Betty. By then, Larry was staying at the house but they'd had a fight and Betty sounded irrational and drunk on the phone. We found her out back butchering the last of five rabbits Larry bought, thinking he was going to start a business. "She looks awful," Lamb whispered to me. Betty was covered in blood, her forehead and one cheek streaked dark red like war paint. At her feet was a bucket of guts and skins saved for catfish bait. She was up to one of Dad's tricks. Fill a can, let it sit in the sun a couple days. Poke holes, tie a line, toss it in the river, and fish next to it the day after. "Look who it is?!" she said brightly, but drunk. She walked toward us with a knife in one hand and a dangling brindle rabbit in the other. "That fucker Larry taught me," she said. "You just hold 'em up and wack the back of the head with the side of your hand." She raised the dead animal toward Lamb. "You people eat rabbit? I'll skin it for you."

"Betty," I said. "Stop."

"Hell," she said. "Conner'll do it. He used to be good with a knife. Isn't that right son?"

Sitting here now with James and Lamb, that old life doesn't seem nearly as distant any longer and I'm stricken with the realization that this confession of sorts will not include Cudge dead in the bathtub.

"That one time," Lamb says, "is why I never pressed you on your childhood. I thought I understood."

"So yeah, Betty's little inside joke about me being good with a knife? Til the end she played that. I was sure she did something to Cudge, but I was fourteen. What would have happened to Sammy and me if I sold her out?"

"Weren't your grandparents alive?" James asks.

"Dad's mother. But after he died…." They understand. "Anyway, the knife. Back then I told them I didn't notice anything missing when I got home, but kind mother must have changed the story."

"And the sheriff never asked you about something like that?"

"Never. And I don't get it." *Was Vale protecting me?*

Lamb reads another index card. "Check again on burglaries, Boy wears UK blue toboggan. Betty/robbery."

The final words make sense only to me. Vale knew, or thought he knew, about Betty and Cudge's heist, a suspicion explained without acknowledgement, and which is thankfully interrupted by James' sleeve accidentally sweeping some of the papers off the table. At my feet, staring up at me from a newspaper clipping is Cudge's face in black and white, the mustached, balding man too familiar to me. He is neither smiling nor stern faced, and if it wasn't for the fact that I can tell he's standing in front of our fireplace mantle, the photo could be a mug shot. Whatever article it was connected to is not attached.

I have to look away because I'm suddenly nauseous with my own brand of vertigo. Cudge's face below me, even in black and white, fucks with my memory; his slobbery ecstasy was something I stared up at, closed my eyes against until he slapped me and insisted I look at him. Cudge above me. Always above me. Not a flat photo. Not dead on paper.

"Conny," James says pointing to the clipping he's reading, "why would he have this in the file?" He hands me the scrap and I immediately know it's not something I care to look at. It's an article about finding my father's body in the river. Just west of Louisville is a long stretch of the Ohio which, in dry periods, reveals an astonishing number of coral fossils. This is where they found the bloated corpse of my father. I make it a point to not talk to people about it, but on the occasions when I do, I try not to sound sentimental. It makes it easier. "I have no idea why Vale saved this," I say, skimming the brief account. It's the first I've known that anything was ever written about what happened. Betty was either protective or thoughtless. I have an opinion on that.

James shakes his head and looks to Lamb for support. "Sometimes you're just a talking block of ice."

I shrug. After Betty reported Dad missing it took just over two days to find him. A woman and her four-year-old grandson were looking at the fossil beds when they came upon his body floating face down and lodged between the rocks. The newspaper says the kid saw him first, asked his grandmother if they could swim like the man in the water. Only In my imagination I can conjure an image of my father like a lolling snorkeler. Betty conveyed so little. When I read about how Dad was found, my first thought is to wonder how the grandmother explained to her grandson what he'd seen.

Next to the article, the paper published a photo of Dad from about five years before he died. It's a black and white, and he is all smiles wearing his favorite shirt, a well-worn hibiscus Hawaiian thing that we called his barbecue uniform. It's a troubling photo to look at because it's been a very long time since I've held in my head for any length of time a happy version of him. But if you didn't know him, like most of the people who would have read that article, you'd think some terrifically cheery man had come to an unfortunate end.

I'm doing my best to pretend there's nothing new to me. "I feel bad for the little kid," I say, handing the article back to James. Before he takes it, I notice writing on the back. One word in pencil: "Pattern?" My face collapses into my hands and I sob. It's that fast. Never in all these years is this something I've considered: Dad went missing; Cudge went missing; and both of them were married to my fucked-up mother. Now, I see Cudge's frozen body, and then, a cloudy image of a child pointing at my father's body in the water. A man in jeans and a torn blue T-shirt and near-gleaming white tube socks. He'd left his near-new shoes neatly paired on the bridge, what I thought was a marker of his leap, or a final gesture to a stranger who might make use of them. But now, of course, that doesn't make sense. My father who picked his teeth with business cards and carpeted the passenger side of his truck with McDonald's bags, the Dad who took me to a memorial service in my Bugs Bunny pajamas and couldn't eat a sandwich without ending up with a mayonnaise smile, he suddenly got tidy at the very moment he was checking out? *Fuck you Betty.*

I feel James' hand on my back, and I look up. He and Lamb are leaning over in a wave of concern. "You get it, right?" I say, tapping Vale's singular query. "He's asking if Betty tossed my dad into the river."

Lamb reaches across James and takes my hand. "He was just thinking out loud. I mean, obviously he never took the idea any further."

And here's when I truly ache, because I can't tell them the version of Cudge's disappearance that's true or not true, that I saw him icy dead upstairs in this house, the place that's supposed to be our family home. Why not just jump a step ahead, pack Lamb's bags in advance, open the extra-key drawer in the kitchen where James could make a three-point shot on the way out? The normal Betty taught me can never be theirs. At the end, she tried to make herself look like my savior, but did she steal my father? I feel her next to me, shrugging. What a mother won't do. Suddenly I feel like an idiot. All versions of happiness are fantasy.

26

I rest my head in the crook of James' arm, one hand laying across his tight bare abdomen. In the dim morning light, from this vantage, his closely trimmed chest hair looks like a silvery field. It's the after moment. James' instincts are spot on as usual, and so the sex wasn't so much passionate as it was enveloping, protective. "I'm sorry," I say.

"It wasn't that bad," he jokes. "I give you a 7."

I try. "I wasn't warned about the six A.M. wakeup call."

"Obviously you were never a boy scout."

My silence belies the question.

"Be prepared."

"I love you." Hand on my naked back, he pulls me tight in as I continue. "And I really am sorry about this Cudge mess."

"Love the man, love his skeletons. I feel better after last night." James removes his arm from around me and props himself on an elbow. His eyes are dark and shining, his expression all kindness. "I mean, it's nothing we can't get through. Remember I told you about Robert?"

"He broke your heart." I've never asked many questions about James' ex-boyfriend with whom he lived for nine years. I know they talk on the phone from time to time, and I know at the end they tried to fix a flagging relationship by opening it up. James was devastated when one of Robert's randoms quickly became the only one, and then moved in just three days after James moved out.

"What I didn't tell you, really, is how I handled our break up. Or didn't handle it. Conny, I didn't give a shit. I was drinking and doing coke and sucking guys off in Cherokee park. I can't even remember their faces. I just wanted to feel good, even for a few minutes, which means I always felt like crap."

"Wow," I say and I want to ask why he's telling me all this but he doesn't give me a chance, drawing a wide circle on my chest and continuing.

"One night I get pulled over, and I'm smashed. The cop goes through the entire line-walking thing, but I don't even know why he bothered. So, they lock me up downtown and make me stay overnight. Five A.M. they let me go, and then I'm standing outside needing to call someone. It hits me. I've pissed off all of my friends. Every last one of them. So even though we haven't talked in five or six months, I call Robert because that's all I can think to do, and when he picks me up, the only thing he says is 'Honey, you look rode.' That afternoon he gets me in rehab. Turns out alcohol wasn't so much a problem as the coke and dick."

"You've never told me any of this."

"I should have, but I guess we both know how shy skeletons are."

"We're fucked up."

"Formerly. That's the point, Conny." James leans his forehead on mine, and I feel a dot of warmth, almost as if the contact itself is a kind of bindi. "There's nothing that's happened in our pasts that's going to change what we are to each other now. I don't know exactly what's going on with Skee coming to town, but I promise, as long as you're honest with me…and Lamb…it will all be okay. I promise."

I nod. It will all be okay if I'm honest with them. Without knowing it, James has just told me it's not all going to be okay. "Thank you," I say as he lays again on his back. I place my head on his chest and listen to his reliable heart and feel him drift off. What do I say to him and Lamb; fun fact, death is a little hobby of mine? Has been since I was a teenager. I day-dreamed about it; Cudge's dying, came up with the kind of implausible acts only a kid would imagine. As if the world was in on it, various methods presented themselves to me, a cornucopia of acts too complicated or too far-fetched to carry out, but in first bloom, wholly possible in my mind. After school one day, I came across a black-and-white rerun, an *Alfred Hitchcock Presents*, in which a woman kills her husband with a frozen leg of lamb, roasts it and feeds it to the detectives as they speculate on what the murder weapon might have been. I imagined my mother doing the same, even to the level of detail that I thought it would more likely be goat, a kid, rather than lamb. I imagined raising the animal myself just for the satisfaction of having part of Cudge's money going to pay for his own end.

There was another a day I sat on a bench facing the Ohio, reading a story in which a man commits murder by stabbing his victim in the neck with an icicle. The weapon melts away and the murderer is never discovered. I thought long and hard about how I might make such an icicle in our freezer. Would I have to freeze something rectangular and whittle it down to a point? That idea reached an early end when I realized before any whittling, I'd have to explain the presence of this object sitting atop the frozen peas and carrots. Then I thought maybe it was a matter of waiting until winter when I could have my pick of weapons from the eves of our garage, but winter seemed too far off. The leaves had only just turned and the river was in its fall mood, moving molasses-like, low from a lack of rain.

Still, I rehearsed the icicle scenario in my head, and not like a thirteen-year-old at play. I was serious. I imagined Cudge sitting on the porch in a white t-shirt, smoking a cigarette. I would approach him from behind, gripping a dazzlingly shiny icicle. I could see his pink scalp and every strand of his sickly comb-over. The metaphors for myself were a jumble. I thought of bullfighters and ninjas, Jedis and vampire killers. But the icicle idea, like the others, eventually gave way because it occurred to me that in winter, Cudge would be wearing a coat and scarf. His neck would be off limits. This is how these thoughts generally petered out, with me searching for reasons not to execute a plan that had too much momentum. It was one thing to want Cudge dead, but I wasn't able to imagine myself seeing it through, had never brought to my mind's eye a vision of Cudge murdered by my own hands. This was something I just couldn't do. I didn't know a morning was coming soon when I'd change my mind.

I worried what it might be like in the winter, our first with Cudge in the house. What shape would our lives take with all those freezing days when me and Sammy weren't able to be outside and away?

Then the world intervened. Gave me a way out. I saw a possibility; maybe a hundred yards down the river a sheriff's car with its large beige star pulled up behind a pair of men sitting on the bank drinking beer. Sheriff Vale crossed one arm over his chest and rested his chin in one hand. One of the men stumbled to his feet and pulled a wallet from his back pocket. The second man did the same. I couldn't hear what was being said, but after a minute or so both men raised their arms in the air and haphazardly made their way to the car where they put their hands on the hood while they were frisked. Vale handcuffed each man and guided them to the backseat of his car. It was when the car drove away and one man looked out the window in my direction that I got the idea. Cudge didn't have to be killed. He needed to be taken away. I might have thought to tell Vale what Cudge was doing to me, how he was treating the entire family. But I was too far down the road for that, and if I said something, and they didn't believe me, then what was I in for, what were all of us in for? It would be my fault. I see it now as the refrain of my young life. And besides, if I tried that, the entire town would find out what had been happening. I would be "that boy." I had to come up with something else. Dead or arrested. I had options.

27

The worst and best thing happened after I saw Vale take away those men on the river bank. I heard Cudge throwing things around downstairs in the middle of the night. "God fucking, dammit," he yelled over and over. "It's us this time." I heard Betty run out of their room and downstairs. At some point after I fell asleep, Sammy had climbed into bed next to me. "What's wrong," he asked? I shushed him with a finger against my lips. Whatever it was, I figured we were just minutes from hearing about it directly. Cudge cussed for a little while longer, and there was one last thud against a wall strong enough that it made the house shudder. "What was that?" Sammy asked. He'd pulled himself tight to me.

"I don't know," I said, which was true, but a thought crossed my mind that Betty was downstairs and maybe she'd been shoved to the wall. We waited for something more, but the house quieted. In the morning, Betty told me someone had broken in and taken her purse and Cudge's wallet off the table near the front. Nothing else. We were just like most of the people who I'd been stealing from. We rarely lock our doors either.

I must have looked stricken because Betty paused to calm me. "Don't worry, little man. They didn't get much. Been a lot of this going around. It's the times." In one stupid coincidence my plan was demolished. How could I make the sheriff believe Cudge had been burglarizing the town if our very own home had been broken into? All that worthless loot hidden in the garage was even more worthless now. And the part of my plan where everyone would have their things returned to them, absolving me of feeling like I was an actual criminal, all that was down the tubes. I was devastated, and, after it sunk in, strangely relieved. I'd done my best to convince myself that my plan would work, but in my heart, I knew it was a desperate, doomed course.

The burglary changed Cudge for a while, through Christmas, past the New Year. He was quiet, spent a lot of time eating sandwiches and pepperoncinis in the living room while he obsessively switched channels on the television. "Hey, little man," he'd mumble to me as I passed, and nothing more. He'd watch game shows and grow maudlin if the person he was rooting for didn't do well. For some reason he insisted on sitting through Lawrence Welk, even though none of the music he listened to on the radio remotely resembled what was sung and danced to on that show.

Sometimes Betty sat next to Cudge and stared into the side of his face, not saying a word as he watched TV. Once I overheard them talking during a commercial. "I still can't believe some fucker came in and took our stuff."

"They didn't get any of our real money," Betty said.

"True enough," Cudge said, but he didn't sound consoled. He was a man used to having his way, and when that didn't happen, he didn't know what to do with himself. In the story he'd told me about driving to Mexico to find his son, it occurred to me, as sad as the situation turned out for him, I had no idea how he acted around the people he was asking to help him. In his own head he was probably a reasonable, loving father trying to recover his son. But from their perspective? I'd seen Cudge's mood swings first hand, and after his wallet was stolen, the newest, broody iteration.

While Cudge was in his funk, the surprise visits to my room and along the road on my way home from school stopped. It all stopped and I started breathing. I didn't have to break into houses, nor worry so much about Sammy. At dinner one night, there was one porkchop left and I reached for it with my fork at the same time Cudge went for it with his fingers. All four of us at the table froze. Such an infraction just a few weeks earlier would have been followed with a "who brings home the bacon tirade," but nothing. He just waved his hand at me as if to say, "it's all yours."

The house was quiet.

28

I leave James in bed and check on Lamb who is also sound asleep, mouth open, silk eyeshades askew. Vale's file in my satchel, I decide to walk to the shop early. If it will fit, I'll slip the file through Jodi's mail slot and hope all is forgiven. The morning is bright and warm. I can almost feel the urgency in the trees ready to leaf out. I have a habit of making sense in my head, coming to a decision, then talking myself out of it. When I arrive in town it looks pretty much the same as it does every morning, except for one thing. Skee's car is parked outside the shop and he's standing in front of the ampersand of "Grayson & Gray Antiques and Collectibles." *Shit. What now?* Returning the file will have to wait.

"Thought we'd seen the last of you when you dashed out yesterday," I say as I approach.

"I'll be out of your hair, young man," Skee says, patting his straw fedora firmly on his head. "Plane tomorrow afternoon." Same hat, different bow tie. This one's green with blue paisley. "Things haven't worked out like I hoped. Called up that Larry, but it took him all but a second to let me know just where we stood. Jodi and I rode around and I did some thinking. Maybe I owe you an apology."

I shake my head. I can pretend to be generous. "If anyone owes an apology…."

"She told me when you were a kid she thought maybe you were up to no good and when I asked what she thinks now…" He pauses and leans on his cane. "Well, she pointed out something I hadn't considered. You stuck around."

"For better or worse."

"I figure if you had anything to do with Cudge disappearing you'd be long gone by now. It's barking up the wrong tree with you. Not even going to bother with that damned folder."

"Very wrong tree," I say, and then I remind myself of my pantry of stolen things, and even now, Vale's file in the satchel dangling at my side. But I feel a soft landing coming on. I suggest we walk toward the river. Skee pops half a pretzel rod into his mouth and apologizes for being a nuisance. He asks about the town. I point to various buildings, telling him what they were when I was a kid. The bakery is gone, so is the beauty parlor. When we get aside Knives-Ammo, I tell him about the bowie knife I wanted for years and that it was a little while after Cudge disappeared before I realized it went missing. I figure it's a useful lie.

Skee is nonplussed at the reminder of this detail. "Vale follow up on that?"

"I'm sure he did. He was like a dog with a bone."

We end up at the bench near the river bank. I brush it off with my hand and we sit, sun at on our shoulders. The river is brown and quiet. "Sammy and I used to come here all the time," I say. "It was our thinking spot."

"I can see why," Skee says.

"As a matter of fact, we sat right here the morning Cudge went missing. We came home from a sleepover."

"Is that so?" He taps his cane around a slow-moving Boxelder bug. "But from what I understand it was damned cold that weekend. If this was your thinking spot, must have been something heavy on your mind that morning."

"It was so bad I thought my eyes would freeze in their sockets." I stretch both of my arms along the back of the bench and stare straight out at the river. *This* is *my thinking spot*. "That's how bad it was. I didn't want to go home with Cudge there."

"But you'd put up with him quite a bit by then. What was special about going home that day?"

"*Nothing*," I say with a sharpness which catches even me off guard. "Nothing was special about that day. You should think about all the times I had to walk through that front door. Add those all up. Eventually it's one too many. You're barely fourteen years old. You aren't a man but you're trying because your little brother is counting on you. That day was my one too many."

"You eventually *did* go home, though." He removes his hat and looks into it as if it's a television and he can see me and Sammy sitting by the river.

"Yes, I did. Sammy was perched right there where you are. Freezing." I point behind us with a thumb. "Friend of my Dad drives up and insists on giving us a lift. So I acted like a man and just accepted the fact we had a shitty life and we were going to have a shitty life."

"And you got home—"

I cut him off. "You know this part."

"I do. But really, did it make it any better? Cudge being gone? Has it ever?"

"*I* made it better."

"What confuses me is how Jodi described Cudge when he first showed up in Orgull. How does a man go from decent to dead? Presumed dead. Your mother wouldn't have married a total bastard. If there's anything you're holding back, please, all I want to know is what happened."

I don't reply and I don't look at Skee.

"Conner, I'm just an old man who made a stupid mistake giving up his son. I'm here with a broken heart. Worse than when first I started searching for Cudge." I hear in his voice he's coming to tears, and a sympathetic world offers a very small maple leaf which glides to his shoulder.

I stand and walk a few feet toward the river, hands in my pocket. Then I sigh and turn. "It was a lie," I say. "Cudge was never a good guy. It was all a con."

"From talking to Jodi, sounds like it was the real thing."

"What can I tell you, Skee? It was just bad. If you're looking for some incident that made him snap, I've got nothing for you. But, okay, here…" I pause and return to the bench. "Your son and my mother robbed her boss for over thirty thousand dollars. Used a gun. And they got away with it. After that, our family was toast. He owned us."

"I'm guessing you never told that to the sheriff."

"And send my mother to jail? What would have happened to me and Sammy?" I wait for a response but nothing comes. Skee simply looks at me as if waiting for more. "So there's your son," I say.

"A hypothetical," he offers, finally. "From my point of view. I didn't know your mother. For that matter, I didn't know Cudge. Couldn't I hear what you're telling me the other way? That Cudge went bad because your mother roped him into a scheme to rob her boss? That *he* was toast after that."

"You could. But if you're looking for a timeline there's a town full of people who would tell you Cudge was a dick long before. I know firsthand that he hit Betty."

Skee brushes the leaf off his shoulder. "And if I take you at your word. That my son was a monster. That he had his foot on your mother's throat. What does that tell me about Cudge's disappearance? About you and her?"

I raise my hands to stop him. "This just went to defcon bullshit again."

"I'm just saying there's another way to hear all this. Even if it was just your mom."

"My mother did not fucking kill Cudge or whatever you're thinking. She was away. Me and Sammy were away. Read the sheriff's report." As I say this, I realize it's sitting right next to me. I realize I'm defending Betty but agreeing with Skee.

He reaches into his pocket and pulls out an index card.

"What's that?"

"There were a few like this. Got it from Jodi. When I dropped her off she went upstairs to get me that file. It was gone, of course. But these were on the floor. A few loose ones." My eyes are locked on the card. "Her father had a lot of doubts about you." He reads the card. "It'll eat him up enough he'll come to, one day. Poor kid." He holds it out in case I want to verify what he's read, but I don't move. "What's he mean by that? Tell you what it means to me, that I ought to get the authorities to take another look at all this."

I feel my face growing red. I want to run. "You want to know?" I shout. "You sure you want to know? You're goddamned son molested me. He fucked me, and not just once. So you know what else? I don't know how, but *he* got fucked. End of story." Skee begins to speak but I jump up and walk away. "Stay the hell away," I yell.

"Wait," he calls, and I stop and turn. His face his blanched, his expression confused. "What are you saying?"

"What does it matter? Your son molested me. Sammy was next in line. Isn't that everything you need to know?"

I can tell he's shaken. Behind him, a barge rumbles along the river. "Please. I have to know." I turn and walk as fast as I can. "Conner," he yells, "I'm at the Galt House. I check out at 11 tomorrow morning. If there's anything…."

I look over my shoulder. He's baffled, not following, the river shimmering behind him.

29

It's one thing to just generally ask around, but I feel like I'm in a vice grip, and I must look it when I practically fling myself into the shop. I'm surprised when I find that James is with a customer. They turn, obviously startled by an entrance that includes the angry ringing of our bell above the door. I try to recover. "Sorry about that," I say, looking at the door jam. "Kind of tripped over myself there." It's the best I can do. James mouths "You okay?" in response, to which I shrug indecisively. No doubt he wonders where I've been.

I mill around, futz with this and that, needing to talk. James and the man are discussing a tabletop ceramic butter churn. After a few minutes I feel like walking over, taking the churn out of James' hands and shoving it into the arms of his customer. When they move on to a coffee grinder, I understand it could be a while.

After a few minutes, the man buys the butter churn and a similar butter crock. I've been half paying attention to the transaction, half thinking about Skee. The customer tells James a story about how he was buying a gift for his mother who'd become nostalgic about her farm days. It's sweet, and, for a minute, takes my mind away. "Wait," I say to the two of them. The man is caught off guard and I realize he is just now understanding that I work at the shop as well. "I have something to show you." It takes me a second, but I find a cream skimmer we've had forever. "Take this too," I say. The man thanks me and says he's spent what he can afford. "No," I say, "just have it."

"There goes the rent," James says after the man leaves. "Big money in skimmers." The store is empty, so he kisses me hello.

"That's why I'm dating an independently wealthy man."

"Oh, Conny," he says, "that's such good news. You finally met someone." He waits a beat and leans against a walnut chest of drawers topped with vintage dolls. "So? You didn't open the shop. I called. Nothing. Now what?"

I don't have to ask what he means. I'd never stumbled through the door Three Stooges-like as I had earlier. "It's just this whole Skee thing. He was out front when I came to open the shop."

"Shit. Wondered where you were. Didn't go well?"

"He outright accused Betty of murder."

"Still?" James says, pulling away from the chest. "Did you tell him about taking the file?"

I get a reprieve. The door opens, jingling the bell. This time it's a couple, the kind that looks like our bread and butter.

"Should I shoo them, or can this wait?" I tell him it can and he suggests that I sit down in the back for a little while, to which I agree.

I hate being in this position. My childhood was chaotic, but James and Lamb have known only stable Conner, no-drama Conner, at least, that was my brand. The very first time James called, we talked for twenty minutes before he asked me out. I'm surprised he went through with it, because I announced how boring I was. He was clearly much more comfortable in his skin than I was, had the whole gay thing down pat. Without even having to think about it, I went into sabotage mode. "Listen," I said, "I have to say something. You're great."

"Yes, you're right," he interrupted, "you do have to say that."

I laughed and continued. "I need to tell you; I don't smoke, I don't do drugs, I'm not on the internet, and I don't have sex on a first date."

James laughed. "Okay, well thanks for the heads up. But tell me, are those supposed to be pros or cons?"

"They're pros in my mind."

"Well, then, tell me more about your cult."

"Seriously," I said. I was sitting on the couch, absentmindedly checking between the cushions for whatever detritus I might find.

"You want to know if that's a deal killer?" James asked. His tone ditched the playfulness, and I thought *shit, I've blown it.* "Or," he continued, "you want to know if I do those things? Or you're trying to weasel out of a date?"

What do *I want to know?* My cold feet were getting cold feet. I chose what I thought was the safest response. "Just needed to make sure I wasn't false advertising."

"Caveat emptor," he said.

"I'm not for sale," I joked. "For rent, maybe."

"There ya go," he said, laughing. "I knew it was in there somewhere. That's all we're doing, kiddo, having a good time."

Months later, I asked about that conversation, wondering what he was thinking as I reeled off my "don't's" list. "I thought you were a little judgmental," he said. "Or that your favorite cologne was called 'Stereotype: for men.' You didn't seem to have a very high opinion of our gay brethren. And you know now that I'd been pretty crazy even not too long before we met. I wasn't struck by lightning."

After a few weeks of dating, he started filling in the details of his life before me. He was definitely more experienced. By the same token, none of that seemed to matter, maybe because his frankness made it all irrelevant. That's where we differed, and what hurt my heart. I played at being frank, but I could never really tell him everything about what Cudge had done to me. Hell, I practically told Skee as much as I ever told James or Lamb. In James' mind I'd been lucky. After my father's death, before Cudge, I'd been rescued by a boy named Mark, my first crush, a partially true story that I made seem whole. I was gay before Cudge molested me. Not because of what he did.

This is what Skee has disrupted, and I feel the truth. I'm fighting to give fourteen-year-old Connor the family he and Sammy deserved. I'm fighting to give my daughter a chance at the life I never had. Revision can happen.

I find myself sitting in the shop's office thinking about what a fraud I am. I remind myself of Lambs' and James' request, that the thing to do is to get it all out and see what they say. Let the chips fall. But we have a baby coming. The new life is built, complete, the scaffolding ready to be taken away. But no.

I want to unscrew my head and replace it with another one.

The door jingles again, and when James pokes his head into the office I am already looking up at the spot where I know his face will appear. "Glass washboard," he says, stepping all the way into the room. In typical fashion he tries to be bright. "I'm a chiropractor. How did you get me into this? But a sale."

"Great," I say. My head is bowed, but I am looking up at him. My eyes sting, feel hot, but I'm not crying. Can anyone love a terrible person? *I want a good life for us.*

"Conny, I don't like this new rough trade you're running around with. You look like shit. I mean, if you can't keep a polo collar straight." He knows I'm in bad shape when I don't laugh. "Aww, babe," he says, sitting on the stool next to me, gently pulling me into him. There's not a second to answer because sirens blare into and past town, and almost as quickly, a helicopter blasts by above us. The phone rings, and James answers. "You're kidding," he gasps, looking at me. "We'll close up and be right there."

30

The three of us, me, my wife, and my boyfriend, stand in front of the television watching a live helicopter shot as it hovers over the dark green water of an abandoned limestone quarry. At the edge, emergency vehicles flash red and white lights. The object of their attention is clear, a white sedan, taillights on and partly submerged in the water, hood first. The driver's side door is swung open like a broken wing. A female reporter narrating the scene identifies Larry as having been arrested. I'm ahead of what comes next because I recognize the car. The reporter says that unconfirmed reports indicate it belongs to a local tavern owner. "Jodi," Lamb whispers to herself, slowly bringing her hand to her mouth. She points as the helicopter shot curves to a different vantage. A body covered in a white sheet is lifted into the swung-open jaws of an Ambulance. This isn't a rescue operation.

And then just a glimpse, but it's all I need. Larry's battered red truck sits in a ditch, the front end smashed against a tree, the result looking like a massive lobster claw taking hold of the trunk. It's a wonder he survived. It's a shame he did. I don't have to wait for the investigation into why he would go after Jodi. I recognize panic as if it were a first cousin.

James looks at me blankly. "Conny, what is this? What's happening?"

"All Hell," is all I can say. He sits and fusses with the cuff of one shirt sleeve, and I hear Lamb sit down behind me. The reporter on television is suddenly a gnat in my ear, so I turn her down. "I told you this Cudge business wasn't a game," I continue. "I told you."

Lamb is looking at the television, one hand at her lips, the other caressing her belly almost protectively. "If that's Jodi…."

"Not if," I say, taking a seat. *Fucking Betty. Throwing this in my lap after all these years.* I can't believe what I'm about to ask for. "This is what I need. The sheriffs will be around for sure. Or some other law. We were with Jodi yesterday, so we have to have the same story."

"Story?" James asks this as if I've requested he place Lamb in a trick box so we can saw her in half. "As in, instead of the truth?"

Lamb runs her fingers over her scalp and looks at the ceiling. "Conner, we didn't do anything."

"Right," I say, trying not to sound too much like a guide who's walked this trail many times for many years. "But I took that folder and Skee more-or-less knows it. He'll say something."

"And you'll say you did," James says. "And we'll say you were stupid and you'll say you were stupid, but Lamb and I know where you've been the last 24 hours. It's no lie to say you were never with Larry."

"You weren't even on the phone," Lamb chimes in, pausing. "You weren't, right? They can check that." The way she says this hurts because I hear in her voice some fraction of doubt.

I place my hands on my face and peer through the bars of my fingers. "No, Lamb," I snap. "I did not secretly call Larry and ask him to kill Jodi. But you're right. That question's going to get asked. And then what happens if we say I took off with a file of notes speculating that I had something to do with Cudge?"

"It's not entirely about you," James says.

"What percentage would you say gives me a pass?"

"Stop," Lamb says pointing at the television. "Just stop. That poor woman is dead." Then she surprises me. "So, what *is* our story?"

But I don't answer that question. I'm looking at the television, at the tree-shrouded quarry where they're pulling Jodi's car up the short rock face. *Oh fuck, Betty.* I take a breath and look at James and Lamb. "I know what happened to Cudge."

31

Larry is helpful, or more accurately, his attorney advises him to be helpful and he listens. Skee and I are sitting behind yellow police tape watching a pair of divers holding on to the edge of a skiff at the far side of the quarry. When they disappear into the water, only the boat and the faintest disturbance of bubbles mark their presence. A half dozen sheriffs stand nearby, and above, two news helicopters film the scene. The detective who questioned me leans between us, her breath heavy with coffee. She has no sense of audience. "If he's down there," she says, "after this many years there won't be much left."

"Excuse us," I say, finding myself surprisingly protective. "Can we have a moment?"

Skee skipped his flight to be here, and he looks ashen. "I'm sorry," I say.

"Hadn't thought of it until just now. There's no body to be found. The boy's a heap of bones if he's down there. Like some damn pirate. Still, maybe I'll have some peace." He doesn't look at me the entire time he talks. "I'll get him a proper resting place back home and let his maker sort out the rest. He'll have dates on that marker." With that remark he turns, and the rebuke is clear. "Get your mother's stone right," he says subtextually, and then literally, after a deep, weary breath, "It's about more than an old man can take in just a few days." He's not mentioned to the police the file. Larry's angry mouth has made it unnecessary.

We both stare at the water which is glazed in spring light, the thut-ta-thutta-thutta of helicopters above, an unwelcome insistence that this is an event larger than two men waiting for news. They have no idea. What neither of us are discussing is what Larry told the authorities, that Betty killed Cudge and put him up to getting rid of the body. All those years of her pretending she thought I'd done something to Cudge and that she was protecting me. All along she was protecting herself.

"That poor woman," Skee says. "Meets me and in a blink she's dead. For what?"

"Would've made more sense for Larry to go after me."

Skee sighs. "Sense is in short supply around here." He taps his cane twice on the ground and continues. "In the car. She put me off you. Said it was your mother that was a piece of work. Her father was barking up the wrong tree. I'm sure I'll be asked."

I inspect the palm of my hands as if I'll find crib notes for what to say next, but nothing. I feel Skee watching me. "What's on your mind, son?" he asks.

Can't get used to that word, "son." Even when Betty was alive those last few years it was my proper name or nothing.

He leans forward on his cane searching for something to say. "Maybe your mother knew she failed you?" he asks.

"Look," I say, running my hands through my hair and feeling like a man on trial waiting for a verdict, "you're talking about the woman who probably killed your son. No need to paint a rosy picture for me."

Skee considers the point and nods. "You've done the right thing here," he says, pointing at the water with his cane. One of the divers has come up to the side of the boat, mask pushed up on his head while he talks to a man at the prow who is speaking into a Walkie Talkie. "We'll know something here shortly," Skee says, pulling out a small black journal from his coat pocket. "I write in this a couple times a day. You know why? Because I couldn't give up the damned past. It got so bad they had to send a lady out to give me counseling. I was a damned tragic old man. I didn't believe the counselor at first, but she was right." He pauses to see if he has an audience. He does. I'm sure I look as if I'm listening to a sermon at a funeral, but at least I'm listening. From back of the journal he retrieves the index cards dropped from Vale's folder. As if saying goodbye, he stares at them, nods, then passes them to me. "Might as well have the complete set."

I know better than to say anything.

"Maybe I'm not the person to tell you this," he says. "I understand. But you have to find a way to let go of the past. Everything that went on with Cudge and your brother, with your mother, and you. Every damned thing you know. All of it."

"Wasn't your entire trip about living in the past?"

He considers the point. "No. This was different. I was trying to fill in a past. Right a wrong. What I thought was a wrong."

"Thought?"

"I can't go as far as to say the boy deserved to die, and it took a while for it to sink into my damned stubborn head, but I understand why you let Cudge go the way you did. Before we head our separate ways, I have one last thing to say. I'm not a wise old man, Conner, but I can tell you, this. For the longest time I tried to pretend that my old life never existed. That I'd never cut my son loose. It was a lot of effort and it amounted to keeping the past on ice. Like these things do, it all came back and nearly pulled me under. If I'd had the courage to tell Myrna about Cudge..." He doesn't finish because I'm fully in tears. Then he does something unexpected. He leans toward me and places his arm across my shoulders, pulls me as close as our chairs and the angle will allow. It isn't for long, but it helps.

Then I tell him. I look behind me and see that though we're not alone, nobody is near. I tell the whole story, but it swerves and weaves. One minute I'm talking about the last time I saw Cudge alive, the next, some other awful things Cudge had done. Back again. I speak and he listens. I'm a mess, damaged and angry. My admissions rush at Skee like a locomotive. I tell him about the petty burglaries, Betty and Cudge's robbery. It all makes Cudge sound as if he was the spoke of a wheel. At a certain point I want to stop, but the ripcord has been pulled.

Skee is stoic.

I work up a head of steam and come to the straw that breaks the camel's back. I am almost breathless. Skee hands me tissues from his pocket. My eyes feel glassy and on fire, and I'm exhausted, gulping and heaving air. I describe Cudge in the shower and a final, disgusting indignity just before he died.

"Okay," Skee says, raising both of his hands. He tells me that he doesn't want to hear the rest, that I must not tell him the rest. Our roles are reversed. Now I'm the one insisting that he know everything. "Don't make me a witness to my own son's depravity," he asks of me. "For both our sakes."

It's as if he's run me straight into a wall. I could barely form the words. "I'm sorry."

"No, son, *I'm* sorry." He's called me that again. This time I don't react. "And I have to say. I don't think this is going to end for you until you put it all into a confession to someone who matters more than me."

"Lamb and James," I say. I am sitting in the chair, hunched forward, head down, arms hung between my legs.

"Or the law, I'd think."

I look up, but not at Skee, because I can't help what I'm about to say next. "I saw him. Dead. I saw Cudge's body in our bathtub."

"What are you talking about?" He leans forward for a look at my face.

"I freaked out and ran, and when I came back the next day, he was gone."

"Dear God," Skee says. "And you never told the sheriff?"

"Because, what about Sammy? Betty was accusing me, but…." I wipe tears from under both eyes. "Not long before she died, Betty took one last stab at trying to make me believe she thought I killed Cudge. She said she'd taken care of things for me." I point to the water. "You see what kind of woman she was."

Skee takes up his cane and rests his chin on it, a white lock of hair laying across his forehead. "I don't know what to make of what you're telling me." Growing quiet, he sits back in his chair before randomly looking around the quarry as if it's almost too much to talk to me. "If you'd just said something when you found him, I'd be reading the boy's marker instead of watching *that*, and waiting for bones." He raises his cane in the direction of the dive operation. "Bones. That's what we're sitting here for."

"I'm sorry," I say again, and I wonder how real any apology can sound when you haven't told everything. I still have part of Cudge's finger in a jar.

Skee bumps my heel with his cane, and I turn. He looks more stern than angry. "What you concealed as a grown man notwithstanding," he says, "if you were sitting in front of a jury, odds are they'd forgive you." He taps the ground a few times and continues. "You were fourteen. A brother, younger still. And Cudge messing with you the way he was. Hell, I don't know what the laws are in this state."

I shake my head and tell him. The news is full of teenagers prosecuted for violent crimes.

"And you have all that other mess about breaking into houses and your mom and my boy robbing that old man," Skee says. "That all true?"

"Yes."

"Lot of consequences in all this." Skee stands, tucks his journal back in his pocket, reconsiders and keeps it out. "You're right about your mother, but that doesn't mean you have to keep on the same as her."

"What are you going to do?"

He offers a placid smile, considers. "What am I going to do? I'm going to see that the boy makes it home and gets in the ground. Now, if by asking that, you want some idea of what *you're* going to do, all I can say is that I intend to know what I knew an hour ago and not a minute beyond because I think it's best if I'm done with all this. I got what I came for. But you? You have a long way to go yet, and a family to raise." It's his turn to walk off. I watch him with that twisted little gait of his, the journal dangling in one hand, the black cover facing back at me like the unapologetic stare of child looking at a stranger.

32

Five months later the trial is nearing. Larry got less helpful. There are pumpkins and cornstalks on our porch, a carpet of yellow and orange leaves in the yard, and a sleeping infant in the downstairs crib. James is at an antiques auction in Nashville and Lamb is meeting with two new clients who've come around just for the proximity of scandal. And Larry? He's being charged with murdering Jodi in the first degree, but for Cudge, they're prosecuting him merely as an accessory. I've given answers to a lot of questions and none of them make Betty look good. When they asked me about the hunting knife they found in the van along with Cudge's remains I told them "Yep, it was mine. Betty convinced me Cudge took it."

Things were shaky for a few weeks, but I've navigated. I've done it. It's taken me some time, but I've pulled it together. I've the satisfaction of knowing Skee has his son's remains, and there's a certain level of release in that fact. But I did learn the lesson. At last I sobbed a final confession. "You're a good man, Conny," James said, concealing anger he would later express with Lamb at his side. Right then he said, resigned, "You should give that man his son's finger. But you can't now, can you? It's too late."

Now I am home alone when a small package and letter arrive in the mail, certified.

> *Dear Mr. Grayson:*
>
> *As executor of the estate of Skeeter Marion Hotter, I'm sad to report that Mr. Hotter passed away on November 3rdth of this year. I hasten to add that Mr. Hotter was largely in good spirits and pain free into his final weeks.*

The purpose of this letter and the enclosed is to execute the matters of his estate in regards to you. Mr. Hotter requested that I express his emphatic appreciation for your part in the recovery of his son's remains. A service was held and the ashes were interred in a plot not far from that of his and his late wife's.

In accordance with his wishes, enclosed please find one personal journal with the inclusion of several pages from another. These represent the entirety of Mr. Hotter's bequest to you.

Yours, Dale Mann
Chief Executor

I half expected to hear from Skee after he returned to Los Angeles, but nothing. I poured my heart out to him, my guilt. He held a lot of cards and used none of them. I was nervous for a long time after that. James and Lamb noticed, but they chalked it up to the general experience of Skee's surprise visit and the fact both of them had really come down on me for concealing so much. The reality of Cudge's body in the quarry hit them hard, but the waters calmed. Now this letter arrives with Skee's journal, a slim, black leather binding, worn, but with a clean spine. Its contents require change, demand it.

The journal has been treated with care. Even though I'm home alone, I'm holding yet another secret object—my life seems plagued by such—and I instinctively head to the garage to read it, that space which is for me part chapel, part shrine. I sit on the floor, back to the window light, and begin to read.

Skee didn't have to, but included with the journal are a separate number of pages from writing he did just before coming to Kentucky. His handwriting is so compressed and thin I have to read slowly, at times holding the journal directly up to the light. What he includes amounts to his estimations of me, of Cudge, of the entire situation. Some of the details touch me deeply, like the sheriff's stash of documents, like the depth of sorrow, real sorrow, Skee feels for having estranged himself from Cudge, and his obvious heartache over losing his wife. I stop. Skee and I are face to face once again, almost as if his ghost sits opposite me in the garage.

Another damned hour I'll be back on the ground. Despite what people say, Southern California is sanity.

I am landing. Cudge and I. His memory. Shouldn't make light. But in a way I am taking him home, as if he's in an urn in the overhead. Of course, home and then all the strange arrangements for when they do send him to me. The plot below mine and Myrna's is Robert's and it's a double, half-full. A new stone with two men's names.

Myrna and Robert, those two would have a stitch over it. Cudge, he didn't do right in his life. His damned soul should feel honored. Look what you just wrote, old man.

I let Conner off the hook. Because I was not equipped to say to him what I believed. I reminded myself I was speaking to a damned fourteen-year-old. Molested. This is not a man trying to protect a fourteen year old boy. He is that boy.

There must be a word for it. I wanted to take him up and hold him. Right there, the man whose mother was responsible for killing my son. He was in tears. Told me everything I allowed. I wanted to hold him.

Halfway home and I know what I should have said to the boy. The man. The man, Skee.

I understand the feeling. The events are different. But I understand. I never told Myrna about Cudge. Never a hint that he existed. All that love and I held back. I wonder if I ever felt quite whole to her. Could never do enough or be enough to make up for what I kept secret.

This is what the boy will face if he doesn't tell what happened. His family will not feel whole. That new child deserves more. He can't be the pig in a poke. Spoke to him about the damned law but not about his heart. I forgive him.

And that is it, the last of his handwriting, the last of Skee. There are more pages in the journal, maybe ten, but they remain empty except for places where it looks as if Skee were scratch starting his pen, and one doodle, a circle resting within a square on the very last page. Skee is right, that if I am to have this family with Lamb and James and Lana, our daughter, I can't pretend any longer. In my future there is no son to recover in some distant state. Everything I need to take care of is right here. But the journal. Now I understand Skee. Nothing can be right unless I am wholly honest with my family. It might be too much for them, but nothing we have can be real unless they know. And hopefully, together, we'll figure out what to do next.

I will tell Lamb and James all of this, and then I will take a deep breath and tell them about coming home to find Cudge dead and frozen in the bathtub. I will tell them the odd relief I felt when, after all these years, Larry confirmed what I thought, that it was Betty who'd killed Cudge. I hadn't, as I sometimes thought, left Cudge to slide down the wall and drown. It will all be out once and for all and we can decide together who else I need to tell before Larry's trial.

As if the world has its own plans for me, I hear intermittent and soft gurgles from the house. Our landline, our lonely dinosaur asking me to trot inside. Without an answering machine I'm able to get to the phone in time. At first there's no response to my greeting, so I repeat myself.

"Conner?" a male voice asks. I reply in the affirmative and he continues. "It's Mark. Do you remember?"

I'm stunned that he asks this because I can't think of a day in the last twenty years I haven't thought of him. My entire body offers a furious pulse as if I've grabbed hold of an electric fence.

"Been watching the news," he says. "I wasn't going to contact you, but the trial is coming up. Are you going to testify? Are you in trouble?" His voice is agitated, much lower than when we were kids, but I recognize it entirely. Still, it's only the fifteen-year-old that I can bring into focus.

"Probably," I say, hurt that even he thinks I might have done something to Cudge. "I mean, I'll probably testify." But I'm more interested in where he's been all these years. Why he never called or came back. Did he ever search for me on the internet? That, and a half dozen other questions seem to come out of me at once.

To all this he simply responds, "I'll be in Orgull tomorrow."

I hesitate. Is seeing Mark again for the first time after all these years something I want Lamb and James present for? Do they really need one more surprise from my past, and right before the trial? I convince myself that the right answer is "no" on both counts, so I tell Mark to meet me at the shop.

He agrees. "And Conner," he says just before hanging up, "I'm sorry."

33

It was a late Friday afternoon, and I was getting our things together. Me and Sammy were staying the weekend with Mark's family because Betty was driving a friend to Cincinnati. It surprised me that Cudge let her go, but when I thought about it I knew why. I'd begged her not to leave us alone with him, and she grabbed my arm. "You can take care of yourself, little man," she said, glaring at me.

So that's what I was doing. I didn't even bother telling Cudge that I'd asked Mark's mother if we could stay. *Fuck him, fuck them both,* I thought. I was going to take Sammy away, and that weekend I was going to figure out how to screw Cudge with all the things I'd been stealing despite the fact someone had burglarized us too. Mark and I would get it straight and by Monday our house would be free of Cudge. I don't know why I thought it would work, but when you're a desperate fucked-in-the-ass kid, raped, not everything you do is rational.

From the window I saw Sammy waiting next to the mailbox, hoping before we left that the postman would bring his box-top water rocket. For a minute I thought I'd have to toss our bags out the window, but then I heard Cudge go into the bathroom and there was my chance. I took the bags and snuck downstairs, but when I got half way across the yard I heard Cudge from the bathroom window. "Where the hell you two going?" he yelled.

"Mark's," Sammy called back before I could stop him.

"The hell you are," Cudge said. It wouldn't do any good to run. Cudge would know where we were. I told Sammy to wait. As I stomped back to the house a half dozen thoughts flashed through my mind.

I couldn't let Cudge touch me one more time and I wouldn't bring Sammy back into that house. I thought about the knife, pictured where I'd hidden it, and I wondered if this was exactly what Betty wanted. Just before I got to the porch I stopped cold. Mark had just come around the corner of the house.

"What are you doing here," I said as he approached. I quickly looked behind me.

Mark was wearing his puffy white coat and a toboggan was pulled down over his ears so that only one red forelock curled in the center of his forehead. "You were supposed to be at our house an hour ago," he said, shrugging. "I just came."

"You could have called."

He shrugged. "I didn't. So, you ready?"

"Give me a second." I put my finger to my lips and pointed toward the top floor of the house. I knew he'd understand.

When I opened the front door, I thought I'd see Cudge at the foot of the stairs but he wasn't there. Instead, I heard the bath running, and as if he had a camera on me, Cudge called out. "Get the fuck up here, Conner."

If he tried anything, I was going to be ready. If he tried to keep us from going to Mark's, I was going to be ready. I didn't know I'd be empty-handed. The knife wasn't hidden with the things I'd stolen. It was in my room, taped to the back of one of my drawers. I thought if Cudge was in the bathtub maybe I could get by the bathroom quick enough to get it. So I pushed past the bathroom and I saw that Cudge was already in the tub with his back to me. "I want your little ass in here, Conner," he said. "Not fucking around the house." He laughed as if he'd made a joke.

"Gimme a sec," I said, trying to sound normal, and then, coming up empty handed, I stomped back to the bathroom. "Where is it?"

Cudge didn't turn. "Where's what?" He dipped his head in the water and re-pasted the long, wet strands of his comb-over onto his scalp. He'd propped the window open so that cold air was pouring in. The hot bathwater steamed, blew sideways. Behind me in the hall, the window was held open with a piece of rebar.

"You know what I'm talking about."

Now he craned his neck around and smiled, water beaded on his moustache. "Oh, you mean the knife. Yeah, you have good taste."

"Why do you do this shit?"

"How about if you come over here and scrub old Dad's back," he said, holding out a washcloth.

I took one step inside to show him I wasn't afraid. "Look," I said, "Mrs. Callihan is expecting us. I told her if we didn't show up by 6 she should pick us up." The last part was a lie.

"Fine. I can tell that Jesus bitch, *fuck no*, same as I can you." He stood up slowly. His penis was partially erect. "Or maybe I'll just let you go. Make me a happy guy and I'll think about it."

"I'm not doing that anymore," I said.

"Sure you are." He began stroking himself. "'Course, there's always that little brother of yours." At that, something came over me and I rushed forward, caught Cudge off guard, and pushed him. He stumbled in the tub and fell backward and hard into the wall. He was wide-eyed and staring through me, as if I'd suddenly gone invisible.

All I could think was *run*, so I was off through the hallway, thudding downstairs. I ran to the back door and outside, where I startled Mark. "Go," I said pointing to the woods. He began to protest but I jabbed toward the woods again. "I'll get Sammy and meet you."

34

I get away. Mark arrives in a red pickup. He parks across the street near Max's, and when he steps out of the car I'm struck by how little he's changed over the years, only slightly taller, and the mop of red hair has turned toward auburn. On his chin is a patch of close-cut soul patch. He's wearing a denim jacket over a brown plaid shirt which fits right in with the fall leaves flickering past his legs like orange flame; with the truck behind him he could be a cigarette ad. I embarrass myself by wondering how I look. When he sees me at the window, he pauses, and though he must know it's me, I understand he doesn't see the boy I was. I'm thicker, taller, all middle-class veneer. I'm running an antique shop, for God's sake. I don't know if any of this even matters, but it must, because I'm all nerves.

From inside, I meet Mark at the door without waiting for the jingle of the bell. We reach for the handles on opposite sides and the confusion causes us to pause and look briefly at each other through the glass. We should smile at the impasse, but neither of us do. Up close, he looks older than I anticipated, large freckles almost notes of music on staff lines running across his forehead. His skin is dark and dry as if he's led a life outdoors.

"Sorry about that," I say, opening the door.

He steps in, nods quickly as if to say, "this is really happening." And then his arms are wide open and we embrace. He's as solid as I remember, and I think I could stay here in this moment forever, but I let go. James and Lamb. "So this is the place," he says, looking around. "Good business?"

"Not bad. A lot of it's online now."

"Never figured you'd stick around this shit hole," he says. Then, catching himself, "No offense."

"None taken. It's a shithole. But my mother gave me the house, and well, it's hard to explain." I point to the ring on my finger. "Doing the whole family thing."

"Damn," he says, "looking at my hand. I thought I heard that on TV, but, you know, it seemed like it couldn't ever happen, right?"

This makes me chuckle. I forget that my life has been broadcast over the past few months, and as much as I've been reported on, I've managed to keep Lamb and James and our daughter out of the spotlight. "It's complicated," I say, unsure of what exactly Mark should know. I take out my wallet and show him the photos inside. "I have a different kind of family. The wife, the kid, the partner."

"Man," he says, rubbing the back of his neck, "complicated isn't the word." And then we're both silent for a few seconds, because what now? He didn't come all this way to hear about my family life. He's here, I'm guessing, because all the news about Cudge reminded him of me, about how he dropped out of my life. He's here to apologize and it's suddenly hitting me that I really, really need to hear it.

Mark takes a seat on a three-legged oak stool and starts to rest his arm on a vintage, unopened six-pack of tab before halting as if it's something precious. "It survived the 70's," I tell him. "It will survive you."

It's clear that Mark is nervous. He rolls a fist in his palm and lets out a deep breath, "There's something I never told you about Cudge and me," he begins. "I should have told you before. Man, I swear I wanted to." I don't want to hear what's coming next, and I'm spared for the moment because Mark nervously veers, tells me that his family moved to Indianapolis and that as soon as he was old enough he left for California and changed his last name. "I was in San Francisco for a hot minute," he says. "But it was the wrong time. It was like the whole city was in mourning. It was an easy time to drop out. So I did." He moved around, changed his name to Dean because it sounded more solid than he felt. He didn't speak to his parents for years, kept track through his grandmother in Indy whom he ended up taking care of. "She never quite got it right.

Called me Dino. But, it's okay. That was two names ago." He shrugs with apology. "I've been that close all these years and I never looked you up," he says. "And you can still call me Mark."

"I've thought about you. How many times have I searched the internet?"

"Dad made me change my last name." He shifts on the stool nervously. "The thing is…Cudge. You were staying at our house that weekend. I told you not to go back. Remember?" I nod. "Before that, when you were coming over, I was waiting outside and you told me to run."

"Because Cudge and I just had a fight."

"I heard you. I thought maybe he'd hit you." Mark is looking directly at me, and I've never seen those blue eyes so pained. "I didn't run when you left. I went upstairs."

"But you were at home when Sammy and I got there."

There's something missing in Mark's gaze, as if he's not present in this moment. "I was pissed off for you. Cudge was sitting on the edge of the bathtub rubbing the back of his head. He was dripping wet, naked, all that weird hair hanging down to one side. He looks up at me and it takes him a moment. He's kind of hazy. 'What the fuck are you doing here?' he says to me. Every bit of me was so pissed, Conner. I really didn't have a plan, so I yelled, 'Leave Conner the fuck alone or I'll fucking kill you.'" He looks at me, every muscle in his face straining, willing me to finish the story for him.

"Don't," I say. "I shouldn't hear the rest." He lowers his head and I go to him, kneel in front of this altar of red hair and plaid. When I reach out and take his hands, I learn a new thing, hot and rough, they have seen so much sun it's the dots of pink skin that look like the freckles; he *has* led a life outdoors. "I'm sorry my life was so fucked up back then. Whatever happened was my fault."

"I have to say it," he says, looking up at me. "Please let me."

I've no alternative. "Alright."

"All the sudden Cudge gets to his feet and rushes me kind of stumbling and I duck under him, but then he's between me and the door and my heart is pounding like crazy and this huge bare-assed man is about to come at me again. Without even thinking I grab this rebar propping the window open and he's almost at me when I swing and hit him in the neck. The sound. It was almost silent, like, dense, you know? Like hitting a wet sandbag. And Cudge curdles over saying something I still don't understand. 'Little fucker,' I think. I throw the rebar out the window and he hits the tub and falls in backward. I remember his head thunking against the hot water handle. He blinks a few times before his eyes close and then he's like wax melting down into the water."

Mark stops and looks at the door. A calico cat I don't know is circling in front of the glass as if it lives here. I go to shoo it away but when I open the door it trots in without regarding me, and heads straight for Mark, curls its body back and forth on his leg. "Not mine," I say as Mark scratches its neck.

"I thought...to pull him up," Mark says quietly. "But I ran. Practically fell down the stairs trying to get out of there. I accidentally knocked off the thermostat. That's why...."

"It was you?" is all I can say.

He nods and there's pain in his expression. "I guess it's the police now?"

But "now" is not what I'm thinking about. If I'd just been a few seconds slower, I would have heard Mark and Cudge. Maybe I could have done something. I remember Sammy was fiddling with gravel when I met him at the mailbox. "Hey," I said, "ready?" I practically dragged him by the collar, but I tried to play it cool.

As we fast-walked, I peeled off my coat and sweater. It was cold and getting colder, but not as cold as it would be in the coming days, and it didn't matter anyway because I felt like I was boiling inside. "Why you doin' that?" Sammy asked.

"Because I'm wearing too many clothes. I'm hot."

He started to take his own coat off. "I guess I'm going to be hot too."

I stopped and slipped his arm back into his coat sleeve, then zipped him back up. "You don't have to do everything I do," I said.

"I can't," he said, smiling with his eyes. "Know why?"

"Cuz I don't have me to take care of."

Now I look at Mark who's watching me, with the calico cat in his lap. "I saw you ten minutes later. Why didn't you say something?" I remember now how quiet we both were at his house all through pizza, but Sammy chattered enough for the two of us. He wanted Mark's mom and dad to make sure they picked up the phone in case his water rocket had come in the mail. And then he was excited because after dinner they were going to turn on *Dukes of Hazard*, which we never got to watch on Friday's because Cudge always had some other show in mind.

When Waylon Jennings started singing about good ol' boys, Mark and I went to his room where he cracked open a window so we could share a cigarette. "What's wrong with you," he asked after taking the first drag and blowing the smoke outside. "You're acting all weird. You have to act normal." In my mind's eye I see now how nervous he was, only then, I thought it was for me.

"Something bad happened today," I said. "I can't act normal. I had a fight with Cudge. I think I hurt him."

"No way." He handed me the cigarette. "You're a kid." He sounded like he didn't understand. "You think it's bad?"

"Maybe," I said. "I keep thinking what if he's planning on doing something?"

Mark crushed our cigarette on the metal sill and flicked it outside and I leaned over to put my head on his shoulder. I ventured further, tentatively. "He was…trying to make me blow him. What am I going to do?"

"Shit. I don't know," Mark said, suddenly frantic. "I don't know. It's really fucked no matter what." He shut himself down, was quiet for a while, and then he asked the question I was afraid to answer. "Has he fucked with you like that before?"

"Not really," I lied, "maybe," and then I had nothing to follow it up with. I was afraid of what might happen if I told him the truth, that it wasn't the first time nor the only thing he'd forced on me. Of all the people in my life at the time, Mark was the natural person to confide in, and I couldn't do it. He would be the first of a list of people in my life to whom I might have turned, who detected hurt in me, reached out, and got nothing for their efforts except my silence, or slim obfuscations.

But now, I owe Mark because he's been carrying around this burden all these years. His act, whether rash or considered, rescued me. I tell him everything I can remember, every violation, every moment of recovery that Mark provided. "I wouldn't be here now if it weren't for you," I tell him.

Cat in his arms, Mark stands and looks out the window, a trio of vintage, gingham dressed Teddy Bears gazing with him. "Got pretty scary, you stealing all that stuff." He pauses, recovering something in his mind. "You ever get rid of that fucking finger?"

I force a laugh and say "of course," though I know precisely where it is.

He walks past me to the door, cracks it open, and gently lets the cat out. "Don't feed her," he says, looking at me with a gentle smile. "She's sweet, but she'll keep coming around if you do."

"I'm guessing it's too late," I say. "James."

Mark nods, takes off his jacket, and returns to the window where he watches the cat scamper across the street and disappear between two parked cars. His shirt hangs untucked and loose, but I can tell he's muscular, healthy. "I'm sorry I let all these years go by without telling you. I shouldn't have let you think it was your mom." He turns to me. "But I was fucking freaked out. I mean, we almost took his body. That was some fucked up shit, and then he's just gone and I have no idea if it was you or your mom, or both of you."

I say what he already knows. "It was her and Larry, the guy on trial." But then I'm without words, find myself looking at Mark without the ability to speak because in this precise moment, it's come together. *Betty, it was you. But not for the reasons I imagined. You really thought I'd killed Cudge. You were protecting me after all. "What a mother won't do for her children," you said, and all I could think, was "bullshit." All these years, and it turns out you cared?*

"What is it?" Mark asks. It's obvious I'm lost.

"Betty…my mother. She thought I killed Cudge. Shit. She told me she protected me."

"And that surprises you?"

"You don't get it. I thought she'd done something and was just scaring the hell out of me to keep me quiet. She was a shitty mother…."

Mark shuffles his feet. "But it sounds like she sorta came through."

"She thought I did it because she asked me to. She wasn't just protecting me."

Mark catches on. "I guess that's why I'm here…. To make things right. The next thing to do is turn myself in."

I place my hands on Mark's shoulders and look at him squarely in the eyes. "Listen to me…Dean, you're not going to do that. It's not your secret anymore. It's ours."

He touches a finger to my lips which I receive as both a kiss and a hush. "I told you. To you I'm Mark and Dean was two names ago." His calm gaze searches me through and I'm certain of what he finds, love and permission. He doesn't have to be eaten up by something that happened twenty years ago. He can go lead his life and I will lead mine, and both of us will hold the memories of the boys we were so we can become the men we must be now. Our pact is silent but clear. He's just a nameless man passing through in a borrowed red pickup.

In minutes he's in his truck which becomes a thrumming cocoon. "Guess this is the goodbye we never had," the man says.

On impulse, I jump into the passenger side. "If you ever need anything…." I don't finish because we both know he's right. This is goodbye.

He looks at me, not quite smiling, but relaxed, then opens his palm to me which I accept with my own. We hold this for just a few seconds, but the warm knot of our hands binds the story within us. "Thanks, bud," the man says softly.

I grin and squeeze his hand with soft correction. "Buds." With that, I release him and step out of the cab, watch as the red pickup carries him away. Years ago, in his mother's car, when he had no idea his parents were taking him from me, he looked at me through the rear window with a sadness I only now understand. Today he does not look back and it feels wholly right. Mark is gone.

There's one thing left to do. From the shop, I retrieve the baby food jar containing the crisp nub of Cudge's finger, lock up, and walk to my bench near the river. The water is calm and low, a gleaming greenish-brown beneath late morning light. My hand tightly holding the jar as if it were a baseball, I listen as a train rumbles in the distance and somewhere in town a pair of dogs bark. Even closer, in the nearby bushes, a cardinal offers its staccato chirping. I wonder if at last I've found normal, if I've now permission to keep the secret of someone I loved from two people I now love.

Soon, our gravel drive will pop with sound and James and Lamb will come in the door with Lana in tow. They will find me near the window, and I will ask them to sit down. I will save my family. Can a father do that? The groceries can wait, I will tell them. One of them will ask me what's wrong, and that will signal the rehearsal is over. I will mention Mark's visit, and I will speak my life to them. "This arrived in the mail," I will say. Before I utter another word, a tableau, the three of us looking quietly at the coffee table on which rests a small black journal filled with sorrow, redemption, and advice. I will say that once, long ago, I found a man frozen in a bathtub and then he was gone. I will say that it's time for a small service around Betty's finished gravestone. And when I finish, I'll grow silent, awkwardly praying that after all this, Lamb and James will stay.

Now, I look at the content of my hand, a murky jar holding the dry kernel of my past. It's a final examination before I rear back and toss it as far out into the slow-moving river as possible where it plops and bobs, concentric circles broken by the mild current. The glass becomes a spark on the canvas of murky water, travels away from me by fractions. I sit on the bench and watch this slow, rocking journey, Cudge leaving at last, becoming the faintest pinprick down river, vanishing beyond bright rivulets, consumed by a vast tributary with a destination that finally I can't even imagine.

ACKNOWLEDGEMENTS

Like each of my previous books, this boat has taken several years to launch. It is in front of you now largely because of a kind, loyal, and tenacious crew. A first appreciation goes to PJ Mark, who, way back, read a "final" draft and wisely advised me it wasn't so final. Andrew H. Sullivan stuck with me after our first novel together, perhaps because I needed help rescuing another kid. A grateful nod to David Groff and Christopher Rice who had coffee with me years ago in Los Angeles and insisted that I write about a terrifying night from my childhood. I'm thankful for my colleagues at Purdue University's Department of English as well as those at Vermont College of Fine Arts, and for my students, who keep me on my toes. Much love and respect to Tom Alvarez, Matthew Brim, John Gosslee, Charles Solomon, and all the spokes of DiTomasos, Dorans, Leungs, Yosts and Thompsons. "And Featuring" Adam McOmber, whose books you must read after you finish mine. Finally, thank you to my second home town, Louisville, a beautiful, complicated city, populated with equally beautiful and complicated citizens who believe in love and justice.

ABOUT THE AUTHOR

Brian Leung is the author of the novels *Ivy vs. Dogg: With a Cast of Thousands*, *Lost Men*, and *Take Me Home*. Among other honors, he is a past recipient of the Lambda Literary Outstanding Mid-Career Prize and the Willa Award. Brian's fiction, creative nonfiction, and poetry appear in numerous magazines and journals. He is a Professor of Creative Writing at Purdue University.

C&R PRESS TITLES

NONFICTION

By the Bridge or By the River by Amy Roma
Women in the Literary Landscape by Doris Weatherford, et al
Credo: An Anthology of Manifestos & Sourcebook for Creative Writing
by Rita Banerjee and Diana Norma Szokolyai

FICTION

Last Tower to Heaven by Jacob Paul
History of the Cat in Nine Chapters or Less by Anis Shivani
No Good, Very Bad Asian by Lelund Cheuk
Surrendering Appomattox by Jacob M. Appel
Made by Mary by Laura Catherine Brown
Ivy vs. Dogg by Brian Leung
While You Were Gone by Sybil Baker
Cloud Diary by Steve Mitchell
Spectrum by Martin Ott
That Man in Our Lives by Xu Xi

SHORT FICTION

A Mother's Tale & Other Stories by Khanh Ha
Fathers of Cambodian Time-Travel Science by Bradley Bazzle
Two Californias by Robert Glick
Notes From the Mother Tongue by An Tran
The Protester Has Been Released by Janet Sarbanes

ESSAY AND CREATIVE NONFICTION

Selling the Farm by Debra Di Blasi
the internet is for real by Chris Campanioni
Immigration Essays by Sybil Baker
Death of Art by Chris Campanioni

POETRY

CPSIA information can be obtained
at www.ICGtesting.com
Printed in the USA
LVHW110054250522
719682LV00014BA/186